Sheffrou's Gambit

Cami Michaels

The Sheffrou Trilogy

I Am Sheffrou

Sheffrou Betrayed

Sheffrou's Gambit

Contents

Author's Note

Welcome to the sci-fi fantasy world of The Sheffrou Trilogy. To enjoy this novel to the fullest, please refer to the glossary in the back.

Thank you,
Cami Michaels

Chapter 1

S heffrou Maashi stood in the semi-obscurity, gaze focused on his opponent, his lean body tense. Clusters of stalactites trickled beads of liquid on the floor of the large, multichambered cave which offered the privacy he needed for training. Arms extended, he bent forward and waited.

Chari, his first Chowli, his bright copper skin subdued in the low light, transferred his weight from left foot to right in anticipation of Maashi's attack. "Go," he told the Sheffrou, "but plan your move carefully before you strike."

Determined not to fumble this time, Maashi watched the other's steps as he moved from side to side. Taking a deep breath, he charged, aiming for Chari's chest. At the last second, his opponent unexpectedly swayed sideways and Maashi sailed by his intended target at high speed.

Chari seized the opportunity. He grabbed Maashi by the waist as he flew by and using the Sheffrou's own energy, he sent him soaring across the room. Maashi's long frame slammed into the rocky ground, his right arm crushed under his weight. A loud gasp escaped his lips.

Chari, straight as a rod, arms crossed on his signature close-fitted black shirt, growled his disapproval. "Not impressed, Maashi. Not impressed at all. We're not here to play games," he said, raising his voice.

"I'm trying, Chari. I'm trying," said Maashi, breathing hard.

"Day ten today and I don't see much progress. You aren't performing at the level expected for a high-ranking Sheffrou. Your counterattack is pathetic. When will I see some decent sparring?"

A grunt escaped Maashi's lips. With much effort, he rolled over on his back. The searing pain from his wrist barred any further practice. He waved with his left hand. "I'm done for the day."

"Fine. Don't come whining to me if you can't make a decent showing in the upcoming ceremony. You know all the Sawishas will be attending and would wish nothing more than to see you embarrass yourself."

Maashi didn't budge from his spot and didn't add anything. It would be useless to argue with Chari. His training methods were excellent, and he was never anything but thoro gh, but his own wrestling skills were average at best. He knew he lacked the aggressivity needed to bring down an opponent. It would take considerably more time to improve his technique and make a satisfactory showing at the competitions.

Maashi rested on his back and stared at the stalactite hanging over his head. It looked sturdy enough but with his luck, it might come crashing down on him.

"I'll be expecting you in the water room," Chari said in a sharp, dry tone. He picked up his folded purple sash from the floor and threw it over his shoulder. It hung on his back and the thin red and pink bands were visible. The purple and red on Chari's sash were a sign he was a tough Multicolor and an accomplished fighter, but the pink and the minute dash of yellow added a touch of gentleness and compassion to his character.

Chari stomped out of the cave and bumped into Maashi's other Chowli. He greeted the younger one with a snarl.

"Watch were you're going, Chopa."

Chopa grumbled in response then noticed Maashi sprawled on the floor. He ignored the taunt and hurried to the Sheffrou's side.

He kneeled beside him and said, his voice filled with concern, "Are you all right, Shonava? You're so pale. Are you hurt?"

"I'm fine, apart from the fact I feel like a boulder dropped on me."

"Sir, let me help you get up." Chopa put one hand under Maashi's shoulder and pulled his right arm.

"Aargh. Wait. Wait." Maashi snatched his right hand away from Chopa's grasp. He dropped to his knees panting and cradled it with his left.

"Sir, your wrist is broken." Chopa hissed, unable to contain his anger. "I can't believe it. Was this Chari's doing?"

"Calm down, Chopa. Don't say a word." Maashi leaned on Chopa's shoulder and pulled himself up. "He's going to be pretty upset if I don't make a good showing at the ceremony." He straightened to his full height, close to seven feet, and inhaled deeply. The pain subsided. Relieved, he ran long fingers through his chestnut hair.

"May I call Sheffrou Chendor? He can help with the pain and start the healing process. I'm sure he's available."

Maashi shook his head to one side. "Not yet. Go. I'll join you in the water room in a few minutes."

Chopa's brow darkened in annoyance. He nodded and left, not without a furtive glance backward to make sure the Sheffrou was all right.

Maashi took a moment to gather his thoughts. He would need to withdraw from wrestling competitions. Chari would disapprove but those weren't important matches. The real competitions, set to be held in a few months, were designed to choose the best candidates for mating, and he knew the Council of Elders was not going to select him in this coming sequence.

So many things had changed in the ten months since the attacks on the night of the Great Eclipse Celebration. As he left the cave, his thoughts wandered once more to the infamous night. His friend Dasho had been severely injured and his pupil Ashani, a young Sheffrou, was kidnapped by the enemy. Not a day went by without Maashi grieving the loss of his friends. He hung his head down and sent a silent plea to the Souls of his Ancestors. Until now, the Black and Silver Guards had been unsuccessful in locating the unfortunate Ashani.

Distracted, he failed to notice that he took a wrong turn o t of the cave and wound up in a tunnel instead of the hallway to the water room. He stopped in his tracks when he realized his error. He turned around and came face to face with a Red Guard, part of the internal security, who handed him a comm nication device.

"A message from the Council of Elders, sir. No response is required from you. I will confirm the delivery." The guard bowed and was gone.

Maashi stared at the device. The Elders never sent messages nless it was of the utmost importance. He opened it. Read it twice. All air escaped from his lungs. His legs grew weak. "No, no, no, no."

Chari stepped out of the shower. He pulled and tied his black pants at the waist, grabbed his sash and shirt, and glanced at the door. The Sheffrou should've been here already. He hated to leave Maashi alone. Many Krakoran attacks had taken place in daytime on a lone Sawisha or Sheffrou. One could not be too cautious. He hurried, finished dressing, and stepped into the receiving room, a large and comfortable one by Chamranlina standards, suitable for a high-ranking Pure Color male celebrating his maturity in two weeks. He stared at the magnificent sculpture of a Shoshan stallion, a gift from Sheffrou Chendor to Maashi. The golden creature, a long-legged antelope with an arched neck, was shown rearing up on his hindquarters with fiery eyes and nostrils flared. The sight softened his expression and his lips stretched in a smile.

Chopa, his brow dark, stood pacing a few feet away. As soon as he saw Chari, he hissed in displeasure. "I don't understand you. Your lack of concern for the Sheffrou is appalling."

"What's ailing you now?" said Chari in a curt tone.

"It's obvious to me that you're not looking out for his welfare. You left him lying in the cave without so much as a glance to make sure he wasn't injured."

"What are you talking about?"

"You will have to check for yourself."

Chari tilted his head and snarled. "I don't like riddles. Where is he?"

"Still in the cave. He said he needed a few minutes."

Chari rushed out of the room and headed towards the cave. He slipped through its narrow opening and avoided the stalactites hanging at the entrance. He glanced around and didn't see Maashi.

The cave connected to many secondary caves and alcoves, and he proceeded to check them one by one. His frustration grew and he grunted in annoyance when it was obvious Maashi wasn't in the immediate vicinity.

Among Chamranlinas, Sheffrous constituted an unusual group. They were part of the elite fertile Pure Colors, but their behavior could surprise even the most experienced Chowlis. When in pain or exasperated by an unexpected event or outcome, they tended to isolate themselves to suffer alone. They preferred to avoid the scrutiny of the ever-watching eye of the monitors present throughout the compounds.

Chari growled, a low grumbling sound. Something had seriously irritated Maashi.

Perhaps he had been too tough on him. He easily forgot that although Maashi had shown resilience and strength of character after the life and death events of the last few months, he never had any taste for fighting. The loss of all his offspring except one, and of his pupil, Sheffrou Ashani, had considerably lowered his charissa, his happiness.

Chari heard something that sounded like a whimper, then irregular, deep sighs. He continued forward and found the source. Maashi stood behind a large boulder, huddled against the wall.

Chari approached him and said, "What's going on? Are you crying?"

Maashi's body tensed, and he averted the other's gaze. "Please," he whispered, "don't mock me."

Chari kissed Maashi's shoulder in a sign of respect. "I am your first Chowli," he stated, his voice gentle. "I would never mock you." He put one arm around the other's waist and noticed his large amber eyes had now lost all color. "What's wrong, sweet one?"

Maashi's lips trembled. "I can't... I cannot...."

Chari put two fingers under his jaw and turned his face towards him. "You can't what? Tell me."

Maashi jerked his body out of Chari's grasp and stepped sideways. He waved his left hand as if to ward off evil spirits. "I can't possibly... I'm not prepared.... I need more time."

Chari's patience was waning fast. He noticed the Sheffrou's trembling. He was close to panicking. "Maashi, we can withdraw from the wrestling. It's not required by law to be recognized as a mature Sheffrou. I'll talk to them. You don't need to get all frazzled." As he spoke, he noticed Maashi's swollen right wrist. He hissed.

"It's not my fault," said Maashi in a defeated tone. "I wasn't expecting this. I thought I was done."

"Why didn't you tell me you broke your wrist? Of course, it's not your fault."

Chari took Maashi in his arms, held him tenderly, and caressed the nape of his neck.

Maashi gulped back his saliva and blinked back tears without much success.

"By the Creatures of the Korr Nebula, what's wrong with you? You're carrying on like you saw a Krakoran."

Maashi shook his head. "It's not that," he mumbled. "It's something else."

Taking Maashi's face in his hands, he said, "Tell me. Tell me what's disturbing you."

The other wiped his eyes, blinked, and with considerable effort, composed himself. He handed him a small device.

"A message? From the Elders?" Chari stared at it, his brow widening in puzzlement. "What is this?" He opened it and read.

His expression changed from bewilderment to fury. "What?" He hissed and stamped his feet, fuming. "How dare they? They can't do this. This is not acceptable."

He pulled Maashi close, licked his neck with a long purple tongue and caressed his back. "I won't let them. I will contest their decision. I'll send an official complaint right away."

Chapter 2

Maashi glided in the crystalline water of his private pool, a brightly lit haven where he enjoyed spending time alone. In this peaceful setting, he could pretend the Elders' appalling request sent two days ago never happened.

As a Sheffrou, member of the third gender, he possessed an intense, unrelenting libido which consumed his life. That libido and the unique capability to produce female offspring conferred to Sheffrous a status close to royalty among the Chamranlinas. But what was considered a gift was also a curse. His excessive sexual impulses required constant attention and stiff control lest they create havoc in his life. The gift was also the source of vile attacks from envious Chamranlinas who often fueled hatred against Sheffrous, especially successful ones like Maashi.

Maashi stepped out of the pool, increased his stunning golden skin's temperature, and the water evaporated creating a fine mist around him. He padded barefoot, silent as a feline, into the adjoining receiving room.

His thoughts went back to a time months ago when in the same morning hours, he swam in the company of Tamara, his human soulmate. Tamara loved to splash in his pool. She called it swimming but it was entirely different from his own smooth gliding in a medium as familiar to him as air was to her. Maashi would entice her in the pool's warm water, floating just a little out of reach. She would giggle and attempt to follow him. When she failed, her high-pitched laugh would burst like a thousand bubbles and echo on the blue walls.

Tamara admitted to being a weak swimmer even among her people and often slid under the surface when she got too excited. Maashi had learned early on that, unlike him, she couldn't breathe under water and for her, the deep pool was fraught with danger, so he never strayed far from her side. One stroke of his long arms would bring him close, and he would hold her head above water and shower her with kisses.

The memory of her wet cheeks against his own filled him with joy. His mouth opened and his lips eased into a rare smile. He missed her curvy body, so different from the long and lean shapes of the females of his species. He missed her courage and sense of humor. Her mental strength and positive outlook had been a beacon of light at a time of deep sorrow, darkness, and pain.

Long before she had announced her decision, he knew she would leave. Living with her own kind was the logical choice. How could he ask her to forsake the chance of a happy life with other humans? He couldn't expect her to endure the severe joint pain she developed from staying in the high humidity of the underground caves where his people lived.

But what kind of logic could explain the way he felt about her? He longed to spend his life at her side, to be able hold her tenderly in his arms, to fulfill her desires....

Instead, although despair filled his heart, he held back and didn't ask her to stay with him on Chitina. He let her slip from his grasp and his heart overflowed with regret. Unwelcome tears filled his eyes and he swallowed hard to control the wave of sadness threatening to envelop him. His body shook from hunger, a hunger he couldn't satisfy. *If only she could have stayed....*

The door chime rang. Chari walked in with a stiff gait and a stern expression. He approached Maashi and kissed his right shoulder.

Maashi quickly hid his distress and searched his Chowli's face for answers.

"I tried," Chari said. His features, black eyes and eyelids, copper skin over a muscular frame, contrasted with Maashi's slender golden body and feline moves. "I have spoken to three Council Elders, and they said that after much deliberating, the Council had reached a consensus, and their decision was final. You will have to successfully complete the first of the Draharma trials." His brow darkened in displeasure.

There was nothing Maashi could say or do. If he refused the trial, he would lose his rank among the elite and, most importantly, the right to mate. Himself asking the Council of Elders to revoke their decision would be improper and would only fuel the rumors. There were whispers that Maashi's mental and physical capacities had been jeopardized after the loss of four Sheffrou friends due to enemy attacks and the plague which killed his offspring. Sheffrou Chendor, a Tousanou, a reputable healer, had vouched for Maashi's mental integrity but there were still Sawishas requesting a trial to test his courage and fortitude.

Chari hugged Maashi and kissed his cheek. "I swear to stand by your side no matter what happens. I have witnessed many Draharma trials in my days and, in my experience, anything can happen."

The sliding door flew open and Sheffrou Tomisho, Maashi's best friend, bolted into the room, wearing a gold shirt with an exquisite wide trouser tied with a cobalt blue sash.

"By the Black Creatures of the Korr Nebula, is this true? Will you have to suffer through another Draharma trial?"

Maashi inhaled deeply and paused before answering. "It would appear so."

Chari took a step back just as Tomisho reached Maashi's side. A head taller than the two, he was an imposing figure and enveloped Maashi in his sculpted frame.

"I'm so sorry." Tomisho's hands cupped Maashi's face, and he landed a passionate kiss on Maashi's lips. He held him for several minutes before easing his embrace. "Stay strong, my friend. This won't be easy, but I have confidence that you will prevail."

"Sheffrou Maashi is strong," Chari stated. "Stronger than others think. He will succeed." With that, he bowed and left the room.

Tomisho plopped his eight-foot frame on the closest couch. He shook his head and said, "I've asked around and everyone agrees that the Elders aren't going to give you a break." He leapt back to his feet and paced the room.

"To this day, I can remember the smell of those red-hot coals." His oval eyes grew bigger and glowed. "The brazier was extremely hot, so much that you could feel the heat more than twenty paces away." He rubbed his big hands together.

Maashi lowered himself on the couch. He too had experienced that terrible heat.

"I thought I was strong, as strong as a Shoshan stallion, but when I saw them choose the gemstone, a diamond the size of the tip of my little finger, and set it on the coals, my heart almost stopped." Tomisho quit pacing, stood rigid, and crossed his arms on his chest.

Maashi lips thinned. "I couldn't watch the first time."

"After that, everything was a blur. I remember being caressed and the pleasure when my member grew big." Tomisho grinned. "Yeah, pretty big...." He rubbed his hands together then his smile disappeared. "Then they brought the gem closer and held it low with those long tongs...."

Maashi exhaled loudly and clenched his teeth.

"The pleasure increased. I was close to reaching climax." Tomisho shook his head.

Silence filled the air.

"All I can remember after that," Tomisho said, "is the smell of burning flesh. My flesh."

Maashi's skin crawled.

Raising his arms high, Tomisho declared, "Between my climax and the pain of the hot stone blazing the tip of my member, I thought I would go insane!" Tomisho grunted. "I was furious. I wanted to scream and hit them." he fisted his hands. "How could they do this to me? What gave them the right?"

"That's enough, Tom Tom."

"I mean, that pain was unbelievable."

"That's enough, I said."

"To this day, I've never felt a pain equal to the one I experienced at the Draharma trials. The three trials."

Maashi sprung off the couch. "Shut up, Tom Tom or, Souls of my Ancestors, I'll slap you!"

Tomisho's brow widened. He looked surprised as if he noticed Maashi's anger for the first time. His shoulders dropped. "I'm confident," he said, staring at Maashi, "that you will succeed." He gave him a quick hug and left.

Bewildered and angry, Maashi stood in the middle of the room, his hands clenched tight. No, he thought. He would not flinch. He would not fail. He wouldn't give them the satisfaction of witnessing his pain.

The day before the trial, Maashi refused to see anyone except Chari. He snapped at his other Chowlis and stayed in a foul mood all day. The inevitable was going to happen, again. How he wished things were different for Sheffrous and Sawishas. Could the Chamranlinas not devise another way to deal with the mating issue?

Centuries ago, vicious fights for dominance between Sheffrous and Sawishas, the other pure color fertile males, had almost destroyed their species until the Elders devised a way to control them all: the Draharma trials. Every Pure Color, Chamranlinas with a unicolor tongue, called Sawishas and Sheffrous, had to complete three Draharma trials, each one more dreadful than the other, to be allowed to mate and maintain their high status. Only those who submitted to years of training had any chance of succeeding in the trials. Failing them meant a lifetime of shame.

He huffed and remembered what Tamara had told him: in the human world, almost half the population consisted of females. So many females compared to his world where males outnumbered the females by a thousand to one. On Earth, there was no need of Draharma trials to gain the right to mate. *What a wonderful world.*

A signal on his computer indicated he had a message. Maashi hesitated. He had instructed Chari to hold all his messages. This one had to be important for him to let it through. He glanced at the color-coded inscription. Sheffrou Chendor wanted to see him.

"Today isn't a good day," responded Maashi.

"This is not a request," said the message.

Maashi produced an annoyed clicking sound with his mouth but responded he was coming.

Chendor's private quarters were located only one hallway down from his. A short walk brought him over. Chendor's guard quickly stepped aside to let him in.

"Shonava Maashi, I'm so pleased to see you," said Chendor. His massive figure, as impressive as ever, moved rapidly across the room to greet him.

Maashi forced a smile and kissed the shoulders of the Sheffrou 6 in a sign of respect.

"Come Shapinka, sweet one, let me meet you properly." Chendor hugged Maashi and kissed his neck with affection. "Join me in the Encounter room. It is my opinion privacy is underrated." He grinned. "One is never too cautious."

Maashi nodded. He didn't want to refuse the Tousanou. He had been instrumental in his recovery when he almost lost his mind after finding that thirteen of fourteen of his youngest offspring had perished in a plague.

Chendor slid through the circular opening of the egg-shaped room located to the far left of the main receiving room. Maashi followed behind. Chendor adjusted the dimensions by pressing subtle controls on the wall beside him to allow them to sit side by side on the carpeted floor. The singular design and the black and gold diamond-shaped forms repeating themselves throughout the walls and ceiling were classic. Only the carpet was a uniform gold color which rippled at the slightest movement. The single light originated from one end and bathed them in its unique soft glow.

Chendor, like all Sheffrous, enjoyed intimate physical contact. This permitted the sharing of Saweya or life-energy between individuals. He held Maashi against his wide bare chest. He took his face in his hands and kissed him. A long, gentle kiss.

"It's true then," said Chendor, releasing Maashi, "You must go through the first Draharma trial. I sense a great deal of unease in you."

Maashi lowered his gaze. The Tousanou had always been able to read his mind as if his thoughts were visible to him like writings on a tablet. He said, "Yes. The trial is tomorrow."

"Your pale skin and rapid heartbeat betray you." Chendor said softly. "Why do you worry such?"

Maashi blinked. Outrage clouded his mind. "Why do you even ask? I never expected to have to go through another one of those humiliating trials."

"Chumpi, sweet one," Chendor put an imposing arm around Maashi's waist, "you shouldn't worry. You have experienced much greater pain in the past few months. This trial is just physical pain, something that will subside after five or six hours. Nothing compared to what you had to withstand."

Maashi understood what he meant but couldn't help feeling panicked at the thought of what awaited him. "Thank you for your confidence in me," he said in a defeated tone. "I hope I live up to your expectations cand everyone else's."

"Shonava, my lord, you are much stronger than you think." Chendor's face shone as he gently rubbed his cheek against Maashi's. He kissed Maashi's neck and, stretching out a lustrous midnight blue tongue, he licked Maashi's quatay, the erogenous markings on his chest.

Intense pleasure flowed in Maashi's body reaching his every cell. His libido swirled in his mind like the coiled snakes of Palarma. He closed his eyes and inhaled deeply.

Chendor held him closer. Maashi's holoma, the fragrant perfume emanated by all Sheffrous when they felt pleasure, surrounded them like a veil. Within minutes, as if under a powerful aphrodisiac, they were drunk with the mesmerizing scent. Maashi swallowed his abundant saliva and his breathing deepened. With Chendor's soothing thoughts reaching deep in his mind, his delight soared. A moment later, they both climaxed and their skin shone a deep blue.

Maashi recovered first and leaned on his back. He exhaled a long-held breath.

"Thank you," he said, "I have been troubled these last two weeks and raged against the Elders' decision. I realize now I should see the whole trial in a different light."

"Sometimes perception is the problem. You have successfully completed Draharma trials before and this one should not unduly distress you. Diminish the anticipated pain in your mind and the pain will be less. You're a powerful Sheffrou 8, Shonava. Don't let this trial intimidate you."

Maashi sighed. "As always, you offer sound counsel. Thank you."

Chendor responded with a smile. "It is a rare pleasure, Shonava."

They hugged one last time gand Maashi left.

On the way back to his quarters, in the calmness of his mind, Maashi sensed a deep disturbance, like a wave traveling in the void of space. The wave struck him with such intensity he stopped in his tracks, dazed. An anguished cry filled his thoughts. A cry which could only originate from a Sheffrou 8. Ashani's life was in peril.

Chapter 3

L eaving the world of the Chamis, leaving her beloved Maashi, had been a heart-wrenching decision, but with the prospect of a life filled with pain, Tamara had been left with little choice.

She gritted her teeth, determined to show strength and courage. Strapped securely in her seat aboard the human ship, she was embarking on a formidable and frightening voyage. The shuttle would rendezvous in two weeks with the main ship called *Innovation*, which would then travel to a human colony on a world called New Earth.

Stay calm. Everything will work out.

Tamara repeated the thought in her head, fighting to control an increasing sense of panic. Shaking hard, she breathed in small gulps of air. She stared at the strangeness of the cabin with its sleek lines in black and white. It felt cold, foreign, unlike anything she had seen before.

Concentrate. Focus. Relax.

She visualized Maashi's slender, gentle fingers on her neck and shoulders, his soft, melodic voice, his warm fragrant body. Then, with his extraordinary ability to enter her mind and shape her thoughts, she remembered how he would transport her to a tranquil and peaceful world where she floated on a vast blue ocean, light as a feather, a gentle breeze on her skin.

"Burn on my mark. Three, two, one, engage," said Patel, the pilot.

Tamara understood they were departing and braced herself, unsure of what to expect. She gripped the armrests as the ship gently vibrated. Her mouth went dry. She closed her eyes. An intolerable feeling of being compressed against the back of her seat overcame her.

Let it pass. Let it go.

She couldn't breathe, like someone confined in a closed space. She remembered being locked in a dark closet as a child. How long it took for her mom to find her. How close to a full-blown panic she had been. A mild jolt brought her mind back into the space shuttle. Tamara opened her eyes and released a long-held breath.

"Burn completed, Lieutenant. We have attained our cruising velocity and we're right on target for rendezvous with *Innovation*," said Patel, using his automatic translator so Tamara could understand.

She frowned as nausea and a metallic taste filled her mouth. She gagged, heaved, and fought the irresistible urge to vomit. Fumbling with the restraints, her hands shook so much she had difficulty freeing herself. "Oh. Help me. Let me go," she cried out with a feeble voice. Her vision blurred and bright spots flashed before her eyes. She felt trapped, crushed by a giant snake coiled around her.

Go. Run before it's too late.

Her breathing became erratic. Her heartbeat drummed in her ears. She finally freed her arms, raised them, and held her head with both hands. Her skull was going to explode.

It was too late.

Darkness flooded her mind. Not registering her surroundings anymore, she dropped limp in her seat. The faint buzz of an alarm sounded from far away; three sharp pings then one long buzz. Then nothing.

"She's waking up, Lieutenant. Her blood pressure is stabilizing." Patel shook his head and furrowed his bushy eyebrows. "I haven't seen a severe panic attack like that in a long time," he said. "She appeared so calm when we were readying for departure."

"Appearances can be deceiving," said Lieutenant Yoon. "She is after all a colonist, and they lack proper training for space travel."

Tamara opened her eyes and noticed the two tall slender humans by her side. Patel, she remembered his name, stood on her right observing the graphs on a tablet located by her seat. He shook his head in disbelief and his long ponytail seemed to fly this way and that in slow motion.

Lieutenant Yoon, his arms moving in mid-air like a puppet held by strings, asked with the help of his translator, "How do you feel? Can you talk?"

Tamara blinked as she tried to understand what had just occurred. "I don't know. I'm exhausted, like I ran a long distance," said Tamara. "What happened?" She turned her head and her hair floated away and slowly fell back down on her shoulders. Gravity. They had some degree of gravity on board. She noticed she was still strapped in her seat, with a small monitor clipped to her right index finger.

Patel answered with his translator. "You had a panic attack and lost consciousness. You should've told us you reacted poorly to 3G acceleration. We could easily have prevented that."

"I've had panic attacks before," said Tamara, "but never like this. I still feel strange, light-headed."

"Keep an eye on her and give her some fluids while I go through the postburn checklist," said Lieutenant Yoon.

"Will do, sir," said Patel. He opened a cabinet on the wall behind him and grabbed a plastic bottle containing a clear fluid. "Here," he said, popping a straw in the top. "Drink some bubble aid. Make you feel better. I'll get the medical recorder and check you out. Several common infectious diseases could be the cause of your panic. A few can trigger sudden drops in blood pressure." He walked slowly, stomping his feet on the metallic floor grid, to another cabinet further down the wall and pulled out a device the size of a cellphone.

Tamara took a sip of the cool liquid and set it in the left armrest. It stuck at the bottom with something similar to Velcro.

"Okay," said Patel, "so where is your chip? Right shoulder blade? Behind your ear?"

"My what?"

"Oh, come on. Your microchip." He lifted the device in the air for a second and eyed her suspiciously. "Don't tell me you don't have one."

Tamara hesitated. "Well...."

"By the seven moons of Potus, you colonists have some serious issues with basic modern science and medicine. I can't believe you don't have a chip."

Hating being treated like an idiot, Tamara responded with a steady voice. "I tried to explain to you before that I'm not from your century. Not even from your world."

"And you think I'm going to believe your bogus story about falling into a wormhole and traveling to an alien world?"

Tamara watched his thick eyebrows move up and down like black caterpillars. From the day she was introduced to the two human astronauts, they dismissed her incredible story of falling into a wormhole and traveling to Chitina, the home world of the Chamis. The humans thought she suffered a state of confusion following a harrowing experience in space.

"Listen, we told you that you're a colonist who was ejected in a survival pod which somehow was retrieved by those aliens. Then they brainwashed you to make you believe they saved you." His tone became louder and louder as his irritation grew. His mouth stretched in a strange pout. "I suppose you don't have the required vaccinations against the Zerilian flu, the Eygorian fever, and the Kona pox."

Tamara was in no mood to argue with the man. She had no idea what he was referring to. She felt wiped out. "I've told you before..."

"No. I don't have time for your fairy tale. You can recount your story to the shrink on *Innovation*."

She raised her hand to stop him from going any further. "I get it," she said. "I need some rest. Is there a quiet place where I can lie down?"

Patel grumbled as he replaced his instrument in the cabinet. He said in a harsh tone, "We're not on Shitango Five here. Just recline your seat for now and nap here. I need to go and help with the checklist. I'll come back later to make sure you're well." He took a few steps toward the front of the room.

Tamara eyed the panel of toggle buttons on her right armrest. She pressed the first one and her legs went up. The second brought her head way down lower than her feet.

"Oh. For Jennifer's sake! Don't you know anything?"

He came back by her side and adjusted her seat to a comfortable reclining position. "Get some rest," he ordered. "Call me when you're ready to get up."

"Thanks."

He glanced back at her, shook his head, and left.

Tamara closed her eyes and took a deep breath. She knew when she decided to leave the Chami world and her alien friends that it wouldn't be easy to adjust to the human world of the future, but never thought her first trip would start with a panic attack and insults from the copilot of a shuttle. She bit her lower lip. *Would she regret her decision to leave her dear Maashi and the Chamis?*

Chapter 4

The day of the Draharma trial arrived. Flanked on each side by two guards and his Chowlis, Chari and Chopa, Maashi, his expression unreadable, advanced in the bright hallway leading to the ceremonial room. The gold crests of all the former Sheffrous and Sawishas who had completed the three Draharma trials hung on the black granite walls, a silent homage to their courage and tenacity. With a seemingly perfect composure on the outside, Maashi's heart raced inside.

His own Draharma trials, a set of three, had been conducted when he reached adulthood over eighty sequences ago. Now, at one hundred and thirty sequences old, the age of maturity, his already exceptional fertility would increase. Unchecked, his libido would reach extremes and be the sole focus of his life. This new Draharma trial, ordered by the Elders, was a stark reminder that controlling his urges and remaining humble was required for his continued acceptance as an honored and privileged member of the Chamranlina society.

In the old days, long before the Chamranlinas were forced to leave their home world Chamtali and establish a colony on Chitina, Sheffrous and the other Pure Colors, the Sawishas, engaged in violent fights to gain the right to mate. At the time, females were numerous and willingly mated with the winners. Today, after years of ruthless attacks by their enemy the Krakoran, no more than forty mature females remained. They lived in compounds isolated from the other fourteen compounds of the colony.

Following the plague that hit the very young offspring months ago, Sheffrous and Sawishas were now allowed to visit and mingle with the females. The new rules permitted bonding with their offspring under the watchful supervision of the Gray Feeders, the sterile males responsible for the care and protection of the females.

Maashi stopped and acknowledged the three guards who stepped aside. The two-paneled door opened revealing a large room with ten-foot-tall vertical banners hanging from the walls. Each banner was adorned with an emblem representing one of the fourteen compounds of the colony. Four guards in black attire and wearing an elaborate gold mask with a unique pattern of colored swirls stood at attention in the center of the room. There, a single chair with arm and leg rests had been placed on the white marble floor. About six feet away, a brazier filled with glowing coals left no doubt about the seriousness of the impending trial.

A shiver of trepidation ran along Maashi's spine. Did he feel disgust? Loathing? He pondered this as he stared tight-lipped at the brazier. Memories of his own Draharma trials were dim. Although drunk with pleasure and shaking with fear, the merciless stare of his mentor, Master Kokin Cronobutin, stood out more than anything else. His likely punishment for humiliating his mentor should Maashi flinch and cry out would have been far worse than the pain of the trial.

A gong resonated from the other end of the room. The striker wore a black mask that didn't cover his mouth or neck. Something about that fact struck Maashi as odd. The guard avoided Maashi's gaze and twice, he stared at the monitors positioned on the ceiling in each corner of the room. Maashi, prompted by the guards, hesitated a fraction of a second before moving forward. On their signal, he removed his chemcha, his protective underwear, the only piece of clothing he wore. Then, they directed him to the dreadful titanium chair.

Maashi inhaled a deep breath and sat down, legs spread. His two Chowlis, Chari and Chopa, stood silently behind him. The rules were clear. No touching or comforting the Sheffrou during the trial. Maashi had to remain still and mute. At the first sign of weakness, he would fail the trial and be covered with shame.

Chari sent him a quick telepathic message. *"Be proud. Be strong."*

A final guard walked in slowly carrying tongs and a diamond the size of the tip of Maashi's thumb. The guard grasped the jewel with the tongs and set it on the red coals.

"We are assembled today to celebrate Sheffrou Maashi Torrenadanga's ascending to maturity," the same guard said. "We honor him with a precious stone. May he wear it proudly as a symbol of courage and strength. May he live to become a wise elder and long enough to meet the grandchildren of his grandchildren." The guard raised his head. "The Draharma trial is an honored tradition established on Chitina centuries ago. Representants of each of the fourteen compounds will bear witness through the monitors and will confirm the completion of this first trial as required by law."

Maashi swallowed hard. The guard took a step towards the stone encircled by the coals. He picked up the searing hot diamond and slowly turned on his heels. "Let us begin," he said.

The gong sounded loud and hollow.

Maashi's breathing increased and his limbs trembled. *I must stay strong. The pain will soon dissipate.*

Another guard stepped closer, knelt beside Maashi, and caressed Maashi's genitals. The Sheffrou blinked and shuddered as pleasure spread through his body. He sensed his member growing and fought to stay calm by inhaling deep breaths. The guard grabbed his member and gently stroked the shaft.

I can't watch this.

Maashi closed his eyes, braced for the pain.

Someone yelled, "Now!" Two guards immediately grabbed Maashi off the chair and held a knife to his throat. Two more seized Chari brandishing a knife in his face. The guard with the black mask aimed a device at each corner of the room. It released a thick gas which quickly spread and obscured the monitors so no one from the outside could see what was happening inside.

"The Sheffrou's life is in your hands," said the guard with the black mask. "If anyone tries to intervene," he shoved a stunned Chopa out of the way and opened the door to the hallway, "we will cut his throat."

As he finished his sentence, the guards dragged Maashi outside the room. He glanced back and saw Chari struggling to free himself. A guard plunged his knife into Chari's arm. "Cooperate or next time it's your throat."

The guard by Maashi's side took off his mask, removed the knife from Maashi's throat, and yelled, "Run with us as fast as you can! Resist and we'll get rid of your Chowli."

Maashi said in a voice raw with anger, "I'll run as long as you don't harm him."

"Run," said the guard.

The guards took off and Maashi, swift on his feet, followed easily. The other guards holding Chari trailed behind.

The group ran for thirty minutes then made a sharp turn to a dust-covered tunnel with a sharp uneven surface. The barefoot Maashi strained behind his abductors. Soon, his sensitive feet were bleeding. At last, they boarded a fast-moving, air-cushioned, underground vehicle. The vehicle charged ahead and gathered speed. After a short ride, they abandoned the vehicle, boarded another one, and zoomed through the wide tunnels.

Maashi was pinned tightly between two guards and couldn't see Chari. He tried to envision in his mind the direction of the vehicle, but all he could determine was that they were headed north.

"Where are we going?" Maashi said. "What do you want from me?"

"Shut up," the guard growled, hatred burning in his eyes, "You'll find out when we reach our destination."

About an hour later, the group disembarked. Maashi was led through a series of tunnels to a small room with a single couch and an adjoining water room. He didn't see where they took Chari.

"Wait here," said the guard, his voice filled with loathing. "The Leader will come to see you later." He shut the sliding door behind him, leaving Maashi naked and alone.

Chapter 5

M aashi sat on the single lounge chair in his detention room, hands spread on his knees, deep in thought. Why did those guards kidnap him and transport him to this remote area? Why did they remove him just before the Draharma trial? The failure to complete it would cost him his reputation and his standing as a high-ranking Sheffrou.

A likely explanation came to mind. Although the main function of the Sheffrous was to produce female offspring, they were considered a third gender and possessed the capability to share pleasure with any living creature. Trained from a young age to respond to both sexes, they fulfilled an important role in Chamranlina society by servicing the males. In a world where females were only available for the fertile Pure Colors, Sawishas and Sheffrous, the Multicolors had no choice but to turn to Sheffrous for sexual satisfaction.

The outskirts of the colony teemed with manual laborers which were supposed to be serviced by Sheffrous. However, these areas were often neglected. The laborers lived in primitive conditions and some Sheffrous found creative excuses to avoid being sent to service them. Perhaps this explained why the guards had decided to snatch him. His upcoming Draharma trial had been all over the colony media and the location of the trial was easily discoverable. If he was correct in his assumption, his release would depend upon his servicing all the workers of the area. He didn't consider his current situation too alarming since this was a habitual task for him.

He looked down and examined the soles of his feet. They were cut in several places from running without sandals in the last tunnel where the ground was rough. Although the risk of infection was small, they needed attention.

The door opened and a broad-shouldered Multi with piercing eyes entered. He tilted his head to the side and scrutinized Maashi's face and upper chest with obvious interest in his quatay. The intricate markings had increased in size and complexity in the last few months, a sure sign he had attained maturity. The Multi failed to bow or approach him to kiss his left shoulder in a sign of respect.

Appearing satisfied with his summary examination, the Multi said, "Follow me. The Leader will see you now. Don't try to escape. The guards will catch you and they won't be kind to you."

Maashi nodded and followed in silence.

They went down a long hallway, through a series of small rooms, then entered a large room with several couches and a central table. Simple blue globes positioned on the floor throughout were the only source of lighting. The walls were covered with the crests of fallen guards who had sacrificed their lives for the colony.

Five impressive Pure Color Black and Silver Guards, eight feet tall with wide silver and black sashes, stood at the back of the cave. A muscular Pure Color Black taller than Maashi walked in through a rear opening and the globes turned white. Maashi recognized him immediately. He had met this one called Dennyvan over twenty sequences ago. Arrogant and ruthless, the guard had disrespected Maashi by refusing to bow and kiss his left shoulder.

Maashi, young and proud, had commented to his Chowli. "Black and Silver Guards are important but not so much that they can disrespect Sheffrous."

Dennyvan had reacted quickly and said, "Young and inexperienced Blues should hold their tongues in front of older Pure Colors."

"A Pure Color," said Maashi, "even a high-ranking one like a Black and Silver will never be chosen for mating."

The insult hit its target. Dennyvan growled and violently shoved Maashi. A major scuffle ensued and Dennyvan pounded Maashi with solid fists delivering a severe beating. A timely intervention by Maashi's Chowlis prevented any serious injury, but the young Sheffrou learned a valuable lesson: he shouldn't let guards intimidate him but should never respond to their taunting. Only mature Sheffrous, much stronger than he was at the time, could confront such adversaries and expect to overpower them. Now, many sequences later, Maashi was confident he could deal with Dennyvan, but he would do so only if a serious situation required it.

Dennyvan's face twisted in disgust at the sight of the Sheffrou. He took a few steps forward then circled him as if appraising a shoshan.

"Why did you kidnap me?" said Maashi in a commanding voice. "Why did you bring me here?"

Dennyvan slapped Maashi across the face so hard that he staggered.

"Shut up, scum," he sneered. "You Sheffrous think everything is about you. Pure Colors, especially the Blues, used to be ferocious and could face any enemy, Krakoran or otherwise. Today, you're all weak and pathetic."

Maashi stared at him for a moment. He couldn't establish any connection with Dennyvan's thoughts. The Leader obviously had been trained to close his mind against intrusion by a skilled telepath like him. "What do you want from me?"

"You should be grateful," Dennyvan growled. "You would be writhing in pain if it weren't for us. We saved you from those ancient Elders and their ridiculous rituals."

Maashi asked again. "Why did you bring me here?"

"You," he spat at Maashi's feet, "are the one responsible for the attacks on the night of the Great Eclipse Celebration."

The guards standing behind showed their approval by stamping their feet in unison. A few spat on the floor, a strong reaction usually reserved for their enemy, the Krakoran.

"That is totally false, and you know this."

"Eight guards died that night, and two were kidnapped by the enemy. They were part of my team."

The Multi and two guards hissed to show their anger and disgust.

"I didn't have anything to do with the attacks," said Maashi. "They were planned under the direction of Master Kokin Cronobutin, my previous mentor."

"Your mentor's plan was to hurt the others to hurt you. Don't you understand? You were the only one protected by a group of Silver Guards while the other groups had little protection. The fact that you survived is an insult to all of us." He tilted his head and said, "But you will make amends. We will make sure of that."

Dennyvan turned to the Multi who stood at Maashi's side and said, "He will serve our purpose. Take care of him. Make sure he doesn't come to any harm." He added, "Tend to his feet. We need him intact."

"Yes, sir," said the Multi.

"What about my Chowli?" said Maashi. "Where is he? What have you done to him?"

"He is safe," said the Leader, "and will remain so as long as you cooperate."

Two guards and the Multi accompanied the unsettled Maashi to his room. Maashi walked in and stopped a few feet away from the door. He turned and stared at the Multi.

"What did your Leader mean by 'make amends'?"

"You will find out soon." The Multi came close to Maashi and caressed his shoulder. His eyes followed Maashi's chest down to his genitals. "But first you and I will meet."

His sly smile left no doubt in Maashi's mind as to what he wanted.

"I've had meetings with Sheffrous like you and I can treat you well. I will be the one taking care of you until we depart."

Maashi's brow darkened. "Where are we going?"

The Multi's smile broadened. "We are going for a trip in space. A first for you, Sheffrou, and to a place you've never heard of. Now, sit down and show me your feet so I can take care of them."

"What is your name?"

"They call me Redden because I have a disposition like a Red, aggressive, short-tempered, and mean."

Maashi slowly sat on the couch. A sense of doom chilled his heart. These Black and Silver Guards harbored a hatred of Sheffrous unlike anything he had seen before. They were trained for combat, therefore capable of everything. Even murder. What was their plan? Why did they need him?

Chapter 6

"Argh! What is wrong with you?" Tamara yelled at Alice, the ship's AI.

"My systems are in working order. Please rephrase your question," said Alice.

"Never mind."

"I don't understand the statement."

Tamara eyed the device and said, "It means ignore."

"Understood."

Tamara shoved aside her floating hair which got in her face all the time. After a couple days on board, she was still figuring things out. The two guys, Lieutenant Yoon, a bland stick-by-the book kind of guy and his pilot Shiva Patel, dark-haired and bushy-eyebrowed, were busy mapping the sector and worked twelve-hour days. They weren't very chatty and mostly left her by herself.

She opened every cupboard in her quarters which was no bigger than a walk-in closet on Earth, and concluded there wasn't any soap, only the wipes she had been using until now. She would have to be content with them to clean herself, a major disappointment after the wonderful showers and pools on Chitina.

"Alice, are there any snacks in my quarters?"

"Food items are confined to the galley which is located on the lower level of the ship to prevent overuse and spoiling."

"Overuse," Tamara mumbled and shook her head. This time, her hair floated above her. *The two guys here are so thin they're not overindulging for sure.*

"I didn't quite get that," said Alice.

"I wasn't talking to you."

Tamara turned around slowly to avoid bumping into the wall with its multiple magnets and Velcro attachments to secure personal items. She had improved her muscle strength after living on Chitina since the gravity on its surface was slightly more than on Earth. However, that hindered her movements aboard the human shuttle because tasks in low gravity required less strength than she needed.

"Alice, I want a coffee, black with two sugars."

"Coffee is a stimulant and requires approval from the commanding officer. It is available only at scheduled times during a 24-hour period."

"Why?" Tamara remembered the many night shifts when she was undergoing her residency in emergency medicine. She wouldn't have survived without coffee. "That sounds ridiculous."

"Excessive consumption has led to coffee being classified as a controlled substance, especially on shuttles."

"Right."

A voice from some intercom she couldn't see said, "Tamara, this is Patel, can you join us in the galley? We are having a mid-day meal."

"The galley is located on the lower level on your left," said Alice.

"On my way," answered Tamara.

She went down the tunnel by holding on to the handrails and got there more easily than in her previous attempts since she bumped the side wall only once. Proud of her accomplishment, she greeted the lieutenant and Patel with a broad smile.

Patel raised his eyebrows and said, "Didn't you complete the training designed to show you the proper way to maneuver inside a shuttle? You almost knocked out the light controls."

"What light controls?"

"That small device over there," Patel said in his most condescending tone.

"I see," said Tamara. "Well, it's intact. No harm done." She flipped a strand of red hair out of the way and added, "What are we eating? I'm starving."

"You have a choice between avocado surprise," said Lieutenant Yoon, "or hot turkey sandwich."

"I think I'll go for the turkey."

"Where are you going?" said Patel. "You are not allowed to eat outside the galley."

"I meant I'll have the turkey." She went to the refrigerated section, opened the glass door, and pulled out a drawer with rows of plastic packets. She chose the turkey one and closed the drawer. The refrigerator door pinged until she shut it.

Since her arrival, she had learned to perform simple tasks on the ship. She rubbed her forehead trying to remember the exact sequence needed to heat the packet in the microwave. *First, press 'open' so that the sliding drawer comes out then put the packet in...*

"Tamara," said Patel who was watching her every move, "you must release the top of the packet before you insert it in."

"Yes, sure," said Tamara, feeling they were treating her like a child. "I was just about to do that." She grabbed the packet and unscrewed the cap, *child's play,* and put it back in the microwave. She pressed 'close' then chose an appropriate time for heating.

One minute later, it was done. She picked up the packet from the drawer and dropped it.

"Wow! So hot," she exclaimed.

The packet didn't go toward the floor. Instead, it flew right in Patel's face. He caught it, somehow popped the cap off, and the turkey squeezed out. Bits and pieces scattered in every direction.

Both men jumped off their seats and bounced around the room in a comical dance to catch the escaped turkey before it hit the instruments on the walls.

Tamara couldn't help bursting with laughter as she watched the two swaying this way and that with their long arms swinging, trying to gather all the pieces.

The lieutenant wasn't amused. Once the turkey was retrieved and he had secured himself, he said in his most authoritative voice, "I have never seen such a display of incompetence and disregard for proper handling of food. Patel will review with you basic protocols used aboard a shuttle. I expect you, Mrs. Walsh, to complete this training to reduce the risk of inadvertently causing accidents on board. Is this understood?"

Tamara stopped laughing. "Basic training. Yes. That's a good idea."

Lieutenant Yoon glared at her. "It is not 'good'. It is essential." The lieutenant left the galley and promptly went to the upper level.

Patel eyed her sideways and said, "I can heat another turkey for you, if you wish."

Tamara exhaled a long breath. "I kind of lost my appetite. Do you have cheese and crackers?"

"We have cheese and something like crackers. Shall I get it for you?"

"Yes, thanks."

"You should eat and then go to your quarters. I would stay out of the lieutenant's way for a bit. I have not seen him this angry in a long time."

"Okay. I mean, yes."

Patel handed her the food and disappeared up the tunnel. Tamara sat down and secured herself. *Was this what she should expect in her new life with humans?*

The cheese was chewy, and the crackers were hard and as tasteless as cardboard.

She thought about the puddings she used to eat on Chitina and how much she complained about them. They tasted so much better.

Chapter 7

"You want me to do what?" Maashi glared at Dennyvan.

Standing face to face in the Leader's bare receiving room, Maashi shook with anger as he waited for an explanation.

They were traveling in space to a designated location for a purpose Dennyvan had refused to disclose. The expected time of arrival was less than two weeks. Although provided with very little food and water, Maashi hadn't been harmed but the low ceilings and bland gray walls of the spaceship made him feel trapped. Worried and suspicious, he didn't know what to expect.

Dennyvan's face contorted in frustration as he said, "As our mission depends on your complete cooperation, I will repeat myself. Once." He balled his fists and eyed Maashi. "You will impersonate an alien. Now, sit down and listen carefully."

Dennyvan waited.

Maashi lowered himself on one of two long reclining couches. Redden, the Multi who had shared Maashi's cell since their departure, stood a few feet away, arms folded across his broad chest.

"The information," Dennyvan said, "would be easier to transfer through saliva, but I have no intention of kissing you to share the details. For months," he continued, "we have been looking for two missing Black and Silver Guards kidnapped by the Krakoran on the night of the Great Eclipse Celebration."

At the mention of the Krakoran, Maashi hissed in disgust. He immediately thought of his young friend Ashani, also kidnapped the same night.

"Our informants have finally succeeded in intercepting communications between a group of aliens and the Rodenegad. As you probably know, we have had previous dealings with them, and we don't trust them. They are a cunning species and have deceived us before," Dennyvan said. "We recently found evidence of a black-market contraband network used as a cover-up for buying and selling of sentient species.

"We know the Krakoran collaborate with the Rodenegad. We suspected there were ongoing prisoner exchanges but had scant information about the inner workings of their system until now. The network is much more complex than we suspected.

"It possesses multiple buyers, called players. All the interested players meet virtually to evaluate the merchandise, mostly aliens kidnapped in the preceding weeks: Luluyan, Chamranlinas, and other species unfamiliar to us. Some are sentient, some not. We believe that's how they can hide the more valuable sentient specimens. They plan a physical meeting in a secret location. At the convened date and time, they proceed with the actual trading. We know for a fact that the two missing guards are among the ones up for the next trade."

Maashi could no longer contain his anger. "Riveting information, but what is my role in all this?" As Maashi spoke, an ominous realization came to mind.

Sheffrous were coveted by the Krakoran above all others.
I would be priceless in this type of market.

A low growl came out from between his thinning lips. "You're planning to trade me for the two guards? Is that why you kidnapped me?"

Dennyvan scoffed. "The thought crossed my mind, Sheffrou, but I'm not callous to the point of getting rid of an individual as valuable as you for the colony. I swore to protect Sheffrous. I will not forsake my vows even though I hate what you represent. You're treated like royalty and are allocated countless benefits while we, Black and Silver Guards, are regarded as expendable." He tilted his head sideways. "Our plan is to complete a transaction involving the two guards initiated by a player some time ago. You will impersonate the player."

Maashi blinked in relief, but his discomfort remained. In his whole life, he had never participated in deception and doubted he could be a convincing alien. The possibility remained that if things didn't work out as Dennyvan planned, the temptation to use him as bait or even for trade would be difficult to resist.

Dennyvan turned and addressed Redden. "Get Kotian in here."

Redden returned shortly with another Multi. Small and slender, Kotian had more yellow and pink on his short sash than any Multi Maashi had ever seen. The bright and unusual combination of colors indicated he possessed excellent artistic skills. Kotian bowed to Dennyvan and directed his gaze toward Maashi.

"Stand, Sheffrou," ordered Dennyvan, "so he can get a good look at you."

Maashi inhaled a long breath and stood. Kotian, much shorter than Maashi, tilted his head to the side and took a few steps to the right then to the left.

"He's the right height," said Kotian. "He should be slimmer, and his posture is wrong, but this can be corrected through training. He will be a convincing Woo-Odong."

Piqued by the Multi's comments, Maashi straightened his shoulders and said, "Your endeavor is futile. I have never heard of or seen a Woo-Odong."

"Don't move." said Kotian. "That's it. That's the posture I'm aiming for. Yes, he'll make a fine Woo-Odong if we can get him to imitate the hopping gait and the screeching cries."

"Good," said Dennyvan. He reached for a console beside the couch, and a life size hologram of a lean figure covered with opaque veils the color of burnt chorila nuts appeared. "This is Supreme Master Woo-Olong-Ti, a well-known player. Your role will be to impersonate him."

Before Maashi could comment, Dennyvan added, "Notice he has amber eyes just like yours, surrounded by dark brown eyelids. The rest of his figure is concealed. That's why posture and a slim figure are so important. Kotian will work with you and if you make good progress, your Chowli will be released to your care. Do you understand?"

"Yes." Maashi said. "But how will this work? Won't the other Woo-Odong know I'm a fake?"

"Patience, Sheffrou. We are working on the details. We are preparing for every contingency. Kotian will start training you today. I will assess your progress in a few days."

As the days went by, Tamara realized there were so many things to learn, so many things to forget. Her life on Chitina wasn't perfect but she felt appreciated, cherished. Here, the two men didn't believe her story, didn't see her as anything other than a colonist, a lesser person in their blind eyes.

Simple tasks aboard the shuttle were fraught with unforeseen difficulties and she often retreated to her quarters to read. She quickly concluded that human history had repeated itself a few times over. Wars, famine, dire consequences of climate changes. There were more natural disasters, hurricanes, monsoons, prolonged heat waves, etc. Earth wasn't a nice place anymore. Resources had been depleted and this gave rise to a space race like never seen before. That's how humans traveled to this sector.

She read about the colonists. They weren't a uniform bunch. Some believed in science and others rejected a lot of scientific facts. Nothing new there. Humans were still the same. Controversies, arguments, fights. Would this lead to other wars in a new world?

Tamara sighed. Her heart longed for Maashi. That night, she dreamed she was back in his arms, his lips on hers, his fingers in her hair. She woke up and tried to sit, forgetting her small space and the restraints meant to prevent her from floating away, and hit her head on the ceiling. Sadness overwhelmed her, and small tears floated and escaped her reach.

I miss you, Maashi. Life is not the same without you.

Hours later, she heard a commotion coming from the ship's control room as if someone was throwing furniture. A loud thud resonated along the hull followed by a disgusting smell of rotten eggs. Not sure what she should do, she held her breath and listened for any other sounds. That's when she heard a strange shuffling like someone dragging their feet along the metal floors.

An instant later, the lights went out and only the AI's blue eye blinked in the darkness of her room. She unfastened the straps holding her and slipped out of her bed. She had no idea what had just happened. Nothing in her basic training had prepared her for this. While she debated what to do next, something blasted the door open and a long, gloved appendage covered by a thick brown sleeve reached inside her quarters and grabbed her. She screamed and fought back to no avail. She heard a faint buzzing and everything went black.

Chapter 8

Training meant hours of repetition until Maashi's head spun. Although Maashi tried his best to recreate the exact posture Kotian was looking for, it never seemed to be satisfactory.

After a long while, Maashi had had enough. He stood, head raised high, unflinching eyes, gaze filled with loathing, and said, "I will stand like this. It seems the most natural stance considering the coverings I must wear."

"Don't move," said Kotian. "It's perfect." He took several pictures in different angles and posted them up on a virtual screen so the Sheffrou could refer to it.

The hopping gait required perfect balance. Maashi's feet were fitted with prosthetics equipped with long talons. The clumsy hopping became even more problematic. A long hop made him lose his balance and fall sideways. A short hop caused him to fall forward and break the prosthetic. Kotian swore under his breath.

Many hops later, Maashi paused and filled his lungs to keep his cool. After a few more tries, he achieved the desired gait.

The screeching cries were tough to emulate. Maashi, like all Sheffrous, had been trained for sequences to stay silent under pressure. Screeching therefore was a completely unnatural reaction for him. Nonplussed, Kotian ordered the guards to bring Chari over.

Chari walked into the room bare-chested with his copper skin gleaming under the light and black hands bound together at the waist by titanium handcuffs. Two guards stood at his side. He nodded at Maashi, and a corner of his mouth stretched into a faint grin.

Maashi was relieved to see his Chowli unharmed.

"Perhaps you need some incentive. Listen to the screeching sound on the recording," said Kotian. "Fail to reproduce it correctly and we will flog your Chowli."

Anger swelled in Maashi's mind, and he missed the cue. Horrified, he saw the guard hit Chari with a thin strip of Hooga plant. A long, red band streaked across Chari's back. The Chowli grimaced and tried to shake off the other guard by jerking his body sideways but to no avail. With muscles tight, Maashi fisted his hands. His lips curled with surging anger. He inhaled a long breath and let out an ear-shattering sound.

Kotian raised his hands and clicked, "This will do nicely."

Chari grinned his approval.

"I will now proceed," said Kotian, "with a minor laser procedure on your eyelids to change their appearance." He signaled to a guard who brought a chair with restraints and a device which he connected to the back of the chair. The device was set on a mobile arm and could be positioned at will.

"What?" cried out a stunned Maashi. "I refuse." A guard grabbed his arm.

Kotian continued without paying attention to the Sheffrou. "The laser will give you a mild burning sensation. We will put a shield over your eyes to protect your eyesight. You may expect temporary blindness. It usually doesn't last more than 26 hours."

Chari roared. "This is unacceptable. You can achieve similar results with makeup." Before his guards could react, Chari hurled himself forward and kicked high and fast. Both the chair and the device crashed to the floor with a loud *clang*.

"Restrain him," Kotian screamed at the guards. "Keep the Chowli under control."

The guards seized Chari and held him tight.

Maashi straightened and assumed a dominating stance. He pinned Kotian with his stare. With his voice cracking with authority like the whip that had recently scored Chari's back, he said, "You will use makeup and the results will be suitable. This should be a basic task for someone with your skills unless I am mistaken, and your abilities are inferior."

"Humph," was Kotian's response. "Very well," he grumbled, "I will use a new makeup formula I have developed. I hope it will hold."

When Dennyvan came by to check on Maashi's progress, he clicked his approval. "Excellent job, Kotian. The eyes are most realistic."

"Thank you," Kotian bowed gracefully. "I think we'll be able to proceed to a full rehearsal of his role tomorrow."

Maashi immediately responded, "I want my Chowli in my quarters from now on."

Dennyvan roared, "You're not the one giving orders, Sheffrou." He glanced at Kotian and said, "Your Chowli will not join you until Kotian is thoroughly satisfied with your performance."

Twelve days later, they approached the space station where the trading was supposed to take place. Maashi learned that Woo-Olong-Ti's whereabouts had been confirmed. As the informants predicted, he was in a faraway nebula where communications were impossible.

The ship used by the Chamranlinas had been modified to look like Woo-Olong-Ti's ship. It emitted the same type of radiation and used the same type of fusion reactors. Its signature emissions in space would be construed as originating from a Woo-Odong ship.

The exchange of prisoners was scheduled to take place aboard a complex and recently expanded space station which controlled arrivals and departures of a multitude of space faring ships. The station was located strategically at the congruence of three solar systems and therefore easily accessible by different routes. It also offered the added advantage of a fast retreat should things get dicey for the players.

The Interstellar Alliance tolerated the illegal trade because it didn't possess the means or the willingness to use force to stop it. It was easier to pretend it was a minor problem than to try to eradicate questionable trading practices which would require costly manpower and equipment, both of which were in short supply in deep space.

The players' ships had the necessary permits to dock with the space station. Designated areas had been programmed for the specific needs of each alien species. From there, the players would proceed through specially designed tunnels connected to alcoves where they would be able to view the goods, in this case the prisoners. The Rodenegad in charge would bring them to a central platform visible from all the alcoves. The trade offered open bidding to all the players and only a few special cases were handled separately.

The night before the day of the trading, Maashi lay awake beside Chari.

"I don't have a good feeling about this whole charade," Maashi said. "I can't shake the idea something will go wrong." He sat up, rested his hands on his thighs, and spread his fingers. "Why does Dennyvan think the Rodenegad will hand over two Black and Silver Guards to a Woo-Odong without anything in exchange?"

Chari sat beside Maashi, one arm resting over his shoulders. With his other hand, he caressed Maashi's neck and let his fingers linger on Maashi's quatay, the erogenous zone on his upper chest. "I heard Dennyvan say the Rodenegad owe an important debt to Woo-Olong-Ti. Apparently, the guards represent only part of the payment." He had found one of the ever-present twigs he loved to chew inside a pocket of his shirt and held it between his teeth. The twig moved up and down with his lips. He inhaled deeply. "We can only hope this information is accurate."

"What if they demand a different trade? What if all that training was a façade to make me a willing participant but their real plan was to exchange me for the two guards?" Maashi shook his head and stared at the floor with disgust.

Chari pulled his twig out. "The thought has crossed my mind" he said, "but it's highly improbable. Dennyvan and his accomplices could never return to Chitina. Charges of treason would be brought against them, and if they tried to escape justice, they would be hunted without mercy."

"I don't think I could survive being a prisoner again."

Chari stared deep into the Sheffrou's eyes and kissed his neck. "I would never let that happen."

Maashi rested his head on his Chowli's shoulder. Overcome by emotion, he held Chari tightly.

Chari took Maashi's face in his hands. "I will be at your side the whole time as your servant, Supreme Master Woo-Olong-Ti." He kissed and hugged him. "Rest, Maashi. Meditate. Clear your mind."

Maashi released him and leaned back on the couch. He closed his eyes. Meditation was a common practice among Chamranlinas to soothe and calm their souls. But now, so many details had to fit perfectly together to obtain the anticipated results. He struggled to find the inner peace needed to meditate. After a moment, he finally cleared his mind. However, clarity of thought facilitated the telepathic process. Within seconds, an anguished cry reached deep within him. He leapt off the couch and stood as if struck by lightning. "A cry for help. It's Ashani. He's close."

Chari whispered, "He must be a prisoner, brought over for the trade. Do not respond to him. I overheard the guards saying the Rodenegad possess devices which can detect telepathic communications if they are powerful enough. This call for help could've been intercepted. It could even be a fake, a ploy to reveal the presence of Sheffrous in the area by the Rodenegad or the Krakoran. Even with the ship cloaked to block detection of our identity, you could become a target. You must remain silent."

Maashi paced the room no bigger than a water room on Chitina, his heart drumming in his abdomen, his senses rendered more acute than usual. His friend was calling. He clenched his fists. Not being able to respond was agonizing.

He only had a vague recollection of his own kidnapping a sequence and a half ago. Numb with pain and anguish at the time, his memory of the ordeal was fragmented. All he remembered was the presence of an helicoidal structure, a hundred fifty feet high with a platform at the top where he stood dazed and confused in front of a group of Krakoran. Then his mind drew a blank.

The trade would happen in just a few hours. *What could he do?* There wasn't any guarantee they would be in Ashani's proximity again. This might be the only opportunity to save him. He had to warn the guards, even Dennyvan. Still treated as a prisoner, it was impossible to reach him now, but he had to inform him of Ashani's presence before the impersonation. He clenched and unclenched his fists.

"Maashi, you should get some rest," said Chari in a soothing voice.

Maashi came to an abrupt stop. He shuddered. He sensed another familiar presence. One he couldn't identify with certainty. Someone else was calling him. *Who could it be?*

Chapter 9

The hours dragged on. Maashi waited. It seemed the night would never end. The next morning, two guards brought a frustrated Maashi and Chari to the Leader's receiving room to be prepped for his performance.

Rattled by what he had sensed the previous evening, Maashi made the guards scramble to keep up with his rapid stride. He cleared the doorway and snapped at Kotian, who had barely opened his makeup kit, "I need to see Dennyvan immediately. It is a matter of grave importance."

Irritated, Kotian said, "You will see him only after you're fully dressed and in your makeup. Do not try my patience this morning, Sheffrou."

Maashi had no choice. He stood in stony silence while Kotian attended to him.

Thick, black makeup on his eyelids and upper cheeks gave Maashi a grave, foreboding look. The eyes would be the only visible part of his body apart from the feet. Veil after veil of opaque brown material hid his figure from head to toe. A slim undergarment, the traditional chemcha worn by all Pure Colors, followed by a second thicker version which would ensure that his large genitals were concealed and protected, and his figure would remain asexual.

Kotian swore under his breath when he realized Maashi's hands were longer than the sleeves and partially visible.

"Damn you, Sheffrou," he snarled. "This is unbelievable. Don't tell me you've grown in the last two weeks."

Maashi could not care less about the changes his body was undergoing. His impatience intensified. He needed to speak to Dennyvan before the trade. He had to know if Ashani was on the list of prisoners. His hands and feet twitched as he fought the urge to push the officious pink and yellow underling aside and demand answers.

Kotian lost it. "Stop moving, Sheffrou or I will have you tazed. Do you understand?"

Maashi raised his voice. "*You* don't understand! Sheffrou Ashani may be present and up for trade. We need to retrieve him. Dennyvan must be told. I need to talk to him now."

Kotian shook his head. "I don't know the Leader's whereabouts and I'm not in charge of sending messages. I've had just about enough of your insubordination." Kotian signaled a guard.

Maashi jolted from his spot and almost fell backward from the electrical discharge. Disoriented by the intense stinging pain, he stood quiet for a few minutes.

"Move again, I'll have the guard shock you once more."

Chari, standing by his side, under close supervision by two stern-faced guards, sent, *"Maashi, don't worry. I have a good rapport with one of the guards. I'll inform him about Ashani and make sure Dennyvan knows."*

Furious but powerless, Maashi nodded. Anger simmered in his mind. Once this rescue was completed, he would refuse to be Dennyvan's puppet.

Upon his request, Kotian's assistant searched in the extensive database they had gathered on the Woo-Odong to get more detailed pictures of their upper limbs. He confirmed the aliens kept their hands/claws hidden with black gloves. With the help of a replicator, Kotian designed a pair for Maashi that looked convincing.

Maashi's feet were covered by a rubbery imitation of Woo-Odong feet: gnarled, yellowish toes with sharp, black talons. The conspicuous feet completed the outfit and Kotian was proud of their effect. He whispered under his breath, "No one will dare question this Woo-Odong's identity after glancing at the feet."

Chari had paid attention to the rumors circulating on the ship. The organizers of the trade sent a communication to inform them of enhanced scrutiny of the players by the space station authorities following rumors of wrongdoing and allegations of irregularities by the Rodenegad. It seemed they hadn't paid the docking fees for all the incoming ships. Also, a recent ruling stated that, contrary to the usual routine, weapons were not allowed inside the station. The guards set to accompany Maashi disguised as Woo-Olong-Ti had to leave them on the ship.

Chari, a silent observer ignored by the guards, overheard Dennyvan's roar when he was informed of the new weapons rule. He later told Maashi that Dennyvan's backup plan if the trade didn't work was to storm the place where the prisoners were held and seize the captive Black Guards.

"A plan fraught with risk," was Maashi's comment.

"Damn the Rodenegad," Dennyvan had yelled, "we'll need to be vigilant and leave as soon as our two guards are in our possession."

One of Dennyvan's spies reproduced a copy of the details of the merchandise available for trading. The prisoners were intermingled among an eclectic choice of goods: new technology gadgets, spaceship components, rare plant seeds and grain, etc. Dennyvan's spy confirmed the two guards were indeed prisoners of the Rodenegad and listed for trading.

Finally, under Kotian's wary eye, Maashi and Chari were escorted to the entrance of a tunnel that led to the official alcove prepared for Woo-Olong-Ti's party. Maashi advanced, his dark robes against the bright background decreasing his chances of detection. His only role was to take a hop forward and signal by raising one arm above his waist when the time came to claim the guards.

Each alcove was designed as an independent entity separate from the others. Their occupants were hidden by a burgundy awning at the entrance and curtains of the same color on each side. Only the Rodenegad directing the trade could see each of the players. The bids were accessible through a virtual screen visible on the wall of each alcove.

The day before, Maashi who had never seen a Rodenegad, was briefed by Dennyvan. "Those aliens are short, stocky," he said. "Their bodies are always protected by a formidable armor resistant to standard short and mid-range weapons. The head is covered by a mask, unique to each individual, made of hardwood sanded to a smooth finish. Rodenegad can swivel their heads more than two hundred forty degrees giving them an unsurpassed range of vision. Incredibly cunning and suspicious, they can easily spot deception."

Maashi had listened and sighed. His performance had to be flawless. Any hint that his identity was false could lead to disaster.

As they were ready to leave the ship, Chari discreetly messaged Maashi. *"Dennyvan said to raise your arm a second time if you see Sheffrou Ashani."*

Maashi blinked to signal he understood.

Chari was instructed to stand to the right and one step behind Maashi. He wore a purple shirt and pants, a sign he was a Woo-Odong slave. Three more guards, a display of Woo-Olong-Ti's rank, walked ten feet behind them wearing all-brown clothing.

The delegation proceeded at a slow pace along the tunnel. Maashi stopped abruptly midway through when he saw the hexagonal platform surrounded by a series of alcoves. Memories of standing on a similar platform in front of Krakoran hunters flooded his mind. His ordeal had started when he was kidnapped a sequence and a half ago and sold to become the plaything of the Master Hunter. He shuddered. Subjected to the indignity of being sexually stimulated by a repulsive creature under the master's command, he had suffered in silence and prayed to the Souls of his Ancestors for strength until his rescue months later.

Stunned by the sight, he held his breath. His heart thumped in his abdomen.

Chari sent, *"Think of Ashani. He needs you to be strong."*

Maashi blinked and inhaled, forcing the air deep in his lungs. He was still a prisoner but this time with an honorable purpose. He hopped to his assigned place in the alcove.

With his senses on alert, Maashi watched the proceedings behind the semi-transparent veils covering his face. He fought the anxiety awakened by being forced to relive moments of his own capture. Thankfully, after months of treatment by Tousanou Chendor, disturbing memories of the ordeal no longer sent him into a state of panic.

His alcove was located close to the platform where the merchandise was exhibited. He therefore had a clear view of the stage. This created a problem unforeseen by Dennyvan's group. The prisoners stood very close to Maashi, and some aliens could potentially identify him as Chamranlina even with the disguise. Also, his Sheffrou identity was a problem. His appearance was well concealed but what about his holoma? If anything stimulated his senses, the pungent fragrance would give him away. All he could do was to stand as still as stone to minimize the risk of discovery.

One after the other, the prisoners paraded on the platform. Different humanoid species advanced alone or in pairs. Some shuffled or stumbled. Maashi suspected the Rodenegad drugged them to keep them subdued. They stood under the harsh light for a few minutes then the stocky Rodenegad in charge of the proceedings hushed them away.

So much suffering. So much misery. Captured in space or kidnapped from their home world, these poor innocent beings were hauled, pushed, and prodded without mercy.

How could this trafficking be tolerated? Why wasn't something done?

Maashi had never heard of or seen some species. A few were transported in clear iridescent bubbles probably because of their need for a special gaseous mix. He saw some Loloyan, a kind of humanoid he knew well. Chamranlinas had rescued and adopted a few after many had perished following a long drought on their planet.

The trade continued for hours. Maashi got restless. He couldn't help but fidget.

Chari sent him a telepathic warning. *"Don't move or you will draw suspicion. Be still."*

"I'm trying. This is intolerable. I can't watch this anymore."

"Maashi, focus on the prisoners. This can't last forever."

Another hour passed with new arrivals, individuals recently captured, recognizable by their hollow stares and aggressive posture. Maashi's hopes of seeing the two guards and Ashani were fading. He let out a long, silent sigh.

The next group came in slowly, as if reluctant to come forward. They were the two guards they were looking for. The first one had a slight limp but otherwise appeared in good health. The second one appeared weak, malnourished. He dragged his feet, eyes glued to the floor. To both Maashi and Chari's surprise, a third Chami followed. Slumped, barely able to stand, and wearing torn rags, he raised his head to scan the players in the alcoves. He paused to look at the Woo-Odong a mere fifteen feet away, blinked, then hung his head down.

In the brief instant when his head was raised, Maashi recognized Ashani. He was elated to see his friend had beat the odds. Maashi knew how much strength, resilience, and determination it took to survive under the challenging physical and mental stress of captivity. His heart overflowed with joy at the sight of him, and, disregarding instructions, he sent him a simple thought. *"We are here."*

Ashani raised his head a second time, scanned every alcove but couldn't pinpoint where the message originated from. His facial expression changed. His eyes widened. The Rodenegad in charge was quick to notice.

Maashi hopped forward and raised his right arm just a few inches above the waist as he had been trained to do. He stood still, his right foot sticking out from under his robes.

The Rodenegad hesitated.

Maashi waited, held his breath.

Something was amiss. The prisoners should already be ushered in his direction. Maashi improvised and screeched a high-pitched cry to indicate Woo-Olong-Ti's displeasure.

The Rodenegad quickly responded. With the help of a translating device on his wrist, he communicated in a language agreed upon by the players. "Our apologies, Supreme Master Woo-Olong-Ti. We are in your debt." But instead of sending the prisoners over, the Rodenegad stepped closer to the alcove where Maashi was standing. His head pointed to Maashi's feet.

Maashi assumed they were the problem. Chari must have noticed since he immediately moved in front of Maashi and partially shielded him from view.

The Rodenegad bowed and said, "It's a pleasure to see your foot has healed, Supreme Master. Your hopping is impeccable."

Maashi understood the Rodenegad expected him to hop again. He was holding out for something. Maashi surmised a Supreme Master would pay no mind to a Rodenegad's wishes. Instead, Maashi assumed the posture favored by Woo-Olong-Ti; the one he had practiced over and over with Kotian. With his head held high and his eyes semi-closed, he stared down and oozed power and superiority.

The Rodenegad had to choose between relinquishing the prisoners or facing the wrath of a displeased player. He bowed to Woo-Olong-Ti. The three prisoners were secured and transferred one by one to Maashi's delegation.

Maashi and Chari blinked in relief.

Dennyvan had clearly indicated that once the trade was completed, they were to depart immediately.

Chari whispered, "We should leave now."

Maashi debated what he should do. His first reaction was to leave immediately and run back to the ship to hug Ashani, but he couldn't shake a deep unease.

A moment later, a forlorn Ashani dragged his tired body a few feet away from him. He raised his head and stared at the figure of Woo-Olong-Ti. His face beamed. Maashi sent him a quick message. *"Look away."*

Ashani turned his head abruptly. The Rodenegad, ever watchful and suspicious, slowly made his way to the alcove in his shuffling gait.

Chari moved closer to Maashi. *"Let's hurry out."* Maashi turned and hopped away as fast as he could but, in his haste to leave, almost tripped.

The Rodenegad paused. His faceless head stared in Maashi's direction. His form made a wheezing sound from deep within. His head pivoted as he gave his attention to the next group on display. He shuffled back towards the platform.

The parade of prisoners resumed.

The next group were two Loloyan who were claimed by a species of aliens who frequently adopted them. Maashi was relieved to see they would be treated fairly.

In the tunnel, Chari said under his breath, "That was close."

Maashi nodded but intense nausea filled his gut. The urge to look back overwhelmed him.

The last group marched in. One which had just been added to the trade.

"Those are humans recently captured," one of the guards whispered as they progressed in the tunnel.

Maashi's breath caught. "Humans?" He glanced in the direction of the platform. There were three humans: two males followed by a female.

He recoiled in horror. *How could this be?* Anger rose in him like a huge dark wave. With his senses on high alert, he filled his lungs and fisted his hands ready for attack.

Chapter 10

Chari caught Maashi by the waist and pushed him forward so hard, Maashi stumbled and almost fell. They charged ahead and crossed the threshold of the large door to the ship. Once inside, they were protected against any aggressive move by the Rodenegad.

Maashi screamed, "I must go back!"

Red and green lights flashed on each side of the massive door connecting the room to the tunnel. An intermittent buzzing alarm resonated to indicate the connection to the space station would be severed in less than ten minutes. Another door opened and Dennyvan leaped into the room.

"Computer," he said raising his voice, "prepare the ship for travel to the coordinates already logged in." Turning to Maashi, he yelled, "What is wrong with you, Sheffrou? Why are you screaming? We have your friend. We have the two guards we wanted. We're leaving now."

"No. No. No," said Maashi struggling to get away from Chari's grasp. "My Chimitanga is out there. We can't leave her."

One of the guards said, "We must leave. Staying any longer is too risky."

"You heard him," said Dennyvan. "We can't take any more risk. We must go now."

"My Chimitanga is out there. She is part of the next group to be traded. We must take her with us." Maashi hugged a speechless Ashani and rushed to the door to the tunnel. "I'm going back."

"Are you sure it's her?" said Chari.

"Yes. We must go. Quickly."

Dennyvan roared. "Damn Sheffrous, I hope I won't regret this," he said, shooting an evil stare at the scrawny Ashani who stood just a few feet away. He spoke to the console. "Computer, delay departure. Hold on to coordinates and readiness state." He pounded his fist in his left hand.

With one nod to the guards, he said, "Leave the rescued ones here and follow them." They rushed to accompany Maashi and Chari who had stepped back in the tunnel.

The delegation advanced once more toward the alcove. This time, Maashi missed a step every few hops. They assumed their positions. On the platform, the Rodenegad in charge of the trade stood, a mere ten feet away, facing the last group. He swiveled his head in their direction, made some strange rumbling sound, then turned his head back toward the new group of prisoners.

No one had claimed them.

The group consisted of three humans: two males, slender and pale skinned, looking unfit for hard labor and one small female who could barely stand on her two feet. She finally collapsed on the platform and stared around with wide, hollow eyes. These aliens were unfamiliar to the players who hesitated to strike a bargain. Hushed sounds could be heard coming from the other alcoves.

The Rodenegad in charge started pacing the length of the platform and his rumblings got louder.

Maashi sent a message to Chari. *"Tell the Rodenegad the Supreme Master can take the two males off his hands if nobody wants them."* Maashi knew that if he showed any interest in the female, the Rodenegad would become suspicious. The Woo-Odong didn't favor females.

Chari shot Maashi a questioning glance. Maashi straightened his posture and lowered his eyes to show contempt.

Chari complied. He stepped forward and said, "Rodenegad, Supreme Master Woo-Olong-Ti is pleased with your concern about his health. The Supreme Master is prepared to save you the cost of transporting the two males back. He can take them to express his gratitude for a mutually satisfactory trading arrangement."

The Rodenegad bowed. "I am flattered by the Supreme Master's concern." He shuffled closer to the female and added, "Perhaps you can also take this one if nobody wants her." Grabbing the female by one of his powerful arms, he lifted her up against his chest. She shrieked and struggled like a small creature caught in a deadly trap. She was no match for the Rodenegad.

Maashi inhaled a long breath. His amber eyes darkened with anger and were reduced to black slits.

Chari, standing close, noticed. *"Careful."*

Maashi didn't respond to the offer right away. He had to show disdain for the female. Suppressing the urge to jump on the platform and rip Tamara out of the Rodenegad's arms, he stood, simmering with rage but still and cold as a boulder on the outside. After a moment, he let his hands drop to his sides. Woo-Olong-Ti would never want a female.

Chari's face and neck paled.

The Rodenegad slowly pivoted his head away to check the other alcoves for any sign of interest.

For a few tense minutes, nothing happened. Then, a loud detonation echoed throughout the trading arena.

Chapter 11

A siren blared so loud everyone covered their ears. Red and yellow warning lights flooded the arena. Lighting in the alcoves and in the dome above the platform blinked on and off. A pungent smell made everybody gag. Puffs of gray smoke appeared. A cacophony of screams, grunts, and growls filled the air.

Stunned, Maashi watched as the Rodenegad's arms released Tamara and her limp body dropped hard on the floor. The alien then collapsed on the platform, his head gone, blown off by some alien weapon. Sticky green mucous oozed from its neck and sizzled, burning anything it met. Bits and pieces of bright yellow twirly pieces of brain material floated in the large room and dropped haphazardly everywhere like hundreds of ribbons at a celebration.

The three Black and Silver Guards at Maashi's side were quick to react. They ran to the platform to recuperate the two human males. Tamara was sprawled on her side at the dead Rodenegad's feet. Maashi hopped to the edge of the alcove. Fear gripped his insides when he realized Tamara lay helpless, terribly close to the oozing Rodenegad's neck. The platform was slowly retreating away from the alcove and easing its way down. He had to retrieve her but jumping with his prosthetic feet was out of the question. He would never make it.

"Chari!" he yelled.

"Stay here. I'll get her." Chari jumped on the moving platform and reached the little female in two strides. He swooped her off the floor and in one effortless leap was back on the platform.

One of the guards cried out, "We need to go back now! The space station security will be here any second."

As if on cue, the platform started sinking faster. Each one of the alcoves retreated further from the central area. Two of the guards jumped back on the floor of the alcove beside Maashi each one holding a human male. The third guard jumped behind them right as the platform jerked and dropped down further away. He missed his jump and caught the edge of the floor of the alcove. He held on for a second then his hands slipped. Just as he lost his grip, two arms firmly grabbed him and pulled him back up. Eyes wide, he nodded to Maashi.

The whole group rushed along the tunnel back to the ship with Maashi hopping along as fast as he could. Smoke started to fill the tunnel. A moment later, they reached the door and leaped across the threshold. To their surprise, a bubble containing a long translucent alien burst open and the alien swished inside the ship. The thick panels slid and closed. The eight locks activated and secured the door.

Dennyvan was standing there waiting for them. He yelled, "Everyone accounted for?"

"Everyone and then some," answered one of the guards as he noticed the strange translucent creature floating near the ceiling.

"Security," said Dennyvan, "establish a forcefield around the floating alien creature on the ceiling in this room."

Dennyvan then issued his orders for departure. "Computer, proceed to the Korr Nebula to the designated coordinates." He pressed on a bracelet on his right wrist and said, "All hands, brace for a rapid engine burst."

Chairs especially designed to hold and protect the occupants were released from the walls throughout the long oval section. Chari handed Tamara to Maashi and made sure he was strapped then sat down on a chair beside him. The guards buckled up the two humans.

Dennyvan and Redden sat side by side.

Blood oozed from Tamara's ears. Maashi wanted to hold her head, but his movements were restricted by the veils. He tore at them in frustration.

"It's all right Maashi," said Chari. He put a reassuring arm on his wrist. "Her breathing is regular. Her color is good."

Maashi, overwhelmed by worry and anguish, couldn't speak. He shook his head sideways in agreement. He held Tamara tenderly hoping she wasn't seriously harmed. He inhaled deeply a few times and sent waves of healing thoughts to her.

Powered by two fusion reactors, Chamranlina ships were designed for rapid launch and extreme acceleration. It took just a few seconds to attain the desired velocity. The gravity inside the ship climbed to a maximum of 3G to prevent discomfort and injury to the occupants. It quickly came back down to 1G and the feeling of being compressed stopped. The mild vibrations slowly dissipated. Everyone took a long breath and exhaled.

Maashi possessed the ability to feel for anomalies deep inside the body. He anxiously palpated Tamara's head with long fingers and decided she had no serious brain swelling or hemorrhage. Reassured by his findings, he nodded to Chari.

Concern about their safety dominated Maashi's mind. News traveled fast through the interstellar media sites and word of the Rodenegad's murder would spread like wildfire. Since the demise of the Rodenegad happened right as the Woo-Odong were concluding the last transaction, they would be among the suspects. His associates would pursue and intercept any ship they thought carried the killer.

Without wasting a second, Maashi questioned Dennyvan, "When will we be out of reach? Will we be safe in the Korr Nebula?"

"Leave that to me, Sheffrou," said Dennyvan. "Our newer needle ships like this one are made of carbon-based materials and polymer matrix. They are designed for extreme speed and stealth. They absorb a wide range of waves across the bandwidth, including electromagnetic and microwaves, providing unequalled protection. We should avoid detection by the Rodenegad but also the Krakoran. I'm not concerned about the space station security. It will take a while before they're able to launch a pursuit. As for the other players, they will scatter like dust in the wind."

The guard saved by Maashi, called Krawl, said, "We should start changing the needle's specs back to Chamranlina characteristics."

"I agree," said Dennyvan, "but don't complete the process until we are in the nebula." Glancing at Maashi, he added, "The Korr Nebula, with its dense clouds of dark matter, will provide satisfactory protection if we avoid sending gamma waves and intense telepathic waves. With two Sheffrous on board, the chance of detection is significantly increased so you and Ashani must be kept separated. Any encounter between you to will be like a beacon in the night sky."

Maashi said, "I must see him once at least."

"Listen to me, Sheffrou," said Dennyvan. "You can't see Ashani and you will refrain from telepathic communication. You will be confined in your quarters in the mid-ship section where the structure has been reinforced with thermoplastics. Your Chowli and your Chimitanga can stay with you. Your Chowli will be allowed to move freely aboard the ship and tend to the two human males."

"You don't understand," said Maashi.

Dennyvan raised his voice. "If you defy my orders, I'll put you in the brig under sedation. We haven't gone through this whole expedition to be detected because you want to have an Encounter with Ashani. Do you understand me?"

"I'm not a child or a fool, Dennyvan," said Maashi. "I won't do anything to put the ship or the crew in jeopardy. Just let me have a video conversation with him once we are safe in the nebula."

Dennyvan tilted his head and grumbled. After a moment, he said, "Only once."

"Thank you," said Maashi.

"What do we do with the two human males?" asked Krawl.

Chari answered. "They're still unconscious from the weapon blast and the acceleration. When they regain consciousness, they will need to eat and rest. I suggest warm clothes and a lot of food. Put them together in the same quarters. I'll check on them when they wake up."

Dennyvan nodded. "I agree. Let's keep them together."

The other guards carried the unconscious humans out.

"What do you think happened to that Rodenegad?" Dennyvan asked Krawl. "No weapons were allowed in the arena."

"When we retrieved the males," said Krawl, "I saw a Serono 95 on the floor a few feet away from him."

Dennyvan grunted. "A Serono 95? These weapons are extremely powerful and have been banned for sequences. How did it get there?"

"I believe the Rodenegad carried the weapon in his armor," said Krawl. "I don't know if anyone took it, or if he pulled it out himself."

"Who shot him then?" said Chari.

"The only ones close to him were the humans," said Krawl. "Could one of them have shot him?"

Chari said, "The two males were further away. The only individual close was Tamara."

"Who?" said Dennyvan.

"Sheffrou Maashi's Chimitanga," said Chari.

All eyes shifted to the human female.

Maashi rose still holding his precious Tamara. She seemed so fragile. A wonderfully disturbing longing filled his heart. "I'll go to my quarters now. I need to get out of these veils and remove my makeup before she wakes."

Dennyvan stepped to Maashi's side. "You performed well today," he said. "How is she?"

"She is stable," Maashi said in a low voice. "We will know more when she wakes up."

"In your opinion," said Dennyvan, "are these humans capable of shooting with the intention to kill?"

Maashi caressed Tamara's cheek with his long fingers. "She once told me to never underestimate humans. That they can kill. They appear weak and vulnerable, but their will to survive is very strong."

"I see," said Dennyvan. He told Krawl. "Keep close watch on all of them."

"Understood," said Krawl. He stood and pointed to the ceiling. "What about this other alien?"

They all looked up at a translucent creature, five feet long and flat as a board. Small blue dots formed a line along the middle and moved this way and that like so many eyes. The creature oscillated in mid-air staying close to the ceiling.

They watched in awe as the creature became so clear it was almost invisible.

Maashi said, "It's reacting to us. I believe it's scared."

Dennyvan said, "Krawl, assess the database to make sure it's harmless and can survive in our environment. In the meantime, keep it under observation in this room. Make sure the forcefield is strong enough to restrain it."

Maashi took a few steps toward the door to the hallway and the creature followed. He came back in the middle of the room and the creature slowly floated back to its original position.

"It's either you, Sheffrou," said Dennyvan, "or your Chim-itanga, but the creature is following. I think you'll have an extra guest in your quarters. Krawl, make sure the creature's forcefield follows all the way to their quarters."

"Yes, sir," said Krawl who grinned. "We should give it a name, don't you think?"

Chari clicked his disapproval. "Let's wait for the human female to wake up. Maybe she knows more about this creature."

"Let's go, then," said Maashi. "I'm ready to change my clothing and especially to get rid of those talons."

Chapter 12

Pangs of hunger woke Tamara. She stretched her bruised limbs and groaned. The events from the previous day flashed in her head: the huge hexagonal platform, the alcoves on the surrounding walls where mysterious aliens hid behind dark red awnings. Her blood froze at the awful realization that she had been for sale like an animal at a farm auction.

It all started that morning when the door of her cell opened, and she stepped out into the corridor. An interlocking mechanism on the floor locked in position and moved her forward like goods on a conveyer. Each group of prisoners was transported on parallel conveyers to the main platform.

The two men with whom she had traveled, also prisoners like her, stood on another conveyer a mere ten feet away from her. Lieutenant Yoon looked exhausted with grayish skin and deep pockets under his eyes. His usually tidy hair hung in a loose knot. Patel's shirt was torn and missing one sleeve. His thick eyebrows were knotted together, and his bloodshot eyes indicated that he hadn't slept well for days. They both stood hunched over in obvious discomfort. The gravity in the arena was much greater than on their own ship; not a problem for her but obviously difficult for them to bear.

The lieutenant took a few labored steps forward and abruptly backtracked when a laser beam shot out and burned the floor inches in front of his foot. He growled and fisted his hands. The conveyer continued to progress forward and brought them to a raised platform surrounded by three levels of alcoves. Raising his head to inspect the surroundings, the lieutenant spotted Tamara.

She waved and called out. "Are you two all right? Are you hurt?"

"We're unharmed," said the lieutenant. "How about you?"

"I'm fine. Do you know why they brought us here?"

Patel answered back, "We received a transmission from the main ship about kidnappings in the sector we were crossing. I think they attacked us and then kept us alive for trafficking purposes. I think this is an auction of some kind and the buyers are hiding in those alcoves."

Tamara looked up and tried to get a glimpse of the buyers, but the burgundy awnings and the low lighting inside concealed their identity. Despair engulfed her. She couldn't believe that they would be sold like livestock. For what purpose? To be eaten? To live a life as a slave or worse? She shuddered. Maashi had explained to her a long while ago that Krakoran kidnapped Sheffrous to keep them as sex slaves. He was sold in a scenario not very different from this one.

Now she sat completely awake in a strange gray room with a low ceiling. She opened her eyes wide. *Did some alien buy her?*

Fear enveloped her. Her limbs trembled. *Where was she now?* She blinked.

Shadows filled the poorly lit room. On the far wall, the now-familiar long translucent creature that shared her cell after she was abducted was immobile, flattened in the corner. *Was it sold with her?* She watched it closely. *Odd. It usually floated about quite freely. Something must have spooked it.*

The smell of warm caramel tickled her nostrils. What would she not give to taste the real thing right now....

Tamara abruptly sat up on her knees. Warm caramel.

Maashi? His body fragrance the Chamis called holoma was unmistakable. What were the odds the alien who bought her smelled like Maashi? Or was Maashi also a captive...in the same room?

She froze. Slowly turning her head from side to side, she focused her gaze on a shape to the right. Someone sat just a few feet away, his bare chest a tangle of muscles, long legs stretched out in front. A little behind the figure, dark robes lay discarded in a loose pile. Tamara gulped her saliva. She had seen an alien wearing those same robes standing close to the edge of the alcove closest to her. An uneasy weight settled in the pit of her stomach. She stared at the bare-chested figure, heart pounding. *Who was he? Was he the alien who bought her?*

He tilted his head sideways. "Good morning, Tamara."

How did he know her name? The musical voice sounded so familiar. Impossible! No. This alien couldn't be Maashi.

She had been kidnapped, held prisoner, and sold. She wasn't going to blindly trust an alien impersonating Maashi.

Keeping her body rigid, she said, "Who are you?"

His eyes, underlined with black and covered with black eyelids, widened. "It is I, Maashi." He stretched one arm out as if to get hold of her.

She shrieked. "Stay away from me." She retreated away from him as fast and as far as she could. She scanned the room for a weapon, anything to fight back if he dared to grab her. She eyed the door. Was it locked? She could make an escape with a mad dash.

"I understand your confusion but there's no need to be alarmed, Tamara." He touched his eyelids. "I apologize. I tried to remove the makeup and even rubbed my skin raw but it's quite impossible to do so." He tilted his head sideways. "Don't you recognize me?"

Tamara hesitated. The voice sounded like Maashi, but this guy wasn't him. First, Maashi had never been very muscular. He was the long and lean type. This alien was all muscles. As her best friend Jess on Earth would say, ripped.

Second, Maashi would never be allowed to travel in space: too dangerous for Sheffrous. They attracted the Krakoran like magnets. He had told her this himself. This one was surely an imposter, unless... he was also a prisoner.

The figure appeared to hesitate. "Computer," he said, "increase light by 50%."

The lights in the room increased to a soft glow.

Tamara's mouth went dry. She could see the striking quatay on his torso and shoulders, the well-developed breasts of a Chami, his long, sculpted limbs, and the familiar, intricate design of the gold bracelet on his right wrist.

"Is it really you?" she whispered. Her words caught in her throat. Her vision blurred from tears that appeared out of nowhere.

"Yes, Chumpi." He bent forward and said simply, "Come."

"Maashi?" She sprang ahead and stopped inches from him. She touched his muscular upper arm with the tip of her fingers, then his broad chest. She caressed his skin as smooth as kid gloves and examined the quatay covering his shoulders and upper back like a wide cape.

His expression softened. The amber of his pupils acquired a rich, warm glow.

She gazed at him with awe. *It was him, but different. What happened?*

"You've changed. You're not the same."

Maashi's lips parted open as if to say something, but he didn't say a word. He blinked and swallowed. She could see him struggling, eyes filling with tears.

She flung both arms around his neck and hugged him. "Maashi," she breathed in his neck, "I missed you so much."

He embraced her and soft moans escaped his lips as tears rolled down his cheeks.

"Forgive me, little one," he said with a soft, rich baritone voice. "I have attained maturity, and it's unacceptable to cry like this but the joy of holding you is overwhelming." Encircling her with his formidable arms, he kissed her temples, touched her cheeks with inquisitive fingers, kissed her jawline, licked her tears. In a voice choking with emotion, he said, "I missed you so. My heart was broken. Not a day passed without my mind reaching out to you."

"Maashi," she cried. She held on to him, pressing her cheek against his.

After a moment, she quieted down and rested her head on his shoulder.

"When I left," said Tamara, "days went by and I started to think that our time together, the feelings I had for you, the feelings I thought you had for me were something I had imagined. How could a powerful Sheffrou, cherished by many lovers, fall in love with someone like me, a woman from Earth, so different from his own kind?"

Maashi tilted his head to one side to acknowledge her words. He handed her a piece of tissue, the size of a handkerchief, to wipe her face.

"The part of my brain that involved logic," said Tamara, "couldn't believe what my heart was telling me. All I know is I was sad all the time and cried a lot."

"I'm sorry you suffered." His eyes changed color to a pale gray, like storm clouds filled with rain.

"There was nothing to look forward to anymore," she continued. "My life had reached a dead end. Depressing thoughts filled my days. Every night, I wished I was back." She wiped her face. "I was cranky and angry. I yelled continually at the two men. They, on the other hand, didn't believe my story about how I got here. They thought I was crazy. They tried to put me on medication, but I refused and felt even more isolated."

Maashi kissed her palms and took her head in his hands. He said in a soothing voice, "You're safe now."

"Are you sure? Aren't we both prisoners?"

"No. Not at all. We are on one of our ships. How I got here is a complicated tale but don't worry, we are both safe."

He pushed away a few strands of her hair. With his long middle finger, he gently felt a prominent bruise on her forehead.

"I examined you yesterday and I see the swelling has improved. Is it still quite painful? Most other cuts and bruises are superficial and should heal quickly."

Tamara grumbled. "I feel like I've been run over by a truck. I'm not sure how I got this bump." She instinctively touched her forehead and felt a bump the size of a quarter.

"The Rodenegad in charge of the auction picked you up and suddenly dropped you. You fell with a hard thump on the floor of the platform."

"What happened to him? I can't remember anything. It's just a blur."

"He was shot in the head and collapsed."

"Wow. Who shot him?"

"We don't know. But, when it happened, the whole arena turned into chaos."

Tamara gritted her teeth. "He got what he deserved," she growled. "I have no pity for that creature. Someone who is involved in trafficking sentient beings should be hung by their balls." She fisted her hands.

Hearing her words, Maashi lifted his head and his brow darkened. "So much anger. This is unlike you." He searched in her eyes. "Tell me. If you could have shot him, would you have done so?"

Tamara considered his question. "I don't know. I hated the creature as much as I could hate someone. But shooting him? I'm a physician by training and killing him would go against all my principles." She paused, pushed back a wayward lock of hair. "I'm just relieved he's dead." Her expression changed. She lifted her eyebrows and asked, "What about the two men from the shuttle? Where are they now? Did you rescue them?"

"Yes, we did. They're safe in their quarters. Chari is keeping an eye on them."

"Chari? He's here also?"

Maashi dropped a kiss on a lone tear just below her eye. "It's a convoluted story. One best transmitted through kissing so, for now, it will have to wait. My mind is swirling with emotions, and I'm unable to keep my thoughts and desires under control, a manifestation of my new maturity." His expression softened. "In the meantime, you will feel better after a warm shower."

Tamara tensed.

I don't know what the future holds for us. I can't let my feelings take over like last time we were together.

She pulled away from him and said, "I'll go. Alone."

Maashi raised his head ever so lightly. "Did I do or say something to offend you?"

"No."

Maashi gazed in her eyes, blinked. "As you wish," he said.

Tamara got up and walked over to the shower. She glanced back to make sure he wasn't following.

If I let him, we'll wind up kissing and then one thing will lead to another.... Leaving him last time almost drove me mad with grief. I can't let that happen again no matter how awful it makes me feel.

Standing under the hot shower, she scrubbed her skin hard even though it stung. She needed to rinse off the lingering smell of the Rodenegad and forget Maashi's glorious warm caramel holoma. Sadness overcame her. Her tears mixed with the water and ran down her cheeks. After several minutes, the jittery feeling inside her subsided. If there was any way to go back with Maashi and live with him on Chitina, she would do so in a heartbeat. Unfortunately, because of the way her body reacted to their underground environment, causing constant coughing and severe pain in her joints, it was impossible to continue living there.

She had to stay strong and not let him get too close. Maashi was like a powerful drug. Just a little would never be enough and, once you tasted it, you couldn't stop wanting more.

Maashi shuddered as he watched her walk to the shower. She stepped lightly on the soft carpet. He suspected her feet still hurt from the cuts she had sustained during her captivity. The

Rodenegad didn't care about the comfort of their prisoners. Providing protection for extremities wasn't a priority.

Her curvy figure and full hips were a reminder of pleasurable Encounters they had shared not so long ago. Yet, it was like a lifetime ago. Saliva filled his mouth as desire surged in his body. He yearned to hold her naked against his flesh. The longing was almost irresistible. His loins felt weak, and his hard member pushed on his chemcha. He licked his lips, swallowed his saliva. *Did she not feel the same way he did? How could she dismiss their time together so easily?*

She had made the difficult decision to leave Chitina a few weeks ago. If she was planning to uphold her decision, he shouldn't interfere with her wishes....

When she was done with the shower, Tamara composed herself. She pressed the controls on the wall and put on the standard khaki shirt and pants worn by Chamis. She went back to the receiving room. Maashi was also dressed in khaki clothes with a short khaki sash. The furniture was rearranged and now two couches were set opposite each other, each equipped with a gray table in the shape of a C.

She settled on the long couch across from where Maashi sat.

He had ordered something to drink. "Would you like a glass of juice?"

"Yes, thank you."

She took the lumi, a tall, opaque glass, and sipped. His holoma lingered like perfume in the air around them.

Maashi was the one who broke the silence. "There is," he said, "the matter of the other creature that followed you when we came back on the ship. Can you tell me more about it?"

Tamara looked up at the creature who hovered without a sound in a corner of the room. "It was a prisoner like me and somehow, we got paired together. Well, at first, I was held in the same cell as the two men and there were two of these creatures." She lowered her head. Her face crumpled. She cleared her throat and said, "We woke up one morning and there was only one of them. That day, we had something extra to complement our meagre meal. A large piece of a dry, crunchy, flat bread." She paused. "But it wasn't bread. We realized after a few bites that it was the other creature they had toasted to a crisp." Tamara dabbed at her eyes with the small towel Maashi had given her earlier.

Anger flashed in Maashi's eyes. His chest heaved. "What unspeakable cruelty. To offer as nourishment a creature which shared the same cell as you, and in front of its companion, is unbelievable."

Tamara shook her head. "I was beside myself with grief."

The door to the hallway opened wide and Dennyvan barged in like an icy gust of wind.

He firmly planted his feet in front of Maashi and stared at the two. "I presume you have had the opportunity to reacquaint yourself with your Chimitanga," he said with a smirk on his face.

Tamara had never seen this one before. Dressed in a black uniform with a thick black and silver belt, thick-soled black boots, he reminded Tamara of a soldier ready for combat.

She watched as he sniffed the air like a beagle. His brow paled, indicating puzzlement. She couldn't hide a little smirk of her own. The Black and Silver had expected the quarters to be flooded with Maashi's fragrant holoma indicating they had been intimate, but the room held no evidence of such activity.

Dennyvan tilted his head and eyed Tamara. He added, "I hope she is worth the trouble."

She shot him a fiery stare. *How rude. Not impressed with the guy, whoever he is.*

Maashi stood and spoke. "My sincere thanks, Dennyvan. Retrieving Tamara was of the utmost importance."

"Umph," said Dennyvan. He tilted his head, opened, and closed his big hands as if waiting for something.

Tamara held back asking who he was. Maashi hadn't bothered to introduce him to her, a significant slight of protocol if this Chami represented the authority here.

Dennyvan's gaze shot upward and focused on the translucent creature hovering under the low ceiling. "What about this floating inconvenience? What do you suggest we do with this one?"

"It's very fragile and quite harmless," said Tamara. "I'll take responsibility for it."

Dennyvan roared with contempt. "You, little Fanella, can't even take care of yourself. You're more of a hindrance than anything else." His brow darkened. He sneered, "We can always use the creature to bargain with the Rodenegad if they catch up with us. We checked in the database, and I understand they eat them. Let me catch it."

Tamara bounced to her feet and stood squarely in front of Dennyvan. "How dare you say that? You're no better than the Rodenegad. You will not touch the creature."

"Move out of my way," Dennyvan took a step forward and Maashi inserted his long frame between the two, inches from Dennyvan's face.

"You heard Tamara," he said. "The creature is harmless." He tilted his head and his voice deepened. "When did we start getting involved in the trade of alien creatures? Chamranlinas are a proud people with a long history of tolerance and respect for other beings. We do not participate in this kind of trade. This isn't who we are. Trafficking of sentient beings is against the basic principles of our society."

With his body rigid and his black eyes thinning with anger, Dennyvan said, "Your principles were easily swayed when you were ready to recuperate your precious Ashani and those humans. We practically stole them from the Rodenegad. We had to run away to hide in the Korr Nebula like thieves. We didn't make any friends that day. We may have to pay for it later."

Maashi said under his breath, his voice filled with veiled threat. "The plan has always been to hide in the nebula. We don't need friends like those players."

The door opened and Chari stepped in. He took one look at Dennyvan and Maashi and said, "Back away from the Sheffrou."

"How dare you give me orders, Ghouli Ghouli?" Dennyvan growled. "You've been causing trouble ever since you boarded this needle."

Chari moved to Maashi's side and said, "Anything that concerns the Sheffrou," he paused a second and nodded to Tamara, "and his Chimitanga, concerns me. Anyone who threatens them will have to deal with me."

"I'll take care of him, Chari," said Maashi.

Ignoring Maashi's words, Dennyvan stated in a grating voice, "The guards will take care of you, CHOWLI. That title doesn't give you the right for insubordination. Twenty lashes should teach you to respect the authority." Dennyvan raised his arm to issue an order on the device on his wrist.

Maashi grabbed his arm. "That will be quite enough, Dennyvan."

The Leader roared and raised his other arm to strike.

A shrill, piercing cry exploded in the room. Its intensity increased until it became intolerable, and they all held their heads in pain. One by one, they collapsed on the floor.

Chapter 13

A while later, Tamara regained consciousness. Her eyes fluttered open. Sprawled face-down on the floor, she moved her head sideways. Her breathing, at first shallow and irregular, got stronger and she inhaled a long breath and filled her lungs.

Thoughts, scattered in her mind like pieces of broken glass, slowly merged back into a comprehensive bundle as Tamara fought to recreate the puzzle of the previous minutes. Her ears resonated with the sound of a thousand gongs. She tried to move her tongue but couldn't, her mouth was completely dry.

Somehow, she had fallen forward and instead of using her arms to break her fall, she had gripped her shirt. With her hands tightly fisted, she struggled to release her fingers. One by one, she mentally released and flexed them to regain proper motion. She used her arms to push on the floor and raise herself to the sitting position. But, as soon as she sat, vertigo took hold of her. The room spun round and round and turned upside down. She dropped to the floor and stayed completely immobile, the only way to avoid the intolerable feeling. Bile rose in her mouth as nausea overcame her. She swallowed the bitter secretion and stayed still.

She tried to remember what happened. Where was she? Who was with her? She tentatively rotated her body and made it to her side. From the corner of her eye, she saw movement. The thin, elongated creature was flying frantically about the room as if in a panic. Its iridescent mantle glowed in shades of pale blue and bright neon green. Puzzled, Tamara watched its erratic movements. Was it reacting to the sudden excruciating sound?

She scanned the room. Maashi was slumped on his stomach, his head resting on his arms. Pink blood trickled down from his ear. She gasped in alarm. All she thought was a possible brain injury.

His lips moved. He clicked something she couldn't hear.

"Maashi?" she called. "Maashi? Can you hear me?"

A soft grunt was his answer. With much effort, he rolled over on his back. He turned his head toward her and blinked. His brow was dark as ink. He whispered, "Tamara?"

The voice sounded as if it was spoken from far away.

"I'm here. I have vertigo. I can't move. How are you?"

"My concentration...is poor. I can't... My mind is not..." He stopped in mid-sentence and moaned.

"I see some blood coming out of your ear."

"Mm," he said. He pushed with his hands and turned to his side. He raised his upper body by increments and managed to sit. The blood from his ears had created a rivulet going down his neck. Touching it, he said with effort, "Strong high-pitched sound waves can damage the inner ear. Sometimes they even cause bleeding in the brain."

"My head feels like it was hit by a boulder," she said. "Do you know what caused that awful sound?"

"I don't."

"The floating creature appears to be panicked. It's zooming right and left across the room."

Maashi lifted his head and focused on the creature. "I see." He stretched his long limbs and soft grunts escaped his lips. "My body feels exhausted like I swam for days."

Chari and Dennyvan stirred. Chari sat up. He held his head in his hands and took a long breath in and out. "What was that sound?"

"I'm not sure," said Maashi. "I can't connect with the creature's mind. I'm unable to say if it had anything to do with the sound.'

Dennyvan grunted and attempted to get up but crashed back down. He held his wrist up and spoke to his device, "Redden, status report."

"A Rodenegad ship is pursuing us. We'll need to increase our current speed to reach the nebula before them."

"Do so," said Dennyvan.

Redden continued, "The computer has detected a high intensity soundwave in your part of the ship. It lasted 3 minutes and went from 172 decibels to 190. Are you all safe? Should I send the ship's physician?"

"Yes, send someone. We'll need an evaluation." Dennyvan quickly inspected the room and said, "Do you know where the sound originated from?"

"It manifested itself only in your area," said Redden. "We don't know what caused it."

Dennyvan raised his head and squinted. "Find all the information possible on the floating creature in the database to determine if it can produce such a sound wave. I'll contact you later." Dennyvan stood with difficulty and wobbled over to the couch. He lowered himself down.

He stared at Tamara and said under his breath, "Harmless creature." He glanced upward and followed its swift movements back and forth across the room. "It's behaving differently."

The creature stopped in the corner of the room farthest from them. It undulated and produced a clear musical sound almost like a harp playing. Everyone watched, fascinated.

Dennyvan said, "We'll need to isolate it in a bubble until we know for sure it had nothing to do with the sound."

The creature's undulations increased. Right then, small bubbles, no bigger than Tamara's thumb, popped out one by one from its tail until there was over a hundred of them. The bubbles clung to the underside of the mantle of the creature. When they stopped coming out, the creature resumed its usual calm floating about the room with the bubbles in tow.

"Amazing," said Tamara, "I think it just produced a ton of eggs."

"One hundred and twelve to be exact," said Chari. "Perhaps it made the sound before it laid its eggs."

"Humph," said Dennyvan. "A reproducing stowaway. One more problem to deal with." He finished his sentence and rubbed his temples.

"I can help with your headache," said Maashi who attempted to get on his feet. He managed to stand on the second try.

"Don't bother, Sheffrou," Dennyvan appeared to push him away by waving his arm but instead, he almost toppled over on the floor.

Maashi caught him just in time. He propped him up with big cushions and sat at his side. He rested his hand on the nape of Dennyvan's neck.

"Wait a few minutes and your pain will subside," said Maashi. "I can't make it disappear, but this should help."

Dennyvan opened his mouth to protest but submitted to the Sheffrou's touch, a sign his pain must have been unbearable. He closed his eyes and inhaled deeply a few times.

"This feels much better." Dennyvan raised his head and stared into the Sheffrou's eyes. "Thank you." With some difficulty, he rose and shuffled to the door. "I'll go and see what's happening with the Rodenegad ship." He shot one last look at the floating creature and left.

Hours passed. Maashi took a shower and came back looking refreshed. He picked up Tamara, keeping her body horizontal, and laid her on the couch. Chari left to find out more about the Rodenegad vessel and to check on Ashani and the two humans.

Exhausted, Tamara dozed on and off. Maashi sat on the opposite couch and reviewed color-coded messages on a virtual screen.

Too many emotions had competed for Tamara's attention in the last few hours. She fell into a deep sleep. Soon a strange feeling of unease infiltrated her mind. She turned on her back. A calmness seeped through her, made her sigh, and stretch her limbs as warmth and lightheartedness invaded her thoughts.

The sensation of calm increased, and her mind opened. She wasn't alone. A presence had infiltrated her brain. She became one with the presence. It compelled her to divulge her most intimate thoughts and desires. She shared how Maashi used to caress her and within seconds sensed the same caresses. A light touch like Maashi's glided almost like silk on her skin, then on her neck, waist, and hip. Soft kisses showered her face and her lips followed by a distinct sensation of being licked.

Such pleasure. It made her giggle like a child.

She moaned and swooned, arching her back. Her whole being relished the intensity of the pleasure. But the tickling changed, becoming insistent, unpleasant, intolerable. She wiggled to get away from the tickling, but she couldn't escape it.

Torture. Pain. Enough. Stop. Stop it. She flailed about and fought to remove the strange presence.

Maashi's voice echoed from far away. So far. "Tamara, wake up. Wake up."

She gasped, opened her eyes but couldn't see. "Where are you?"

"I'm right here," he said.

She focused on his voice and the tickling and licking stopped. Drained by the odd experience, she stirred and stared around her with astonishment.

Only a dream? So vivid. So real. How could this be? She wiped the beads of perspiration on her forehead. Her heart thumped in her chest. She sighed in relief. *Finally over.*

A sudden moan from Maashi startled her. He was holding his head and rocking back and forth. His face and neck were pale as alabaster. He fell sideways on the couch.

"No! Maashi? Maashi. Snap out of it."

She gave him a big shove. Nothing changed. "Maashi!" she yelled. His breathing slowed, became erratic. She needed to get help. Fast.

She pressed on the buttons on the floor. *Yellow for help.* "Chari. Come quickly. There's something wrong with Maashi. He's in trouble."

Seconds later, the door slid open, and Chari sprang into the room. He immediately went to Maashi's side, followed by Dennyvan and two guards. He tried to stir him, but his breathing remained shallow and his color as pale as Chitina's moons. "He's in some kind of trance."

He turned to the guards. "Help me lift him in the shower. Cold water should revive him."

Dennyvan joined the three and they carried him to the water room where they turned on the full jets.

Tamara called out to him like he had done for her. "Maashi! Come back to me."

Maashi struggled and grunted. He fought and pulled against the guards. They sat him down on the cold white marble of the water room floor. He mumbled something and stared around with fearful eyes.

"You're safe Maashi. You're safe," repeated Chari. He put his arms around his waist and kissed his shoulder. Maashi responded. He hung his head low, and his shoulders sagged. "Thank you for rescuing me," he said. "The stimulation was unbearable. I thought I would die."

Right then a speck of light flew in front of Tamara. Another small creature, the exact replica of its parent zoomed by. Soon, the room was invaded by the little floating creatures. The parent undulated freely in the room producing a pleasant humming.

Tamara watched, her mouth agape. "Well, how about that?"

Dennyvan shook his head. "We should've caught the thing before it had offspring. Now we'll have to catch them all and isolate them. I'll send a team to take care of it."

"Please be gentle. These creatures look so fragile," said Tamara.

Dennyvan growled, "Supervise them if you're so concerned."

Chari said, "I'll help and keep an eye on the Sheffrou. We need to be wary. This is the second strange occurrence in the presence of the creature since we've been back on the ship."

Chapter 14

Dennyvan's patience was quickly reaching a breaking point. "What do you mean you don't want to talk about it?" His baritone voice increased in volume until it seemed the whole receiving room with its strange purple walls vibrated. "I told you I don't want to kiss you! Just tell me what happened." With his brow now dark as coal and his thinning black eyes, his anger increased and consumed him.

Standing a mere five feet from him, Maashi looked away and fisted his hands. "It's not something I want to share."

"I have enough problems trying to deal with the Rodenegad without having to deal with your attitude, Sheffrou. I'll need answers soon. I must know if there is a possibility the floating creature is responsible for producing the unbearable sound we were subjected to the other day, and I want explanations on your recent loss of consciousness."

Dennyvan took a step back and scrutinized Maashi up and down. "You're changing. You're getting taller and more muscular. I swear it must be Dompati."

"This is unlikely," Maashi said, dismissing the possibility with a wave of his arm. "I'm just feeling less stress and I eat more." The last thing Maashi wanted was a surge in hormones to alter his emotions and behavior. He was already disturbed by

Tamara's presence and the fact he couldn't show his affection toward her.

"Nonetheless," said Dennyvan, "I've requested assistance from two other ships since the Rodenegad are still following us. They're slower than we are but are relentless in their pursuit. I demanded to the head of security on Chitina to send an experienced Sawisha to deal with you."

"Whatever happened the day I lost consciousness," Maashi said, "it's over now. I don't want to talk about it."

"How do you expect us to protect you if you won't disclose what almost killed you? I was present and I saw how pale you were. You were powerless to fight off whatever had taken hold of your mind."

Dennyvan took a step towards the door and said, "I hope for your sake this is the last of it. I can't afford to lose a Sheffrou," he grunted. "I should've asked for backup as soon as we had two Sheffrous on board and one female Chimitanga." He shot a malevolent stare towards Tamara.

She frowned and stared right back at him.

Dennyvan ignored her and addressed Chari. "See if you can get either of them to talk," he said. "I will assign three guards for constant coverage of those two." Straightening his shoulders, he stormed out of the room.

Maashi sat down and held his head in his hands. Untethered emotions swirled in his mind.

Tamara watched him closely. She leaned back on the thick dark purple couch.

Chari sat beside Maashi. "It's been two days, Shapinka. You need sustenance. Don't you want to drink some choun at least?" He kissed his shoulder affectionately. "I'm sure you're thirsty."

Maashi stirred as if he was going to reply then just shook his head sideways. He squeezed Chari's hand. He kept his lips tightly closed as if a terrible secret would escape if he didn't.

The door slid open, and the guard called Krawl, the one Maashi had saved from falling when they rescued the humans, walked in. He bowed to everyone, slowly approached Maashi, and kissed his right shoulder. Maashi nodded and looked away.

Krawl said in a low voice, "May I stay at your side, Shona-va?"

Maashi, his head still turned away, said, "You may."

Krawl sat close but without touching the Sheffrou. He nodded in Chari's direction.

"Maashi," said Chari. "I'll leave the room with Tamara for a few minutes."

Maashi glared at him with brazen eyes. "Do not," he said, "annoy her with questions."

Chari answered. "Of course not." He glanced over at Tamara who rose and followed him out. "It's okay, Maashi. Don't worry."

They went to another room further down the corridor, Chari stepped aside and opened the door to let Tamara in.

She sat on a couch, grabbed a light blue cushion, and held it in her lap. He settled on another couch close by.

"I like this room," said Tamara. "This whole darn ship is gray or purple, floors and walls. It gets depressing after a while. The big turquoise and blue cushions in here add some color. Don't you think they go well together?"

Chari took a small twig from the inner pocket of his shirt and said, "Yes, they do."

He pressed some controls on the floor and two lumis ap-peared on the side table, containing a dark blue liquid. He offered her one. "I hope you'll indulge a little and drink with me. I know I need a moment to relax. These last few days have been trying."

"I agree," she reached out and took the glass he offered. "No alcohol, right?"

"No. Not a drop," Chari smiled. "The Sheffrou would not approve. He would reprimand me."

How easily this one smiled, contrary to all the other Chamis on this ship. From what she had observed, most of them were Black and Silver Guards, and they probably never smiled.

From the start, Chari had been different from the other Chamranlinas. He was a Multi with purple dominant which meant he possessed a few other colors including some red and pink and a dash of yellow. Maybe that's what set him apart. That and his Ghouli Ghouli physical traits: his stunning copper skin, his eyes circled by black eyelids, and his coal black hands.

She took a sip of her drink. "Not bad. Not too sweet and just a little tart." She inhaled and prepared for a barrage of questions. "I guess you want to know what happened to me the other day just before Maashi got in trouble."

Chari set his glass down and inserted the kego twig between his lips.

Even here, he found one of his favorite twigs. He sure loves chewing on those.

Chari ran long black fingers in his unruly raven hair. "Let me be blunt. I need to understand what happened to both of you. My function is to protect the Sheffrou and you." He rubbed the glass gently between his hands. "I must admit that since that strange reaction, that trance, he has been disturbed. I'm concerned that he is in pain, and because of that, trusts no one. Sheffrous learn from a young age to hide strong feelings to avoid being bullied by Pure Colors and this ship is home to quite a few Black and Silver Sawishas, the strongest Pure Colors. So he cannot divulge his pain and I'm concerned it will increase."

"There's something I don't understand. Why did you two get on this ship?"

"The Sheffrou and I were kidnapped to take part in a plot to retrieve two Black and Silver Guards kidnapped months ago on the night of the Great Eclipse Celebration."

"The same night when the Sheffrous were kidnapped?"

"Yes, that same night." Chari looked away. He took a long sip of his drink.

"Why was he disguised with those dark veils?"

Chari lowered his head. "It's a strange story but suffice it to say that Maashi was coerced into impersonating an alien player, a Woo-Odong called Woo-Olong-Ti, who buys and trades aliens. This stratagem enabled us to rescue the two missing guards and Sheffrou Ashani, which was an unexpected bonus. You and the two humans just happened to be there at the right moment."

"I guess fate reunited us," said Tamara in a soft voice.

"Tamara, I think the Sheffrou's pain could degenerate into something more serious. I want to know what caused it to help him deal with it."

Tamara cleared her throat. "It's not that I refuse to help but, how can I say, it was a very private experience."

"In that case, we could communicate by a kiss, and I'll be able to better understand what happened."

Tamara raised her hands in alarm. "No. I don't want to do that."

"As you wish." Chari crossed his legs and swallowed a gulp of his drink. He put back the twig between his lips and stared at the floor.

Tamara inhaled a long breath. "In my world," she said, "there's something we call modesty. It is a common concept and can be found in all cultures." She paused. "I guess you could say it's a state of mind." She paused. "Let me explain. It's considered improper or immodest for a person, especially a woman, to be naked in front of a man unless they are planning to be intimate. In most societies, women will be punished, put in jail, or fined for showing their bodies. In extreme cases, the penalty is death."

Chari pulled out the twig from his mouth, stood, and paced the room. "Are you telling me that my request for a meeting with you months ago was something that is totally unacceptable in your society?"

"Yes," Tamara nodded. "A meeting involves you and I getting naked and touching each other's body. That was out of the question. The only time this happens in my world is when a woman is having an Encounter with her sexual partner or in cases of assault or rape."

Chari's eyes widened in surprise. "I can assure you I would never attack a female and the intent wasn't to have an Encounter."

Tamara chuckled and held back a smile. "I didn't think so."

Chari settled back on the couch. "I'm curious about your meeting with the Sheffrou. How did he convince you to accept?"

"That meeting happened in the very first few weeks following my arrival here. I had explained to him at length that I fell in what we call a wormhole and was transported to Chitina. I didn't know then that Chitina is far away in space and time from my world. All I can say is that I understood the meeting was extremely important for him and it also seemed to have a special symbolic meaning. I accepted the meeting when he explained that this wasn't a sexual encounter. I wanted to cooperate with his request because I thought this would ensure his cooperation in my search for a way back to my family on Earth."

"Tragic circumstances," said Chari. "There is no way back. That wormhole disappeared like dust in the wind. That's why the Sheffrou calls you Ishkibu, the traveler. You were pulled out of your world and landed on ours and couldn't get back."

"That's right," said Tamara. "It took me a long time to accept the fact that I was never going back home." Tamara set her lumi down on the table.

"Tell me about your experience the other day," said Chari in a low voice.

Tamara glanced at him with a timid grin and said, "What I was trying to say is... one doesn't disclose intimate desires and sexual fantasies to others unless they are very close, like lovers."

"Did your experience involve desires and sexual fantasies? That's something which could explain the Sheffrou's reticence in sharing this, even with me. That and Dompati."

"Dompati. I'm not familiar with that word. What does it mean?"

"Dompati refers to physical and mental changes associated with full maturity."

Tamara chuckled. "I must agree with Dennyvan on the physical changes. Maashi certainly looks different."

Chari held his glass as if about to take a sip but stopped mid-air. "He'll need more than one Chowli to deal with his increasing libido."

"Increasing?" Tamara said with a mocking tone. "I think it's high already. I watched him the other day. He reminds me of an elk in mating season. Everything seems to set him off."

"If it's Dompati," said Chari, "it will increase another ten-fold. We need to get back to Chitina as soon as possible. This needle will soon be overwhelmed with fragrant holoma, and the males will go wild with lust. That's why Dennyvan requested a Sawisha. He wants an experienced Pure Color to shadow the Sheffrou. He knows my presence won't be enough to contain him."

"Wait. I'm not following you. What is a needle?"

"The ship is called a needle."

"Why do you say contain Maashi?"

"He will feel urges like he's never felt before and will be tempted to have Encounters with all the males on the ship."

Tamara shook her head with a scornful look. "That'll be interesting. Is that normal behavior for Sheffrous?"

"Yes, for those undergoing Dompati."

She took a sip of her glass. "All this energy and so few females on Chitina."

Chari shrugged. "That's why the Fanellas are kept in well-guarded compounds."

"I don't agree with that," Tamara declared in a harsh voice. "Their freedom is restricted. They're treated like prisoners."

"This is a debate I'm not willing to engage in. But I must warn you; you'll need to be ready for advances from the Sheffrou."

Tamara just smiled. *I wouldn't mind.*

"Right now, I need to know more about your recent experience with sexual fantasies. Perhaps Maashi was subjected to intense sexual stimulation and that compounded his Dompati energy and increased his libido."

"It's difficult to explain. I fell asleep and that's when I felt a presence in my dreams. It infiltrated my thoughts and uncovered what I enjoy the most sexually. Things I have never shared with anyone. Some details only Maashi knew...." She inhaled deeply. "Fantasies that he sensed and sometimes fulfilled when we had an Encounter. That presence assumed the role of a lover and I felt things that were so intense, so vivid, I can't imagine how they were possible." Tamara took her head in her hands and rubbed her forehead. "But this experience was also different." She took a deep breath, "A real partner knows when to stop the kisses, caresses, etc... When the pleasure reaches its peak, it will last a few minutes and then, it will subside, and your body will return to its resting state. The panting and the rapid heartbeat slow down, and you recuperate. In the medical field, we call it the resolution phase."

Chari nodded sideways. "Your description is accurate. We experience something similar."

"The day this event occurred; I was sleeping. I sensed this presence, this entity, and the stimulation was powerful, relentless. I couldn't make it stop." Overwhelmed with the memory, Tamara's voice choked. She clenched her hands together. Her eyes filled with tears. "It was unbearable, like torture. I was going out of my mind." She burst into sobs.

Chari went to her and held her gently. "Oh, Chumpi. Don't cry. You're safe now. No one will hurt you." He held her against his shoulder and blurted out, "If this happened to Maashi, I must stay by his side. He might be in danger."

Chapter 15

F ive days had passed since the incident involving Maashi and Tamara. She spent most of her time with Lieutenant Yoon and his pilot.

With his thick brows moving up and down like hairy caterpillars, Patel stated with much emphasis as he usually did, "The Rodenegad are messing with the wrong aliens. We should soon rendezvous with *Innovation* and when we give our report, the commander will take appropriate action. They will be sorry they attacked and kidnapped us."

"Don't get carried away, Patel," said Lieutenant Yoon, "I'm sure they will attempt intimidation first and then, if necessary, a show of force." He looked relaxed and confident with his hair pulled in a bun on the top of his head.

"Either way, they won't get away with this without losing some feathers."

"To think we were close to being sold," Tamara said with a scowl. "I just can't wrap my head around it."

"Wrap your head?" asked Patel.

"I mean I can't believe it," explained Tamara. Some common phrases from her century were totally foreign to those two who were 570 years ahead in time. She had gotten used to their expressions, but they seemed not to catch on to hers.

Both men nodded in unison.

Tamara marveled at the fact that those two possessed the same mannerisms. *They must have spent a lot of time together in space.*

"Hey,' said Patel, "I heard the thin floating creature had some hatchlings. Or whatever they call them."

"It sure did," said Tamara. "One hundred twelve of them."

"Incredible. I wonder if it's male or female," he said. "I guess we'll never know."

Tamara pursed her lips. "It doesn't really matter. However, it's going to be difficult to figure out where it's from. Even Maashi can't connect telepathically with the creature. I don't know what the Chamis are going to do with them."

"Maashi?" said Patel. "Is that the one they call Sheffrou? The one who's always accompanied by another with bright copper skin and black eyes like those rodents? I can't remember what they're called."

"You mean raccoons. Yes, it's him."

Lieutenant Yoon said, "I thought the Black and Silver Guards were impressive but the one you call Sheffrou has a noble appearance. With his towering height and his calm but intense expression, he stands out from all the others."

She agreed. He wasn't the Maashi she had known. Taller, all muscles, broad chest covered by an impressive quatay, he told her he had reached maturity. Chari called it Dompati. Did that explain his poise and composure when he spoke? His musical voice had changed to a warm baritone. The sound made Tamara's heart flutter. And that was without mentioning his holoma. His fragrance followed him and lingered where he stood like an exquisite perfume. It was so tantalizing that one whiff was all it took for Tamara to shudder with desire.

The door opened and Chari came in. He shot a quick nod to the two men and said to Tamara, "Sheffrou Maashi would be pleased to see you if you have time."

"Now?"

"Yes, Tamara." He stepped back and the door opened.

"Is everything okay?"

"Yes. Let's not make him wait. Shall we?"

Tamara's pulse quickened as she entered Maashi's quarters. Her legs felt like gel, and she pinched her waist to bring her mind back to reality. It wouldn't take much to be engulfed in Maashi's charm and succumb to wild yearnings. She needed to keep her cool. That wasn't going to be easy. Chari led her in and quickly took his leave.

Maashi rose when she entered and said in his lovely voice, "Please, come and sit with me for a little while."

He was wearing a cream shirt open wide showing off the complex quatay on his chest which had spread to his shoulders and neck. He pointed with his long middle finger at the couch opposite his, filled with bright cushions of all sizes.

Conscious of his seductive holoma, Tamara took a seat and smiled.

What caused him to turn into such a hunk?

Her head swayed as if she had drunk champagne. She decided she had to go on the offensive because very soon, she would surrender to his inviting arms. He would do whatever he wanted with her, and she would be a willing partner.

"It's a pleasure to see you Maashi. I'm glad you recovered from your unpleasant experience. Chari said we're entering the Korr Nebula, and he says we'll soon be safe."

Why am I rambling on like a teenager?

Maashi sat down and spread his hands on his knees. "I'm pleased to see you. We haven't had a chance to be alone since you came aboard the ship."

"I know. We've been busy right and left."

"As I remember, the first day you kept your distance from me. May I ask why? Am I just a memory for you?"

Tamara expected the question. She braced herself and said, "I left you to try a new life in the human world. You know this was the best decision." Her mouth suddenly felt dry. She took a breath. "I see now your circumstances haven't changed. You still have Chowlis, and you spend a lot of time with the other males. I'm not sure how I feel about all that. I know I missed you terribly and I..." *I'm still in love with you.* Her words choked in her throat.

This was going to be a challenge.

Maashi pressed controls on the floor and a glass of water appeared on the minuscule synthetic table beside him. "Have some water." He extended his arm, and she took the glass.

"I understand your dilemma," he said. "Living on Chitina was difficult on many levels. Your health suffered and you were distressed by the fact that I had to share my time with many. I couldn't be with you as much as both of us would have liked."

Tamara took a sip and cleared her throat. "I don't want you to think I'm not grateful for being rescued. I just can't start something that will lead to nothing but an impasse." *Again. And break your heart and mine.*

"I see." Maashi lowered his head and stared at his hands. "I wish circumstances were different, but some things are out of my control."

"I wish they were different also." *If I could, I would go with you in a heartbeat.*

A chime rang. Someone was at the door. Maashi pressed on the controls on the floor to his right and the door opened. Redden strode in with a confident air, accompanied by a guard. Chari followed right behind them.

Maashi rose and stared at Redden. He stood silent for a moment. His face settled in a mild expression.

Redden eyed Maashi and said, "By express orders of the Leader, your friend Ashani will be transferred out to another needle as soon as it gets here. Dennyvan wants to minimize any interaction between the two of you because of the risk of attracting Krakoran entities while the needle is pursued by the Rodenegad."

He turned to leave, then pulled a small messaging device out of his inner pocket. "It's for you, Sheffrou. From the Council of Elders."

He handed it to Maashi and left.

Maashi stood with the message in hand and paused.

"Do you want me to leave? Maybe it's something private?" said Tamara rising from her seat.

"I'm sure it's not that important. A reprimand of some sort," said Maashi. He threw the device on the couch.

Chari tilted his head sideways. "May I read it?"

"Go ahead. I already know the Elders are not pleased with me."

Chari pressed on the device and read it. An ugly hissing sound came out of his lips. He said, "You need to read this now."

"What's wrong?" said Tamara.

Maashi took the message and read it. His eyes widened. He stared at Chari. "They can't be serious. Two hundred lashes?"

Chari nodded. "It's as close to a death sentence as they can give."

Chapter 16

Redden yelled, "Shields are gone! First degree alert!" Red lights alternating with purple ones flooded the control room.

Dennyvan, his face set in a scowl, roared, "All non-essential personnel, seek shelter in your quarters! Guards, prepare for an assault."

"Possible intruder alert, deck five," said a guard manning the main console.

"Krawl," said Dennyvan to the broad-shouldered guard a few feet away from him, "take a few men and go to deck five."

"Yes, sir." Krawl signaled three others who were already arming themselves with hand-held weapons. "We'll try to take them alive," he said to the others, "but if they become a danger to you or the ship, you know the rules, they must be neutralized." He exited into the hall with his group.

"You and you, secure the guests," said Dennyvan to a security team who had just stepped in the control room. "Don't let anyone come close to a Sheffrou."

"What about the two humans?" asked one guard.

"Confine them to their quarters," said Dennyvan.

"The human ship is coming within range," said Redden.

"Send an encrypted message," said Dennyvan. "Tell them we have rescued their two males and we're under attack by the Rodenegad. Any assistance is appreciated."

"Sir," said the guard at the console, "we have two confirmed intruders on deck five."

"Containment protocol, deck five," said Dennyvan. He talked to a device on his wrist, "Krawl, did you get their coordinates?"

"Got them," said Krawl. "We're on our way."

"Sir," said the guard at the console, "the coordinates are within 100 feet of reactor one."

"Damn," said Dennyvan. He brought his wrist closer. "Krawl, they're going for the reactor."

"Understood," said Krawl.

"Watch out for possible Serono 95 weapons," said Dennyvan. "They might be carrying some."

"Yes, sir."

"Monitor the intruders' position," said Dennyvan to the guard at the console.

"Sir," said Redden, "shots fired on deck five. The reactor is compromised. We are at risk of a cascading fusion reaction."

Dennyvan roared, "Initiate reactor ejection protocol!"

Redden punched in a series of coordinates on his panel. "Reactor one ejected."

"Krawl, status report," asked Dennyvan.

No answer.

"Sir," said the guard at the console, "I have contained the two intruders with level 3 forcefields. Sending coordinates now to Krawl."

"Good," said Dennyvan. He added, "Krawl, report."

"Sir, the fire alarm went off on deck five. I can't reach Krawl," said the guard at the console.

Redden said, "I can try Kenn, another one on the team."

"Do so," said Dennyvan.

"Kenn here."

"Report," ordered Dennyvan.

"Krawl has been hit. One Rodenegad is dead. His head has been blown up. His own Serono 95 is on the ground a few feet away. The other Rodenegad is contained. We are modulating the frequency of the forcefield around him. He is boxed in."

"Excellent. What about Krawl?"

"We're bringing him to the medic. He's been shot in the chest. Life signs are weak. I'm sending you the exact coordinates of the Rodenegad we have captured."

"I've got them, sir," said the guard at the console.

'Keep a close eye on him," said Dennyvan. "If he attempts anything, flush him out in space like garbage."

"Yes, sir."

"Redden," said Dennyvan, "get Sheffrou Maashi. Bring him to the medical unit." To Kenn he said, "I'm on my way." Dennyvan stormed out of the command center.

Maashi followed Redden at a brisk pace down the hallways. He only mentioned that a guard named Krawl was in critical condition.

He entered the area and was immediately brought to an isolation room in the back. An acrid odor of burned flesh permeated the air. Dennyvan and a few others were behind a glass panel and spoke in hushed voices with the medic. Krawl lay semiconscious on the gurney, his face contorted with pain. Half his chest had been blown to pieces by the Serono 95.

The medic in charge informed Maashi about the status of the guard. Maashi glanced at the patient and fought to keep his emotions in check. This was the same guard he had rescued when the platform was moving away from their alcove back on the space station.

Like all Sheffrous, he had been trained as a physician and could provide valuable assistance in medical emergencies, but he had little practical experience. Watching the guard struggling and fighting for each breath was almost too much to bear. He couldn't help but think about his friend Dasho who had suffered severe injuries inflicted by the Krakoran.

Krawl was extremely weak. Blood loss was minimal because of the severity of the burns, and the vital organs had been spared, but the whole right side of his chest was missing. The AI device in position right above his chest had been activated and it had started the process of rejuvenation. Sadly, the process would take days and would save the patient only if he stayed alive long enough to complete the healing.

Maashi's role was to keep him alive and minimize the pain and anguish. Sheffrous had healing powers well beyond any other Chamranlina and their saweya was exceptional, but Maashi had never healed anyone with such extensive injuries. Doubt crept into his mind. What were his chances of succeeding given the severity of the wounds? Would he be up to the task?

He requested a seat to avoid spending energy on anything besides healing the patient. He held Krawl's face in his hands and whispered to him. "It is I, Maashi. I will help you."

The others left one by one. Maashi, alone with the patient, gently opened Krawl's mouth and touched his black tongue with his long middle finger to facilitate telepathic contact.

"I am here. Let me into your thoughts and let my mind connect with yours."

With senses on alert, Maashi waited for a response. The tongue moved ever so slightly. He gently grabbed it and pulled it out to better access it. He opened his shirt, exposing his quatay and upper chest and bent over Krawl. He lay flat over Krawl on the side still intact, skin against skin, his head resting against the guard's neck.

Maashi then stretched out his own long, royal blue tongue and thoroughly licked the other's tongue and face. He then twirled his tongue around Krawl's tongue and reached for his mind.

"Pain. Pain. Burning pain."

"It is I, Maashi, here to help you."

"Burning. Pressure. Dying."

"Help is here. Share the pain. You will live."

Hours passed. Krawl's condition remained critical. Maashi continued his watch, transferring all the energy he could. After twelve hours, Chari came and sat close to Maashi and rested his head on Maashi's back.

Chari reached out to Maashi, *"Are you all right?"*

"My energy is good. Stay with me."

"I will stay as long as you need me."

The next day, Krawl's vital signs stabilized and gradually strengthened. New flesh appeared in several places on his burnt chest. Chari left and came back with a tall glass of choun and, to Maashi's surprise and elation, accompanied by Sheffrou Ashani.

Maashi disentangled himself from the patient and fiercely hugged and kissed Ashani.

Chari grinned and said, "I told Dennyvan that if he wanted his guard to live, he should let Ashani see you. He had no choice but to accept."

The joy and happiness of holding him made Maashi's saweya gush with energy.

The thin Ashani, overcome with emotion, smiled with tears running down his cheeks and fiercely kissed Maashi's neck and face. He whispered, "I thought I would never kiss you again. I lost hope and prepared my mind to die." He held back sobs.

Maashi kissed him back, a long warm kiss. "Never lose hope, Chumpi. No matter what happens, fight to stay alive. We would never have stopped looking for you until we found you."

Chari said, "Time is short. Drink this, Maashi, before you return to your patient."

Maashi lightly touched his Chowli's cheek in an unspoken thank you and drank the warm choun as fast as he could.

"I've got to take Sheffrou Ashani back," Chari said. "I'll join you later."

Maashi nodded. He squeezed Ashani's hand and said, "You're such a joy to behold. Rest for now. I will try to see you later."

"Of course, Shonava," said Ashani. "Seeing you makes my heart dance. I'll be waiting."

Maashi watched them leave, then turned to Krawl and licked his face. He clicked softly and caressed his cheeks. Such displays of affection were not permitted with a Black and Silver Guard unless he was having an Encounter with the Sheffrou. However, in exceptional circumstances, any pleasure experienced by the patient increased his chances of survival, so Maashi kissed him without restraint. Hopefully, the patient wouldn't remember much. Maashi was convinced that if Krawl ever mentioned his tender licking, the other guards would mock him without cease.

The ship's medic paid a visit twice during the night to check on the patient and the Sheffrou and arrived a few minutes later.

"Shonava, the patient's vitals are much stronger," he said, "and the healing process is well under way. I commend you for your efforts."

"I agree," said Maashi. His mouth eased in a tired smile. "I'll stay for another day at his bedside. If he continues to improve without complications, he will pull through."

Chapter 17

The needle had finally reached the Korr Nebula. Two Chami ships were closing in and would soon reach them. Tamara joined Maashi and Chari.

"In light of the incredible rescue of Sheffrou Ashani, and the remarkable recovery of that guard," said Tamara as she munched on dry cereal, their version of popcorn, "do you think that the Council will reevaluate its decision to punish you? Surely, they can reopen your case and forego the punishment." She sat with her feet propped up on a couch close to Maashi in his small receiving room.

Maashi reclined on the high-back couch and spread his hands on his knees. "My actions were what you would normally expect from a Sheffrou. I haven't performed anything extraordinary."

"Still, they can revise their edict," Tamara said with an energetic tone. "To this day, I still don't understand why they wanted to punish you in the first place. I'm starting to think these old farts are slowly losing their marbles."

Chari sat on a couch adjacent to Maashi wearing an olive shirt with short sleeves. He had dropped the black attire he usually wore. "Too many Black Guards on this ship," he had explained. His copper-colored arms showed his toned muscles, he pulled out the kego twig wedged between his lips and said,

"Farts? Marbles? Sometimes what you say is incomprehensible, Tamara. However, I sense a derisive tone."

Rolling her eyes, Tamara raised her voice. "I'm just saying they aren't making rational decisions."

Chari laughed heartily. "I couldn't agree with you more. I've been saying this for many sequences, but our society is averse to change and puts a lot of faith in tradition. In this case, although it may sound illogical to you, from the Council's point of view, the fact that the Sheffrou didn't complete the Draharma trial as ordered is a huge insult. This entails consequences."

"But Chari, he was forcefully removed right as they were going to complete the procedure. Maashi said so himself. He explained everything to me the other day. Right?" She glanced over at Maashi who didn't contest her words. "It's not his fault. He didn't do anything wrong. Can't they understand that?" Tamara took a mouthful of popcorn and produced a loud crunching sound.

"Tamara," said Maashi, "the Elders don't listen to tall tales. From their point of view, the kidnapping by the guards could have been staged. Bribes have been used before. Stranger things have happened. Centuries ago, when Pure Colors were all required to complete the Draharma trials, some resorted to creative stratagems to avoid them. Today, the Elders stick to the facts, and the fact is, I have not completed what they ordered."

"That's so unfair," said Tamara with a pinched expression. She popped a handful of cereal in her mouth, readjusted her position, and tapped her foot nervously on the floor.

Chari said in a sarcastic tone, "Justice and fairness aren't involved. The Elders want to show that they still have control over Sheffrou Maashi as he reaches maturity. I believe the Council has been manipulated by Sawishas who are envious of Maashi's status and power. I follow the media and they have exhibited a load of malicious comments."

Tamara bent forward. "Why do the Sawishas hate Maashi so much? What has he done to them?"

"The events that occurred the night of the Great Eclipse," said Chari, "and the loss of Maashi's offspring have given his opponents the advantage. The ones who hate him manipulate the facts, create a false narrative, and put them in a different light. Once doubt is planted and left to grow, it takes on a life of its own and no matter what happens, it will persist in one form or another."

"You're right about that.," Tamara huffed. "We've had the same problem trying to keep the facts straight about vaccines. False statements by people who take advantage of the public's fears destroy any chance we have of getting the facts straight."

Chari added, "All they're saying is he's guilty of something."

"Come on," said Tamara in an exasperated tone. "Are you talking about the kidnappings of the other Sheffrous, Ashani and Tomisho? The true culprits have been exposed. Maashi's mentor, Kokin Cronobutin and his assistant, whatever his name is, were found guilty and sent to the mining compounds."

"Noolin," said Maashi.

"Yes, sorry," Tamara shot a kind look at Maashi. The circumstances surrounding the loss of his offspring remained a source of overwhelming grief for him.

"Even Dennyvan hates Sheffrou Maashi and what he represents," said Chari. "He told us that by increasing Maashi's protection on the night of the Great Eclipse, the other Sheffrous and their guards were left vulnerable. Consequently, more guards were killed, and that's how two members of his team were kidnapped."

"Tsk." Tamara shook her head. "I could care less about Dennyvan's opinion."

Chari continued. "As for the offspring, the Elders made a poor decision in refusing to inform Sheffrous of the plague."

Maashi looked away and swore under his breath.

"And since Maashi was chosen for mating with all the Fanellas for two sequences in a row, he obliterated any chance of mating for the Sawishas."

"How so?" asked Tamara. "I've been told only Sheffrous were chosen for mating these last few sequences."

"If the mating," said Chari, "is unsuccessful for the first two choices, a Sawisha can be picked as a third choice."

"And Maashi was successful every time." She sighed. "I get it now." She shook her head. "They should've just been happy he fathered a lot of children."

Maashi said in a defeated voice, "It's best to let it go, Tamara. Anger and resentment aren't the solution. With time, the Elders may reconsider the punishment."

Chari plugged his twig back in his mouth and chewed hard on it. He glanced toward Maashi who had lowered his head. He pulled the twig out and threw it on the table by the couch. He leaned forward, came shoulder to shoulder with the Sheffrou. "We can still appeal their decision when we get back to Chitina."

Maashi clasped his hands together and made no comment.

The three of them sat in silence.

"Chari," said Tamara, "you mentioned something earlier about the floating creature. What were you saying?"

"I said the crew can't locate the floating creature or its off-spring. The needle's computer has confirmed that the creature isn't aboard the ship."

Maashi raised his head and said, "I used to feel its presence but not anymore."

"That makes no sense," said Tamara. She rose and paced the room. "How can it survive outside the ship in the emptiness of space?"

"Actually," said Chari, "we are traveling in the Korr Nebula and there are a multitude of particles including hydrogen molecules in this area. There are also large pockets of dark matter. The creature could use that for energy. We know very little about it, and we have previously encountered beings who survive in deep space."

Tamara slowed her steps and said, "Let's suppose it has left the needle." She pointed a finger at the ceiling. "How did it get out of its confinement? Did it have the offspring with it?"

Chari's eyes widened. "The only possible way it could have escaped was when the two intruders came in. No. Let me rephrase this. When the reactor core was ejected, the creature could have been ejected at the same time. The crew has reviewed the recordings of what happened on deck five. There is one view where the creature with its offspring is clearly visible, but we can't see it in the subsequent views. However," he said, "I fail to see why this captivates your attention so much."

"I have a hypothesis. You'll think it's crazy but hear me out. I'm putting two and two together and I think I've solved the mystery of what happened to the Rodenegad in charge back at the space station. I heard the guards mention the investigators haven't found what and who killed him."

Maashi said in a gentle voice, "Come and let me kiss you. I will understand your theory and it will be a lot easier than going back and forth with this discussion."

Tamara's face brightened with a broad smile. "Nice try, Maashi. But no, I can't kiss you. I must be extra careful around you these days. This Dompati thing makes you as hot as a hot tamale. You're like a cat waiting to pounce on a mouse and swallow it whole."

With eyes wide, he raised both hands and presented his palms. "I assure you that my intentions are honorable. I won't take advantage of you."

Chari burst into laughter. "Shapinka, she's right to be wary. Having an Encounter with you right now is like playing with explosive material. I should know." Chari's lips eased into a mocking grin. "I hear Shonava Benshimu is on his way here from Chitina and can't wait to be transferred aboard this needle and have a meeting with you. His nonstop praise will entice Black and Silver Guards to request Encounters with you."

Maashi tilted his head sideways. He brushed off some imaginary speck off his pants. "That can't be true."

"I can confirm it. You should have seen Dennyvan's face when that big green said something to that effect in a virtual chat. Dennyvan almost choked on his drink. You can see this for yourself on the recordings."

The Sheffrou's mouth stretched in a timid smile. "You're a devious one, Chari. Are you concocting something behind my back? Are you encouraging the Pure Colors on board to request an Encounter with me?"

"Not in so many words," Chari's black eyes glowed as he made a sweeping gesture with his arm. "I may have pointed out that the needle has plenty of occupants that could benefit from your surplus of energy."

Maashi looked at Chari in mock outrage then whispered to Tamara in a gentle voice, "Don't believe everything Chari says. I would hate it if you were offended by this type of discussion."

Tamara, standing a few feet away, giggled. "Don't worry, Maashi. I'm not offended. As a matter of fact, I'm enjoying this."

He shook his head in disbelief.

Chari bent over and ordered a drink by pressing the controls on the floor. "Anyone else would like a drink?"

"I'll have one, thank you," said Maashi.

"No, thanks," said Tamara. "I'll stick to my fake popcorn."

Two tall lumis appeared. Chari handed one containing an emerald liquor to Maashi and raised his own glass. "To your successful return, Shonava."

"Mm," said Maashi. "Thank you."

They both took a sip by dipping their long tongues in the opaque glasses.

"I must tell you," said Chari, "that your successful intervention with Krawl has spread all over the media and Dennyvan's attitude towards you is changing. He might be willing to put in a favorable comment on your behalf to the Council of Elders."

"Your efforts are noted, Chari." Maashi raised his glass to his Chowli.

Tamara abruptly sat down and said, "All I'm trying to say about the creature is that it was present when that filthy Rodenegad was killed back at the arena, and it was also on deck five when this other guy had his head blown off."

Both Chamis looked at her like she was delirious. Maashi took a long sip of his glass and set it down.

"My theory is simple," said Tamara, "The creature can produce damaging sound waves. We all experienced it the other day. What if it could produce a killer sound wave and direct it towards one specific individual? And Chari," continued Tamara, "you said that the Serono 95 recovered in the hallway hadn't been fired. It was the other Rodenegad who fired at Krawl. So how did this first Rodenegad get his head blown off since the guards here never used their weapons?"

Chari clicked in approval. "At this point, your logic rings true. I will convey your theory to Dennyvan and to the space station agents who are conducting the investigation of the murder of the Rodenegad in the arena."

"Thank you." Tamara shoved the last of her popcorn in her mouth. "Now," she swallowed, "do you know how to find the creature if it's in space, and what is Dennyvan going to do with that other Rodenegad they're keeping prisoner?"

Maashi produced a rare smile. "I must applaud your persistence, Tamara. Your words have given me some ideas about the subject that I plan to share with Dennyvan."

Chapter 18

M aashi's Dompati or attainment of maturity produced some noteworthy physical and mental changes. His height now reached seven and a half feet and he could rub shoulders with the tallest Black and Silver Guards on board. His voice had kept its musicality but became a deeper baritone. Whenever he experienced pleasure, his intense holoma permeated the air around him with an irresistible fragrance.

Maashi had enjoyed Encounters with Sawishas and Multis on board the needle, but his libido seemed unquenchable. Satisfying his partners, watching them climax in his arms brought joy and pride. However, the thrill was brief, and he constantly needed more. He roamed the ship in search of partners to share his energy with.

His mind absorbed new information with unparalleled ease. In the closed environment of the needle, he expanded the reach and scope of his already impressive telepathic skills. He could identify and locate each and everyone on board individually. He could hone in on a particular individual and connect with his thoughts. This ability came with some unwanted side effects. He had to learn how to block the myriad trivial thoughts from others because they could overwhelm and confuse him.

Ignoring the water restrictions aboard the ship, Maashi took a long invigorating shower. He missed his daily swimming in the cold waters of the underground caves of Chitina, competing for hours with the fastest swimmers. The absence of his friend Dasho weighed on him. Thirty sequences ago, he and Dasho accompanied by their Chowlis, used to ride together and play chitutu, a high-energy water sport, for hours at a time. Afterwards, they often spent an evening chatting and laughing at the local Lantilica, a gathering place where they enjoyed a slow drink and tasted the seasonal delicacies. Following a long day of activities, they found solace in each other's arms in the Encounter room.

Stepping out of the shower, Maashi walked over to his receiving room and settled on the gray couch. Sad memories continued to torment him.

There was a time when the elite, Sawishas and Sheffrous, could go freely to the surface of Chitina. They rode across the desert for hours atop the tall and swift Shoshans brought from their home world Chamtali. Maashi was a skilled rider and was often chosen to represent his compound at the most prestigious race of the sequence two weeks before the Great Eclipse Celebration. Maashi smiled as he recalled the most recent race. He came in second behind a young Sheffrou with a booming laugh called Tomisho. They met and became inseparable.

He rose and paced the room like a feline in a cage as he remembered the anger and helplessness he had felt after the attacks the night of the celebration when the Sheffrous were on their way back to their quarters.

Four Sheffrous, all close friends, were impacted the night of the Great Eclipse. His best friend Tomisho and Ashani, his pupil, were kidnapped by the enemy. Tomisho was rescued a few months ago but circumstances had prevented them from seeing each other more than a few times. Ashani had been rescued with the two guards, but he had seen him only briefly since then. Dasho, another close friend, was severely injured and lived like a recluse. Shoban, his mentor, was killed.

After the Krakoran attacks that night, his world changed, never to be the same. More guards, more restrictions, more danger. Shoshan riding was limited to just a few outings closely supervised by the Red Guards.

Maashi paused and sat on the couch. He bent over and rested his head in his hands.

He reflected on his own future. Would there be a time in his life where he would enjoy the calm and stillness of meditation without memories haunting him? A time of peace and serenity without fear of an attack?

For now, his only objective was living every day making sure his libido didn't run wild like a Shoshan stallion in rut.

Pleasure had always been the most important thing in his life. Yet now that he was free to indulge as much as he wanted, something was missing. He felt like someone who ate a whole meal, had a full belly, but still hunger gnawed at him. Day after day, he had been in the arms of his Chowlis, Chari and Chopa, who had traveled on the needle, the big green Benshimu, and all the Pure Colors on board, except Dennyvan, and there he was, overcome by a strange longing. A longing he couldn't shake.

Just a few more days and the space station investigators would complete their task and leave. The Black and Silver Guards were eager to go back to Chitina. However, Maashi was less than thrilled. In fact, he contemplated his return with dread, uncertainty, and anger.

How dare the Council punish him for something that was out of his control? There was no indication that the Elders would relent and change their decision. He couldn't think of a way out of his predicament. He spread his hands on his knees. Two hundred lashes were a lot of lashes. Chari called it a death sentence. Maashi was convinced he could survive, but at what price? Knowing what he was going to face on his return and this continuous sadness were almost too much.

Often, when sorrow threatened to overcome him, his thoughts focused on Tamara. This time, instead of bringing joy, thinking of her only brought more sadness. Her departure for the human ship was imminent. That fact made his head spin. He leaned forward and took a long breath to steady himself. He clasped his hands together as wave after wave of pain washed over him. He had come to the inescapable realization that her departure was the one thing he couldn't change and couldn't bear.

When she left for the first time, he encouraged her to join the humans and start a new life among her own kind. It was the right thing to do. Alas, he had underestimated how much ache this would cause him. He suffered in silence knowing she had to leave or be subjected to terrible joint and muscle pain if she stayed on Chitina. Now, she was readying to go for a second time, a final time, and this tore him apart.

Maashi closed his eyes. *Maybe the solution was dying from the flogging on Chitina. At least, this unbearable ache would cease. Was this what fate had in store for him?*

Tamara washed her hair using a ton of shampoo-like cream and then rinsed it off with the help of the warm water jets. She had gotten used to the showers on board the needle and enjoyed them thoroughly. Chamis treasured water and this was reflected in their marvelous water rooms present even on board their spaceships.

She used a fuzzy towel to wipe and dry her skin. Feeling refreshed, she chose a new outfit with turquoise borders, the color worn by young Sheffrous. Maashi had always said she was a young Sheffrou and treated her as such. He liked to call her Ishkibu Sheffrou: the traveler.

She scrutinized her reflection on the black marble wall and sighed. She would be leaving soon, and her world would be turned upside down again. The human ship was going to drop her to a colony on New Earth and that's where she would start her brand-new life. She anticipated challenges. This wouldn't be easy. Doubt crept in her mind. *Would she fit in this colony?*

Walking back to her receiving room, she considered the decision to leave the Chamis and especially Maashi. Her love for Maashi was as strong as ever. He had changed but in a good way. He looked more mature and at the same time (was that even possible?) more seductive. She grinned at the memory of a group of male performers on Earth. She loved to watch them. They were funny and entertaining. He reminded her of them, sexy, alluring without taking themselves too seriously.

Standing there, her thoughts filled with anguish, Tamara couldn't help it and bit her nails. She would give anything to be with Maashi for the rest of her life. She didn't care if he had lovers or Chowlis, didn't mind that he was a Sheffrou, and his libido was through the roof. He loved her. She loved him. She knew this without a doubt. That was enough.

She sat on the plush couch, sadness overcoming her. Tears rolled down her face and she let them drop and soak her shirt. Powerless to change what couldn't be changed, she waited for the tears to dry. Her energy had dissipated. Feeling empty, she reclined and held a pillow in her arms. She let her mind drift away. A dreamless sleep enveloped her.

Chapter 19

The door to Tamara's bedroom opened without a sound. Maashi entered and slid to Tamara's side like a feline on the prowl. He stood and watched her steady, regular breathing as she slept.

Senses on alert, he inhaled her delicate fragrance, tilted his head back, and closed his eyes to savor it. He knelt by the couch where she lay. His own holoma diffused in the room like fine mist over a tranquil pond. He held back from touching her. Instead, he let his desire blossom into an intoxicating potion until his body quivered with need.

How could he have been so blind? She, the little female, the gentle Ishkibu, was the one he craved, the one he hungered to touch and hold, the one who haunted his soul. The only one who could quench this relentless longing. Why didn't he see it sooner?

He thought of his favorite Fanella, Ileana, his soul mate. She had shared many Encounters with him, and he had bonded with her like no other, until the plague. The wretched sickness had killed his offspring, thirteen little females, except one, Ileana's first daughter.

The news about the plague had been kept hidden from all the Pure Colors, Sawishas and Sheffrous. When Chari revealed to him the truth, risking the wrath of the Council, he refused to believe him. Mad with grief, he transgressed all rules and went into the female compound to see Ileana, mother of two of his daughters. That's when he faced the sad reality.

How could he blame Ileana for her fury when she saw him? Losing a child was horrible. How can one recover from such grief? Sorrow had made her blind. The Gray Feeders, coerced under heavy penalty by the Elders, told the Fanellas he was the one carrying the evil plague. His impure body had enabled the sickness, and it killed the young females. One by one they died.

Ileana was convinced he was foul, tainted with death since all his offspring had succumbed including her youngest daughter. Only the oldest of the two clung to life but inched closer to death with every breath. When Maashi went to see the Fanella, he begged her to believe his innocence. Instead, she flung insults at him, slapped him, and the bond between them shattered.

Maashi closed his eyes. His heart heaved with sorrow. Life would have taken a different course if it hadn't been for the plague. So many innocent lives lost. Little Fanellas that he never had a chance to meet.

If Chari's latest prediction was right, about the Sawishas banding together to destroy him and his reputation, he would never mate again. Ever. Of the fourteen little Fanellas he fathered during those two memorable sequences, only one, Ileana's oldest daughter, Shalina, would carry on his genes.

Maashi watched as Tamara turned on her back and took a long breath. Deep in her dreams, she smiled.

If the Elders refused to forgive him, he would be punished with 200 lashes until he was within a finger's breath from death.

With his life in jeopardy, what prevented him from breaking all the rules?

Mating with a female of another species was forbidden, punishable by death. Faced with the possibility of dying by flogging or living the rest of his life under the crushing burden of shame, what could stop him now from sharing everything with the little female?

His amber eyes grew bigger and shone. He had made his decision.

Tamara moaned and turned. She sensed someone was close and opened her eyes.

"Maashi. I didn't hear you come in. I was just resting a bit after my shower."

Why did I think I could just disregard my feelings for him? He's changed, became a charming hunk, one I can't resist.

She sat up, stretched. He was so close she could feel him purring like a feline. It gave her goosebumps. "What brings you here?"

"How are you today, Chumpi?" His eyes caressed her face.

"I'm feeling better now that you're here," she said, glancing at him sideways. *What a gorgeous fragrance.*

Maashi tilted his head. He took a long strand of her auburn locks and let it slide between his fingers. "So soft, so silky. I've always loved your hair."

"And so long," said Tamara. "I used to keep it short but now it has grown and hangs down below my shoulders."

Maashi smiled. "Does it never stop growing?"

"I don't think so but the longer it gets, the more slowly it grows." She smiled back at him. "How about you? Does your hair grow longer?"

"We are born with very short hair, and it grows slowly until it reaches the appropriate length unique to each one of us. Then, it stays that length."

"How convenient," Tamara forced a laugh. His holoma swirled around them like a protective cloak and made her skin tingle. All she wanted to do was inhale the tantalizing aroma and lose herself in his arms. She hungered for the forbidden fruit.

Why did he have to be the rescuer? Why did fate bring them together again?

He raised her head by putting his long middle finger under her chin. "Your eyes are red. You've been crying."

Tamara groaned. She turned her head away, raw emotions threatening to explode. "I'm not pleased about what's going to happen to you. There's something terribly wrong about the whole thing."

Maashi whispered, "You shouldn't worry about that."

Tamara quickly wiped a tear rolling down her cheek. "You once told me Sheffrous were among the elite, were the most important Chamis in your world. Why would they order you to be whipped like a vulgar criminal to the point of endangering your life?"

He looked away. "I don't believe they will actually go through with that order."

Tamara shook her head, letting her auburn strands fall forward, partially hiding her face. "Chari is convinced they will execute the order." She clenched her hands. "There must be another way. A way to avoid this."

"This isn't the first time I've transgressed rules. I've always been able to escape harsh punishments."

The door opened and Dennyvan stomped in the room with Redden right behind. "What orders? What punishments?"

Tamara jumped off the couch and planted herself right in front of Dennyvan. Hands on her hips, she spoke in a forceful voice, "Has no one ever told you that you can't just barge in a room like that, especially in a lady's room?"

"Little Fanella, get out of my way." With one sweep of his muscular arm, Dennyvan pushed her aside and Tamara went flying over to the couch.

In a split second, Maashi jumped on his feet, inches away from Dennyvan's face. "You will not touch her," he roared, "or I will make you regret it!"

"Don't make me laugh, Sheffrou. You're no threat to me."

The punch to Dennyvan's face came so fast he stumbled backward.

The stunned Leader growled, then erupted in laughter and rubbed his jaw at the same time. "By the Black Creatures of the Korr Nebula, hail the protector of the little Fanella."

Maashi produced a low warning hiss and his eyes darkened to black slits.

Redden stood impassive like a granite boulder.

Dennyvan raised his hands. "Before you get all worked up, I have a few questions for you and the Fanella."

The door burst open. Chari entered. He eyed Dennyvan and Maashi and stepped to the Sheffrou's side.

Dennyvan ignored his stare. "Welcome, Chowli. Join our little meeting."

"This isn't the place or time to get into an argument," said Chari. "There is much to discuss."

Tamara stood. "Let's hear what you have to say, Dennyvan."

Dennyvan nodded at her. "First let's all sit down. Redden, stand by the door. I don't want anyone to interrupt us."

Chapter 20

Dennyvan sat and leaned back on the closest couch. "What are the orders from the Council?"

Maashi lowered his head, keeping his lips tightly closed. Tamara could tell he wanted to be anywhere but here, facing Dennyvan and his shame.

Chari tilted his head, sending a questioning glance toward Maashi who nodded once.

"The Elders," said Chari, "no doubt under intense pressure from Maashi's detractors and other Sawishas envious of his position, have decided to punish him for fleeing from the Draharma trial they had demanded."

Dennyvan sat closer to the edge of his chair trying to conceal his interest. "What's the punishment?" he said, brushing his shirt with the flick of a finger as if the matter was beneath him.

Chari said, keeping his voice low. "Flogging. Two hundred lashes."

"What?" Dennyvan's head whipped backward, and he howled. "They cannot be serious!"

Tamara's gaze locked on him. She watched in awe his black tongue swirl in his mouth. His yellow teeth were longer and sharper than Maashi's, indicating he was much older. *Not ap-*

pealing at all. She grimaced. *Kissing him would be seriously disgusting.*

When Chari's only response was to glare at him, Dennyvan's brow widened, and he clenched his jaw. "Have the Elders lost their minds?" he said with an ugly grin. "We are talking about a Sheffrou here, not some hostile Multi guilty of a crime."

When Maashi and Chari showed no reaction to his comments, confirming the gravity of the Elders' demands, anger replaced hilarity. Dennyvan fisted his hands and raised his voice with growing irritation. "My guards are trained to bear harsh physical punishment. Blacks and Silver guards and Reds are prepared mentally and physically for battle, but Sheffrous possess no such training. What on Chitina do they hope to accomplish with this flogging?"

Dennyvan rose from his seat and paced the room. "The Elders are powerless to control the Sawishas. They surely know Sheffrou Maashi didn't leave of his own accord. We are the ones who kidnapped him!" he roared. Turning to Redden, he said, "Find more about this. I want to know who is behind these orders. It might be a conspiracy, someone trying to get back at me. I want all the details."

"Yes, sir." Redden snapped to action and sprinted out of the room.

"Now, we must address our other problem." Dennyvan sat back down. "We have lost track of the Rodenegad ship. It was following us till a few hours ago, then it vanished. We can't find any trace of it. No reactor residue. Nothing."

"I conferred with the two humans on board," said Chari, "they have contacted the human ship *Innovation.* They're also baffled by its sudden disappearance. They confirmed the Rodenegad vessel disappeared right after they traveled close to a large asteroid about 30,000 miles away." Chari straightened his shoulders and his black eyes glowed in his copper face. "We should investigate that asteroid. As far as I know, the last coordinates we had on the elongated creature showed it was headed towards it."

"Could the ship be hiding behind or inside the asteroid?" asked Tamara.

Dennyvan nodded, "That is the possibility we are exploring. The asteroid should be solid, a mix of rock and ice crystals, but we scanned it and there's a large hollow section inside. We have tried to map that section, but it has proven a difficult task. It seems to be changing its composition every thirty minutes or so."

"Is that asteroid big enough to hide a ship?" said Maashi.

"Compared to other asteroids, it's huge," said Chari. "One hundred miles long and thirty miles wide, large enough to hide several ships. I've seen the coordinates. It could serve as a meeting place for the Rodenegad."

Maashi spread his hands on his knees. He clicked softly. "Thirty minutes," he said. He tilted his head to one side. "Thirty minutes...."

"What is it?" said Chari.

"When I was a captive of the Krakoran, I often heard the number thirty."

"Could this asteroid have something to do with the Krakoran?" said Tamara.

Dennyvan grunted. "The asteroid is large, but the data is inconclusive. I can't confirm at this time if it is being used as a meeting place. But I agree this would be a clever way to hide ships."

Tamara jumped from her seat. "Maybe it's some kind of rendezvous point between the Rodenegad and the Krakoran."

"You have a lot of imaginary ideas, little Fanella," said Dennyvan with a dismissive wave of his arm. "We know the Krakoran live in another world, parallel to ours. We have been seeking a portal of some kind to pursue them in their world for centuries. We have never been able to find any clues."

"That's it!" exclaimed Tamara. "A portal. You've been searching in the wrong places. This asteroid might be concealing a connection of some kind between the two worlds."

Dennyvan grinned. "I'm starting to understand why the Sheffrou finds you so entertaining. You are a source of endless ideas and conjectures."

Tamara said, "When all the obvious possibilities have been explored, you need to examine the ones that appear unlikely or impossible." *A famous human saying.*

Crossing her arms on her chest and furrowing her brows, she looked up at Dennyvan. "You must open your mind, entertain new theories. It's possible a portal has been there all along but if you cannot visualize the possibility, then you won't find what's right there in front of you. It's like in medicine, most diagnoses are obvious, but occasionally, you're dealing with a rare disease. You must keep all options open to diagnose rare conditions."

Dennyvan clicked a few times as if mumbling to himself. He rose and headed for the door, "We'll continue to investigate the asteroid but unless we find any solid evidence the ship is in there, we'll be on our way back to Chitina."

Maashi was restless the rest of the day. He decided to go lie down for a while. He told Chari and Tamara he needed to sleep so they both left. A weight, heavier than usual, rested on his shoulders. He tried stretching, moving his arms up and down, rotating his shoulders, but nothing helped.

He settled on one of the long couches and put his arms by his side. His thoughts drifted. Images from the long months of capture by the Krakoran swirled in his mind.

The Krakoran restrained their prisoners in a coffin-like structure made of a clear rigid material. Immobilized for days, he would lie naked with only his thoughts to keep him company,

Maashi struggled for long months alone with his two jailers, the little worker and the big worker, who were free to tease and torture him.

The little worker was the smart one and controlled the bigger creature. They both looked as if they had sprung from a diabolical nightmare. With a hard red and brown exoskeleton, eight legs, and a tail ending in a sharp stinger, they scurried about, intent on doing their hellish deeds. The little worker communicated with Maashi with a form of telepathy. He called Maashi Talinda.

With time, Maashi learned that Krakoran couldn't feel emotions. They hunted other beings and used them to elicit strong emotions for their enjoyment, like what Tamara told him humans do when they watch videos or movie. Tantalizing fear, gripping horror, or unbearable pain were sought after. But pleasure, especially intense, mind-blowing pleasure was the thing they treasured the most.

Krakoran had hunted Chamranlinas for centuries for this reason. Their preferred prey were Fanellas and Sheffrous, which they regarded as invaluable.

The transfer of pleasure was simple. The little worker used an appendage with soft bristles to caress Maashi's genitals. Maashi, stuck in the clear casing with only his face and genitals free, couldn't escape the stimulation. The worker continued until Maashi showed signs of intense pleasure. He watched for changes in breathing, eye dilation, and discrete moaning. When Maashi was close to climax, the little worker called for the Krakoran whom he addressed as His Excellency the Master Hunter.

The Krakoran would establish contact with Maashi with a long filamentous tentacle and feel Maashi's emotions as if they were its own. He would stretch his amoeba-like body, glow intensely, and wave after wave of fluorescent fluid would flow in his tentacles. Daily visits by the Krakoran with intense sharing of pleasure ensured Maashi's survival.

The recollection upset Maashi so much he bounced off the couch and ran to the water room. He threw up copious amounts of fluid. To this day, even fragmented memories were hard to bear.

Maashi inhaled deeply. He stared at the low ceiling of his water room. He sat on the floor and gripped his legs, overcome with anger. Why did nature curse Sheffrous? Why was pleasure such an essential part of their lives that without it they couldn't survive? Some Chamranlinas envied Sheffrous because their days were constantly filled with pleasure, but Maashi saw reality from a totally different perspective. Pleasure controlled his life and the lack of it could bring forth terrible misery.

Recent changes in his body were clear indications he was attaining maturity. Controlling his libido became paramount. This wasn't an easy feat aboard the needle. He had experienced urges all his life, but now, they had the power to control his mind.

Maashi went back to his couch and drifted off to sleep in a world invaded by amoebas and crawling creatures. A sensation of being flat and floating came to him. He recalled the long flat creature that Tamara was so fond of. Images formed and swirled in his mind. Light and darkness competed in an immense void. A massive arch carved in solid rock framed a world filled with intense white light. The light pulsed every thirty minutes. He woke up eyes wide with dread.

Chapter 21

Maashi sat up so fast he almost fell off the narrow couch. He stared at the walls of his receiving room in disbelief, gathering his thoughts. Was it possible the floating creature had communicated with him in his dream? To show him a portal?

Everything had felt so real. With its long thin form hovering close, it was as if the creature hung right above him. He even heard its faint humming. Could the massive arch he saw be the gateway to the world of the Krakoran? Or was it his mind playing tricks? Could he trust the strange creature or was it manipulating him?

Finding the portal to the world of the Krakoran had been the lifelong goal of hundreds of Chamranlinas throughout the centuries. The discovery of the threshold to their world would be an incredible find.

Maashi had spent so many restless nights wondering where his friend Tomisho was held after his capture by the Krakoran. He would have given anything to reach him. Destroying the portal would change the future of the Chamranlinas like no other event had done before, not even leaving Chamtali, their home world, to come to Chitina. *Could it be done?* The immensity of the thought overwhelmed him. *Was it even possible?*

Was his desire to find that portal so strong it affected his dreams? Was he a victim of his own wishes? Perhaps the need to avenge his time as a prisoner pushed his mind to extremes?

The light had been so bright. The heat it produced burned his skin and his second eyelids had instinctively shut to protect his eyes from the glare. But how could he be sure the vision was real?

A chime indicated someone was at the door. "Enter," he said.

Tamara bolted into the room. She was still wearing her sleeping clothes, what she called her pajamas. Maashi smiled. They were pink and made of finely woven clothing which kept her warm at night. She couldn't stand the cold. His tolerance was much greater. He never paid attention to heat and cold but knew she couldn't stand it.

"Maashi," she said in an excited tone, "you'll never guess the dream I had last night. It felt so real."

Shared dreams were uncommon but not unheard of, especially in kindred spirits. Her alien mind was close to his. "What was your dream about?" Maashi stood and swept her into his arms. She smelled fresh like morning dew. How he wished she was naked against his skin.

Tamara giggled. She kissed his neck and cooed. "Put me down and I'll explain everything."

Maashi set her down gently on the couch and sat right beside her. A warm wave rolled over him. Saliva flooded his mouth. The desire to kiss her was almost irresistible.

"Remember how we talked with Dennyvan about a portal with the Krakoran? Well, I saw an immense arch in my dream. Could it be the portal?"

Maashi brushed his lips against her neck.

The door opened and Chari came in. He grinned. "I'm not surprised to see you two together." He sat opposite them and observed them with obvious pleasure. He moved his lips in his characteristic fashion as if he had a little kego twig in between them. "Is there anything I should know?" he said with a cynical tone.

Maashi chuckled. "Only that I took a nap, and a strange vision came upon me."

Chari ran his fingers through his unruly coal black hair. "A vision?"

"An immense arch with a brilliant white light?" blurted out Tamara.

Maashi nodded. "Yes."

"Was the flat creature present in your vision?" asked Tamara.

"Yes, it was," said Maashi. "I even heard the sound it made."

"Do you think that flat creature sent us the same information? Maybe it's trying to contact us."

Chari let out a low hiss. "I think that creature is dangerous. I don't like the fact it can reach into your minds this way."

"I think it's attempting to send us a message," said Tamara.

Chari looked at her, then at Maashi. "Whatever the case, I checked out the latest information about the asteroid. We are convinced the Rodenegad ship is hidden inside. There is a long narrow passageway that leads to a large hollow area, much bigger than would normally be expected inside an asteroid."

Tamara's face lit up. "Perhaps it has been designed that way on purpose," she glanced at Maashi, "to hide ships or a portal."

Chari stared at Tamara. "You have such a vivid imagination, Tamara. You see things that don't exist except in folklore." Chari crossed his arms on his chest. "Nonetheless, I think you two need to disclose your vision with Dennyvan. We'll see what he says."

"Have you gone mad?" Dennyvan hit his closed fist in his other hand. "You don't have the slightest idea of how ludicrous what you're proposing is, do you?"

Tamara was the first to react. *Men were so dense sometimes.* "I know this sounds far-fetched but—"

"I will not grant an answer to that ridiculous plan. We cannot go in a battle in tight quarters with an alien ship. It is too risky and especially with a Sheffrou, his Chimitanga, and two humans that have just been rescued. For all I know, we could be sucked into this portal you're talking about and sent across the universe."

Tamara pushed on. "What if we sent a shuttle to investigate? We could confirm the existence of the portal, then find a way to blow it up."

"What? I will not send my men on a suicide mission. That is out of the question."

"How about a drone then?" Her face became animated with excitement. "Yes. That's it. A drone with a bomb."

Everyone looked at her, eyes wide with disbelief. Even Dennyvan's face contorted in an ugly way. That's when Tamara realized that she was talking to Chamis, supposedly trained for combat but geared for peace, trying to avoid direct conflict as much as possible. *I guess that's why they were never able to defeat the Krakoran.*

Dennyvan rose from his seat in silence. He stared at her as if seeing her for the first time, "I have heard enough. As soon as we finish transferring those two males to the human ship, we will return to Chitina." His words had a dead finality to them. He glared at Maashi and Chari and turned to exit the receiving room.

Anger simmered in Tamara. She stood up. "I'll be in my quarters."

As she finished saying the words, she felt a fluttering beside her like huge butterfly wings. She looked over her shoulder and opened her mouth in surprise to scream but no sound came out.

A Rodenegad materialized and with one powerful scoop of his long arms grabbed Tamara's neck and Maashi's forearm. Dennyvan roared into action and slammed the creature's helmeted head with a powerful blow while Chari bolted ahead to hold Maashi.

The creature shook violently. Maashi jerked back his arm until his shirt sleeve ripped. The Rodenegad lost its grip leaving a large gash on Maashi's arm then it disappeared, carrying Tamara with it.

The whole incident lasted less than ten seconds.

Pushing Chari out of his way, Maashi screamed. "Noooooooo! How could this happen? How is this possible?" Fury blinded him. He tore off his mangled shirt, paced the room like a trapped feline, and with long fingers pulled at his hair.

Standing a few feet away, Dennyvan's eyes thinned with anger. He raised his wristband close to his face and listened to a transmission from the control room. "Sending security to your coordinates as we speak," said the voice.

"Understood," answered Dennyvan. "See if you can find where that Rodenegad came from. Increase shields to maximum."

Maashi's head shot up and he glared at Dennyvan. "Why weren't the shields up? Why put us at risk?"

"The Rodenegad ship had gone out of range so we assumed it could not transport individuals," said Dennyvan in a somber tone. "The shields weren't at full capacity."

"It was out of range for us but not for them," said Chari with sarcasm in his voice.

Dennyvan shot him a hateful look.

"Sir," said the voice from the control room. "We have the coordinates, and we can confirm the Rodenegad ship is located inside the asteroid."

"Thanks. Dennyvan out."

Maashi straightened to his full height, his head almost touching the low ceiling. His mind calculated possibilities of rescue. "It's our turn to pay the Rodenegad a little visit. When can we leave?" said Maashi, his jaw set and a determined expression shadowed his face. There was no doubt in his mind that they would go and save Tamara.

"We are not leaving," said Dennyvan stressing every word. "I will confer with one of the other needles and then we will devise a plan to retrieve your Chimitanga."

Maashi cocked his head to the right. "Do you understand that there is a strong possibility that a portal exists inside the asteroid and that the Rodenegad will rush to trade or transfer their prisoners if two needles try to intercept them?"

Dennyvan's brow darkened, and he said, "A possibility is not a certainty, and the Rodenegad may or may not contact the Krakoran. Remember, we have no proof the portal exists. It is safer to wait for the other needle."

Maashi fisted his hands. "The safest course of action isn't always the best."

"This is my decision, and I don't want to hear anything more from you, Sheffrou."

Maashi hissed but held back any further comment. It would be futile to argue with Dennyvan.

Two guards reported at the door. Dennyvan turned to leave. He stopped and said, "Do not try anything foolish, or I will put you in the brig."

Maashi took a step back and crossed his arms on his chest.

When Dennyvan had gone out, he said, "Leave me, Chari. I want to be alone."

Chari sighed, nodded, and left the room.

Maashi sat down and held his head in his hands. *How could this happen?* He thought of Tamara and how lost and afraid she must feel. Anger gripped his insides. *What if she was hurt?*

He swallowed his saliva and inhaled a long breath to stop his shaking. He couldn't let his emotions cloud his mind.

After a little while, he opened the virtual screen of the ship's computer. He searched for a few minutes until he found what he was looking for, basic and advanced shuttle operations and an extensive map of a large sector of space comprising their location.

Chapter 22

Maashi glanced at Chari sitting on the couch opposite his. "What do you think?" He had made his decision and wanted to find out what was his Chowli's position.

Chari crossed his legs and pondered the question, chewing on his twig. "Let's have a drink." He clicked on the controls beside him and a carafe and two lumis appeared on the synthetic table beside the couch. He poured himself a generous portion of his favorite green liquor, filled one for Maashi, and handed it to him.

Maashi leaned back on his own couch and rolled the opalescent glass in his palms to warm the liquor.

They both sipped in silence for a moment.

Chari pulled his twig out. "There are pros and cons of course," he said. "Loss of life. Perhaps our own lives."

Maashi set his glass down on the other table beside him. "By all the Black Creatures that have ever existed, we can't waste this opportunity." He emphasized the statement by leaning closer to his Chowli. "We must find Tamara. We can scan their ship for a human signature and look for the portal. This may be our only chance to destroy it."

Chari swallowed a generous gulp of his drink. "If the portal really exists. And even if it does, we may not be able to annihilate it."

"No," said Maashi, his voice resolute. "Not we. I am the one who must act." He raised his hand to silence any protest from his Chowli. "I will find the portal and destroy it. So many Chamranlinas have suffered and died under the yoke of the Krakoran. The kidnappings have gone on for centuries, even before we moved from our home world Chamtali to our current colony on Chitina." Maashi spread his hands on his knees. "Our lives would be so different if it weren't for the enemy's threat hanging over us."

With eyes glowing, he added, "I've asked myself a thousand times, why did I survive being kidnapped by the Krakoran when so many courageous Pure Colors have died? Now I know why. This is my destiny. This is why I was spared."

Chari raised his arm in protest. "Maashi, you're getting carried away. It seems like you're attributing some divine purpose to the fact that you survived being kidnapped by the Krakoran."

"Throughout the ages," added Maashi, "Sheffrous were bred and nurtured by the colony for a purpose. The Elders hoped Sheffrous would further the population by producing more Fanellas but also find a solution to escape the wrath of the enemy. Many have tried and failed. Now it's my turn to prove myself. My fate wasn't to die then. It is to destroy this portal and free our race forever from the reach of these monsters."

Chari's lips stretched into a mocking grin. "A speech worthy of foot stomping." He shook his head. "Are you sure you want to do this?"

Maashi's decision was made. He stared straight ahead. "It's my life, my choice." His eyes narrowed and their amber color darkened. "I'm not going back to Chitina with my head down, my face hidden in shadows, for a punishment of 200 lashes. I will not be treated like a criminal because the Sawishas envy me."

"The risk is too great. I can't let you do this. You don't even know for sure if the portal is real. Your desire to destroy the connection to the enemy is so great you have visions. It may all be a mind trick." Chari set down his glass. "My function is to protect you. The Council would put the blame on me if anything happened."

Maashi rose from his seat. "I must try. I will free Tamara and destroy the portal. It is the honorable thing to do." He stretched and glared at Chari with revulsion. "I have put my trust in you but now I see I was mistaken. I always wondered why the Council of Elders sent you to the Burned Zone. You were the Leader of the Rebellion that rocked the foundation of our colony more than sixty sequences ago. Twenty-three Ghouli Ghouli and Multis lost their lives during the two sequences it lasted. Many of your coconspirators were served with 100 and 200 lashes but you were spared. You negotiated with the Council and somehow persuaded them to send you in exile to the Burned Zone without further punishment."

"That was uncalled for." Chari's black eyes thinned with anger. "What are you implying?"

"Honor is a strange thing, Chari. I believe nothing is more important than destroying the connection between our world and the world of the Krakoran. I also believe that what you did after the Rebellion, twisting the truth, finding a loophole in the law to avoid physical punishment when your companions were flogged was dishonorable. Your reputation has been smeared and you have carried this dishonor since then."

Maashi paused. "It took me a long time to understand why you didn't have any friends. Just a few acquaintances here and there. I thought that somehow the Multicolors treated you differently because you were a Ghouli Ghouli. But after I met them, I surmised there was something different about you. Now, I think I know what it is."

The punch came so fast that Maashi never saw it coming. He blinked and quickly refocused but before he could move, Chari grabbed him by the shoulders and rammed him against the wall. "Talitanfe," he uttered to the computer, ordering it to stop recording.

"Listen to me, SHONAVA Maashi," Chari growled, his face an inch away from Maashi's. "You may be a mature Sheffrou but that doesn't give you the right to insult me. You probably would've done the same. Do not presume to pass judgement on me."

Maashi hissed. The sound was low and menacing. "Let me go, now."

"I can't. My function is to protect you from bad decisions. I won't let you throw your life away."

Maashi gathered his strength, his muscles tensed under his skin. He roared and freed his arms from Chari's grasp. He punched him in the stomach then rained blows on his head. Chari backed away and lifted his arms to protect his face. Another punch hit his stomach with such intensity he dropped to his knees. Maashi, overcome with fury, kicked him until he collapsed to the ground.

Taking in a long breath, Maashi signaled the computer with his left arm and summoned tape and ties. He quickly taped Chari's eyes and mouth shut and secured his wrists and ankles. He signaled the computer again and a large rectangular compartment made of woven fibers appeared propped alongside the wall. He lifted the unconscious Chari and settled him in the container. He closed it, placed a few big cushions on it, and revoked the Talifante order.

Maashi paused and called Redden. "I need to stretch my legs and I can't leave my room without an escort. Would you like to join me? Perhaps you could send the guards away."

Redden thought highly of himself. He would be flattered by Maashi's request and never suspect a ruse. Maashi quickly changed his clothes choosing a dark olive color for shirt and pants and a dark gray for his sash. He exited the room without a sound. As he expected, the guards were nowhere to be seen. His long stride carried him swiftly down the hall in the direction of the back of the needle where the shuttles were located.

Chapter 23

The teletransport had acted like a blow to Tamara's head, and she blacked out. When she came to, she opened her eyes and slowly raised herself on her elbows then sat up on the floor. Two things confirmed that she was aboard the Rodenegad ship. First, the smell. The rotten egg smell was unmistakable and overpowering. Second, the semi-obscure detention cell with mirrored walls and a cold floor. Night or day, the lighting never changed much.

She moaned and rubbed her forehead. *Back again. How nice.*

Her thoughts immediately went to Maashi. *Was he also captured?* Everything happened so fast she couldn't be sure.

That alien had grabbed her like a doll made of cloth. Her neck was sore. She stretched her muscles and her legs. The waiting began. It might take a few days, but she was sure someone would come. She had to stay alert and in shape. Keep her hopes up. Not that she had anything else to do. She rose and paced around the small room no bigger than a walk-in closet.

Moans and soft crying could be heard. There were others. Humans? Possibly.

Maybe the Rodenegad had a full load of prisoners. They might be planning to trade them soon or send them to the Krakoran. *What a horrible thought.* She remembered hearing that if a prisoner wasn't useful to the Krakoran, they were given to their workers as food. She shuddered with fear and disgust.

Maashi, you better hurry. I need to get out of here asap.

Chapter 24

"Bring him in," said Dennyvan. He sat in his black chair in the conference room with crests of Black and Silver Guards who died with honor hanging on the purple walls, his wide brow hiding a penetrating gaze.

His assistant Redden stood by his side. He rubbed his big hands and nodded. "Right away, sir."

Minutes later, Chari walked into Dennyvan's receiving room. Wearing olive clothing and his purple and pink sash, he shot a suspicious look toward the Leader. He came forward, stood a few feet away from Dennyvan, and crossed his arms on his chest.

"Have a seat, Chowli," Dennyvan pointed to a couch across from where he sat. He waited until Chari was settled and said, "I want to know what happened between you and Sheffrou Maashi yesterday evening. You were fortunate we found you in that box. You were still unconscious. Why did you get into a fight with Sheffrou Maashi?"

Chari's hand reached for his inner pocket for his kego twig but stopped mid-way through. He leaned on the back of the couch and spoke slowly rubbing his jaw, "What happens between the Sheffrou and me is not for anyone else's ears."

Dennyvan tilted his head to one side. "The Sheffrou has taken command of one of my shuttles. He is going to the asteroid when I specifically told him not to leave. Whatever disagreement we had before is now irrelevant. He is my responsibility. He is under my protection. I want answers."

Chari lowered his head. He ran his fingers through his ebony hair.

Dennyvan's patience was running out. "I'm waiting," he growled.

Chari sighed. "As you know, Sheffrou Maashi harbored strong feelings for the human female. When the Rodenegad abducted Tamara, he became distraught to the point he lost all logical thinking, and his emotions dictated his actions." Chari glanced over to Dennyvan to determine if he believed him.

"Continue," said Dennyvan, his face set in angry mode.

"He vowed to go after her. I tried to stop him and made the costly mistake of underestimating his anger and determination. His Dompati has increased his strength and aggressivity. I had been training him for weeks to face Pure Colors should he run into challenges on Chitina but did not anticipate his fury when I told him he couldn't leave and risk his life in a fool's quest." Chari moved his lips as if he wanted to add something but hesitated.

Dennyvan leaned forward and said, "Computer, Talifante," He stared at Chari. "What quest? What is it you're not telling me?"

"I should add that Sheffrou Maashi had visions. This started just recently. Every time he got a few hours of sleep, he would see a dot in space that stretched into a complete circle. He was convinced it was a portal, some cosmic connection between our world and the world of the Krakoran. He mentioned it to you also. Even though I insisted that there wasn't sufficient proof it existed, that it could be just some hallucination or a figment of his imagination, he hissed at me for not understanding." Chari took a deep breath and his hand reached for his painful broken ribs.

Dennyvan's expression changed. He rubbed his hands and said, "Many rumors have circulated about a gateway to the Krakoran world. Prisoners we rescued talked about a portal of some kind. No one really believed them, but I know for a fact that the Krakoran we pursued managed to escape our ships more than once. They were right in front of us and then they were gone. We suspected they traveled to a parallel world we couldn't reach."

Dennyvan stood and paced the room. "Perhaps that portal really exists. I will contact the other needle and investigate this further." His gaze rested on Chari. "Why didn't you go with him?"

"My job as Chowli is to protect Maashi. I didn't believe him. I wasn't going to let him risk his life to find a portal because he had a vision. We fought." Chari lowered his head. "He gave me a thorough beating."

Dennyvan's eyes thinned. "He did." Nodding, he said, "Good for him." He raised his arm and said to his bracelet, "Computer, resume recording. Helm, plot a course for the asteroid at moderate speed. Engage." He stared at Chari with dismay. "Consider yourself fortunate if the Sheffrou agrees to keep you as Chowli." With that, he stumped out of the room.

Chapter 25

Maashi sat at the controls and ordered the computer to plot a course to the asteroid. Piloting a shuttle in real time, he surmised, wasn't that different from simulations.

Like all Chamranlinas, he had been trained to pilot different types of flying vehicles, including spaceships. Two hundred sequences ago, the Chamranlinas had to escape Chamtali, their beloved home world plagued by earthquakes and extreme volcanic activity. Since then, preparedness for unforeseen events, droughts, floods, and even massive attacks by the enemy, was required for everyone. The fact that Chamis lived long lives meant that even the most inept became proficient in basic training.

He grabbed the console with both hands and breathed deeply. His emotions were reined in by a tight rope threatening to snap if he let them take over. *Was Tamara still alive? Was she safe?* At this distance, trying to locate her position aboard the enemy ship was close to impossible. He couldn't sense her presence and not knowing her condition tore him apart. He exhaled a long-held breath.

Conflicting thoughts boiled in his head. Although he had a plan, Maashi wasn't sure it would work without glitches. Experience had taught him there were always some. Tamara's safety was foremost in his mind, but he couldn't let that distract him from his first goal which was to find and destroy the connection between this world and the Krakoran world. If the visions were accurate, and he was convinced they were, the portal was deep inside the asteroid.

Maashi loathed the Krakoran. They had hunted his people without mercy and had brought his species close to extinction. His hatred awakened now that he saw a possible solution for his people. He swallowed with difficulty the bile surging in his mouth.

The shuttle approached the asteroid from underneath and easily rose and slipped through the large fissure Dennyvan's men had discovered between two massive rock formations. Maashi switched to manual controls and piloted the craft himself. Using only the ship's thrusters, he avoided the many obstacles along his path. Jagged outcroppings threatened to hit his small craft and boulders floated about freely, no doubt recently broken off by the Rodenegad ship. The alien ships, built with a composite metal, were almost indestructible and traveled with ease amid space debris and asteroids of all sizes.

Maashi hugged the irregular walls with dexterity and slowed his speed to minimize the chance of detection. The mouth of the cave was narrow but the cave itself could hide a flotilla of vessels.

The Rodenegad ship loomed ahead. Instead of a sleek design like the Chamranlinas' ships, theirs were huge and composed of multiple sections attached to a core mid-section. He planned to board it like a small creature which has hopped on the back of a large one. As he focused on the spaceship growing larger and filling the viewing screen, his lips stretched into a spiteful grin.

If his visions were right, he would sever the connection between his world and the world of the Krakoran forever. Clenching his hands in a rare display of anger, he called upon the Souls of his Ancestors to give him strength and stand with him in this perilous endeavor. Success would free his people at last and he would walk with pride as a mature Sheffrou.

The stakes were high. He might lose his life. Possibly endanger Tamara's life.... But failing to destroy the connection was unacceptable.

Maashi refocused on the task at hand. Now within closer range, he scanned the interior of the Rodenegad ship in detail and located a place devoid of obstacles and far removed from the command center. Teletransportation was a simple affair but executing it in enemy territory had to be flawless otherwise several things could happen, all with negative outcomes.

He had to be taken alive....

He searched for Tamara's vital signs, found her, and memorized the coordinates. Luckily, she wasn't too far from where he would materialize. His heart drummed in his abdomen. He surmised the last time he was so wound up was when he had just been kidnapped by the Krakoran. He inhaled deeply then entered the coordinates for transport in the computer, confirmed them, then pressed the controls. In less than ten seconds, the transport aboard the Rodenegad ship was complete.

The pungent odor of sulfur confirmed he had beamed on board successfully. Senses on alert, Maashi proceeded ahead. He had verified the gas composition before beaming on the ship. The twenty-two percent oxygen and two percent helium levels were acceptable.

In Maashi's opinion, Rodenegad ships were designed in a most peculiar fashion. Mirrors and bright metallic surfaces covered every surface, including walls and ceilings. For reasons Maashi couldn't understand, the Rodenegad enjoyed watching their reflection from every angle. The endless mirrors created an illusion of infinity and any alien brazen enough to board the ship rapidly became confused and disoriented.

Maashi counted his steps, turns, and registered the overall direction he was traveling. He walked up to a shiny metallic door and for the first time in a long while, stared at his reflection. Instead of the young Sheffrou he remembered, lean and swift of limbs, a tall muscular Chamranlina stood, a portrait of determination and purpose.

He stared for the briefest of moments, but it was enough. A dot that morphed into a line appeared on the mirror behind him. The line spread open and the stocky shape of a Rodenegad stepped in. He immediately pressed the sharp edge of a blade on Maashi's neck, and a mechanical arm grabbed his waist. The alien pushed the blade harder, and it grazed his skin. A warm trickle ran down Maashi's neck.

"Don't move, execrable," the Rodenegad sputtered, "or I will end you."

The hatred in the alien warrior's eyes as seen in his mirrored reflection iced Maashi's blood. Maashi had learned their language when he impersonated the Woo-Odong-Ti. The smell of fear and loathing emanating from the creature filled his nostrils. Any attempt to resist would get him killed.

Maashi couldn't help remembering Dennyvan's warning: 'There is a 99% chance you'll get caught and they won't spare you. They don't want mature Sheffrous. They only want the young ones.'

He heard a hissing sound and sensed a prick on each side of his neck. The world disappeared. His mind slipped into a state close to unconsciousness. He collapsed face down on the floor.

Only a minute area in his mind continued to register the voice of his aggressor.

"I gave him enough to drop a bull shoshan," the warrior's voice a sputtering of words. "He should be out for hours. Time sufficient to secure him for transport."

"Leader," said another Rodenegad who had appeared, "do you think the Krakoran will take him?"

"Certainty is not present, but I won't waste the opportunity to make a deal."

"Why not take the specimen?" said the second Rodenegad. "This one is healthy."

The warrior said, "This one is mature. He can resist training. Telepathic abilities increase with age. Can be used to kill. Now, stop questions. Help me secure him."

Maashi heard scraping sounds like metal rubbing against metal. Then nothing.

A while later, Maashi regained consciousness and felt his breath on the cold metallic floor. He was resting on his side, hands cuffed together in front of him and bound to a metal belt which circled his waist. The words of the two Rodenegad floated in his mind and assembled themselves like pieces of a puzzle. Maashi's eyes thinned, he clamped his jaw, and waited. His plan was coming together.

Chapter 26

A single reddish dot floated in deep space. No, the exact color was magenta.

In Maashi's dream, a minute later the dot divided into two, then four, then eight, and so on. It created a line that curved and continued to elongate on both sides. After fifteen minutes, a half circle formed. He watched, mesmerized, as the line stretched until it joined at the bottom and produced a full circle, considered the perfect form in Chamranlina culture.

Thirty minutes. That's how long it took for the circle to form. Once completed, the circle's center started throbbing, one pulse per second. Maashi felt like he was observing a phenomenon in an accelerated fashion. The time he experienced in the dream was discordant with the time of the event. He understood the number thirty was crucial.

Maashi repositioned his long frame to make himself comfortable on his cell's cold metallic floor. He didn't understand why the Rodenegad had removed all his clothes except his chemcha, his undergarment. The cold didn't bother him, but he was used to thick mattresses overflowing with plush pillows. He groaned in displeasure.

Every time he reached a dreamlike state over the last few days, the same vision invaded his mind, but never as vivid as he had just seen it. Maashi struggled to make sense of what he saw.

Does the circle represent the portal? His intuition told him yes, this was the portal. *Then what are the thirty minutes about?*

His internal clock suggested five days had elapsed since his capture. The Rodenegad jailer had removed the metallic belt from his waist and although his wrists were still bound together, he could move his arms in front of him. The jailer brought some sulfur-tasting water daily but no food. He would drink some of the fluid, but the awful taste prevented him from emptying the bottle with a long, curved neck. He grew impatient, wrestling with conflicting ideas on how to leave his cell and travel through the ship without arousing suspicion.

He had the sudden feeling of being watched. He glanced at the ceiling and spotted the elongated flat creature he had seen in Dennyvan's ship. It was floating and undulating freely as if expecting a response.

"You're the one who sent me the vision, aren't you?" Maashi's voice sounded a little high pitched due to the presence of helium in the air. He felt ill at ease and didn't make any move to avoid upsetting the creature. He couldn't forget it had almost killed him before.

The creature undulated faster.

"It's a vision of the future, isn't it?"

The creature stilled, its many eyes grew darker, then in a fraction of a second, it disappeared.

Maashi remembered how last time it had disappeared, the crew couldn't locate it on the ship. Perhaps it could materialize at will, whenever and wherever it wants. Perhaps it could travel through time and that's how it knew the future....

Maashi stretched, catching sight of a small flat device, no bigger than his thumb, in between his legs. The jailer must have dropped it. He recalled the alien had last been inside the cell hours ago and the device wasn't there before.

Maashi looked up at the ceiling. *Did the flat creature bring it?* Although puzzled, he wasted no time scooping up the device. It was the same one the aliens used to open the mirrors and travel throughout the ship. He stood and cautiously pressed the device on the mirrored wall behind him. As if in cue, a dot formed, stretched upwards and downwards forming a vertical line that separated the mirror into two panels. Maashi stepped out of his cell. Still holding the strange device, he touched his handcuffs and they unlocked. Maashi caught them before they dropped on the floor. He refrained from gasping. Hope filled his mind.

Taking a quick look around, he visualized the ship's layout, and advanced in the direction of Tamara's cell keeping a wary eye for any change in the mirrors.

Coming upon a hexagonal area, he paused. Six mirrors stood before him. Only one led to Tamara's cell. The others could be traps or expose him. To find the correct door, he closed his eyes and used a sense he was beginning to familiarize himself with. All substances and especially living beings emitted waves as unique as fingerprints that traveled through matter. The closer you were to the source, the stronger they felt. As a mature Sheffrou, Maashi could detect them and pinpoint their source.

Maashi stood still and cleared his mind. He stared at the chosen mirror. Hesitated. This sixth sense was still new. There was a slight possibility he was wrong. If so, the Rodenegad would recapture him and make him pay for his escapade. Memories of indescribable pain came to him. Their cruelty was surpassed only by the Krakorans'. He held his breath, pressed the device on the mirror, and watched the dot appear and stretch vertically into a line. Two sides opened.

Tamara jumped up from the floor and squeaked. "Maashi! What are you doing here? Where did you come from?"

Her high-pitched voice sounded like she had eaten a mouthful of whistli berries. Those berries were an endless source of hilarity when he was a youngster because they changed everyone's voice.

"Quickly, step out before the mirror closes," he said, extending a hand.

She took his hand and stepped out of her cell. The mirror reformed immediately behind her.

"Why are you wearing only a chemcha?" Tamara's eyes widened and instead of jumping in his arms, she stayed where she was transferring her weight from foot to foot. Maashi felt her shyness. It reminded him of a young Sheffrou intimidated by the imposing presence of an older Sawisha.

All he wanted was to take her in his arms and feel the smoothness of her skin on his. Instead, he froze and refrained from approaching her. It was obvious his scant attire made her uncomfortable like months ago when they had just met. In his world, wearing clothes was optional. He should have remembered that clothing was important to her.

"Forgive my appearance. The aliens removed my clothes, and accessing the computer to find suitable coverings is too risky."

"I'm sorry. It's just that you look different and..."

"Do I look offensive to you?"

"Of course not. It's just that you've changed and..."

Maashi noted her dilated pupils and the blush spreading across her face and neck. She held her hands tightly together as if afraid to touch him. He smiled inwardly. His presence stimulated her senses, and her body reacted in a positive way. One couldn't ask for more evidence that she was pleased to see him.

"Tamara, I'm happy to have found you but you must leave this ship. The Rodenegad will soon connect with the portal and transfer the prisoners to the Krakoran. Come, follow me."

"No. We must free the other prisoners first. There are other humans here. I've heard their voices. We can't leave them." Her eyes filled with tears.

Maashi hissed softly. She was right; he couldn't leave without the others. However, every minute counted. Time spent roaming the corridors increased the risk of being discovered.

Maashi's brow widened. "Where are they?"

"All the mirrors down this way contain prisoners," Tamara said. "Can't you open the other mirrors the same way you opened mine?"

Maashi blinked and nodded sideways. He raised his hand to activate the device on the next door.

"Wait," Tamara said. "Let me stand by your side so they will see me when you open the mirror."

He proceeded to open all the doors and was surprised to see how so many had been caught by the aliens. Every time one came out, Tamara put a finger on her lips to ask them to remain silent and showed them the way down the hall. The humans, wearing simple clothing consisting of a shirt and pants, were tall and even thinner than Lieutenant Yoon and his assistant, Patel. Unfamiliar with Chamranlinas, they were wary of this new alien and some looked terrified. Tamara had to quickly shush them before they cried out in alarm. Thankfully, they didn't show signs indicating they had been tortured.

Once all fourteen of them were out, Maashi gave them their instructions. "You must all leave. I will lead you to a shuttle. You must travel away from this ship and reach deep space as quickly as possible. There is a human and a Chamranlina ship in the vicinity to render assistance."

Tamara translated into simpler sentences as needed.

As they prepared to leave, Maashi noticed there was one last unopened mirror. He approached it. That mirror wasn't there before. He was certain of it. Was it a trap? He tried to access the interior but couldn't get a clear picture in his mind. His eyes thinned with concentration. Something was wrong.

"Tamara, you and the others step back twenty paces. I'm not sure this one leads to a prisoner."

He put the device against the door and opened it.

A Chami stepped out. Behind him stood a Rodenegad with one long arm around his neck and another holding an impressive, serrated knife pressed on his waist. One look and Maashi recognized the Multi, one of his own guards.

Maashi hissed. The Rodenegad pressed the knife harder until pink blood surged from the guard's side.

Maashi didn't dare make a move. How could he free the Multi without a fight? The other humans stood a few feet back, unable to help. Maashi's anger funneled his energy. His mind reached and grabbed the enemy's thoughts, harnessed them. "Hot. Burning. You're burning," he said.

For a moment, nothing happened. Then, the alien took a step back and his hold slipped just enough for the Multi to jerk away. Maashi jumped ahead and rammed the Rodenegad against the wall.

"Help me contain him, Rowni," Maashi said using all his weight to keep the enemy pinned.

The Rodenegad seemed to have recuperated from his trance-like state and used his massive size to push the two Chamis like they were dwarves fighting a giant. Still holding his knife, the blade swung in the air coming within inches of Maashi's face.

"Hold his arm!" Maashi yelled. He searched the Rodenegad's sleeves and retrieved another device. He clicked at Rowni in the Chami language. Using all his strength, Maashi tilted the Rodenegad's head backward to cut his air giving them the advantage. The two Chamis used their combined weight to keep the enemy off balance and pushed him back step by step towards the cell. Then, with a final, mighty effort, they shoved him into the cell. Maashi closed the mirror.

Straightening, they looked at each other.

"Shonava?" the guard clicked. "Is it really you?" He kissed Maashi's shoulder and hugged him.

Maashi closed his eyes, savoring the hug which felt like a brisk intake of fresh energy. He kissed the Multi, leader of his own security team, kidnapped by the Krakoran months ago.

Muffled exclamations from the humans brought them back to reality.

Maashi said in English, "We must go to the shuttle."

A dark-skinned human stepped forward and said, "We know the way."

"Take this device to open the mirrors," said Maashi handing him the device he had wrestled from the Rodenegad. "Leave now. Don't make any loud sound on your way there, especially no banging. The Rodenegad can detect movement by vibrations carried by metal. Use thrusters only when you fly away from the bulkhead of the ship," he said. "Can you pilot the shuttle?"

"Yes, sir. They're all pretty much the same," said another who looked up at Maashi without flinching. "But we'll need codes and passwords."

Maashi tilted his head to the right. "I can transfer them to your thoughts." Maashi paused. "To accomplish this, I must perform an act called sliva which is quite effective but may seem inappropriate."

The first human who spoke squared his shoulders and crossed his muscular arms on his chest. "What do you mean?" He squinted in Maashi's direction. "Will it be painful?"

Maashi glanced at Tamara, standing at his side. She nodded.

"He's going to kiss you," she said. "It might be pleasurable and make you uneasy, but you'll get all the information you need." She looked up at Maashi. "Hurry."

The brown-skinned human dropped his arms to his side and said, "Do it."

Maashi stepped forward and cupped the male's face with his hands, bent down, and kissed him. A long, soft kiss.

The man took a deep breath. He blinked several times as if dazed, opened his mouth to say something then closed it. He cleared his throat. "Numbers and codes. Right. They're all there."

"I also showed you the best way to get to the shuttle," said Maashi.

A few others mumbled with impatience. One of them said, "We should go now."

"Yes," said Maashi. "You too, Tamara."

"No. I'm staying with you."

"You must go. I plan to destroy the portal that connects to the world of the Krakoran; a dangerous objective and it may put my life at risk."

"If we die," said Tamara. "We die together."

Maashi knelt in front of Tamara. His voice sounded almost feminine in the environment, "I will join you when I'm done. I promise."

"I know the odds. I'm staying."

He felt a sudden surge of anger. So many had died staying by his side or trying to save him. She was so small yet so determined. Now, he had no choice; he had to succeed at all costs.

"Let's go then." Turning to the humans, he said, "Good luck."

Maashi's group ran down one corridor while the others ran the other way.

Chapter 27

Tamara saw how Maashi reacted when she refused to leave with the others. His eyes were dark with anger and the color drained from his face and neck, but she had made up her mind. He came to save her. She was determined to stay at his side until the end.

As they progressed along the mirrored hallways, the trio stayed on high alert for any hint of a Rodenegad. The strong sulfur smell made Tamara gag, and she started coughing. The more she tried to suppress it, the more she coughed. Maashi touched the shoulder of the Multi to tell him to halt and bent down towards her. He slipped two fingers under her chin. His metallic handcuffs were carefully lodged in his other hand so they wouldn't dangle and make a sound.

"Let me kiss you. Just a little kiss to relieve your cough."

She had no choice. Her coughing could alert the Rodenegad. Maashi could relieve it, but he would easily uncover her runaway feelings for him. She trembled at the thought.

What if being a mature Sheffrou meant his feelings for her had changed? She would gladly get a beating from the enemy rather than find out he didn't care for her.

Her anguish must have been visible because Maashi whispered something to the guard then he raised her face to his lips. The kiss was gentle, and she barely felt it but the message he transmitted was clear, *"I love you too."* He retreated, kept his gaze downward, then stood.

"Come, Shapinka. We must make haste."

He had called her Shapinka, Precious one, a meaningful term for the Chamis, a sign of deep affection. Tamara breathed more freely, thrilled that his feelings for her hadn't changed. And he had sent a clear message to the guard; she was important, and he was bound to protect her with his life. With her coughing under control, they pressed on.

They came to a room the size of a conference room, big enough for twenty people, with a large, bright metallic counter located in the middle, a shiny island in a sea of mirrors. There were two doors easily recognizable by breaks in the mirrors covered with a slate gray material with vertical characters. They were oddly shaped and overlapped with each other reminding Tamara of the Korean language. She could only guess why these strange Rodenegad surrounded themselves with so many reflective surfaces when they themselves looked more like robots with helmets on their heads and covered by dull, brown clothing. Was their own world shrouded in darkness?

"The device doesn't work on this console," said Maashi, his eyes dark with consternation. He applied it on all of them until he succeeded in activating one smaller surface. This one worked like a camera and showed a picture of the space outside the ship. Maashi proceeded to rotate the lens and made a 360-degree tour of their surroundings. He came to a sudden stop. A magenta dot up high on the screen had just divided itself in two.

Maashi's expression changed from one of surprise to one of concern as he watched the dot dividing once again in four. "We have 28 minutes to execute our plan."

He stared at Rowni who said, "Understood."

Maashi searched the room feverishly for another key to access to the main console. He tried lever after lever, but the console refused to turn on.

Tamara studied the rows of similar signs for evidence of patterns. A carved V was set at the beginning of every row which flowed left or right, up, or down. The game of Scrabble came to mind.

With stern looks on their faces, the two Chamis clicked away as they tried to solve the problem. She watched them and her anxiety grew. Why weren't there any Rodenegad in this room? They must have cameras to detect any abnormal activity aboard the ship. They would surely show up soon. Maashi and the Multi had no weapons. She didn't think the two could tackle more than one Rodenegad at a time.

What would they do if more than one appeared?

With her heart thumping hard, Tamara scanned the room. Perhaps they had overlooked something. She leaned back against a counter and felt a tap on her shoulder. She pivoted and didn't see anything until she looked up and saw the long floating creature. Her breath hitched.

Why was it here? Was it going to attack them?

"Maashi," she said in a loud whisper. "Look up."

He raised his head and slowly reached for the Multi to still him.

Tamara said in a gentle voice, "Are you here to help?"

The creature undulated faster then stopped. Hide. An instant later it disappeared.

"Take cover," said Tamara.

How could anyone hide in a room full of mirrors? Tamara remembered that the Rodenegad's head rotated on its axis but prevented them from looking downward or upward, so she crouched on the floor. Maashi and Rowni did the same.

A slit appeared in the middle of the mirrored door on the left. It opened and a Rodenegad shuffled in. The alien, built like a steam engine, huffed and wheezed his way in.

As soon as the door closed, Maashi and Rowni jumped him.

Rowni was immediately thrown. Pink blood oozed from his side staining his shirt. Somehow Maashi attacked the Rodenegad sideways and managed to hold onto its waist and arms with a Herculean grip.

"Quickly! Cuff him!" cried out Maashi.

Rowni struggled back to his feet and grabbed the handcuffs Maashi had dropped. He cuffed one of the alien's wrists then, with Maashi's help, brought the other arm behind his back and closed the handcuffs. Working together, they shoved him to the wall and held him there. Maashi's eyes bore down on the alien's faceless mask. After a few seconds, the Rodenegad crumpled to the floor.

Tamara approached the alien who had gone silent. "What did you do?" she asked. "Is he dead?"

"Unconscious."

Maashi felt along the folds of the alien's sleeves and retrieved a V-shaped device.

"That's the key we need to turn on the console," said Tamara in an excited whisper.

"We have only 22 minutes left," said Rowni. "Hurry."

Tamara pointed to a spot on the counter where several rows connected. "There, insert the V there."

Maashi nodded. He pressed the V on that spot. Rows of signs toggled upward, and the whole surface came to life with bright dots. He punched in instructions, but Tamara could see something wasn't right. His brow was dark. With eyes fixated on the screen, he tried different signal combinations. None seemed satisfactory. He paused and ran his fingers through his hair, a gesture Tamara knew well indicating severe frustration.

"One of us must stay here to ensure that the command to release the explosives is carried out," Maashi said in a low voice. "There isn't any other way."

"I'll stay, Shonava. You go with the Fanella."

"Unacceptable, Rowni. You've just been set free. I will stay."

"I'll stay too," said Tamara with conviction in her voice.

Maashi hissed. He opened and closed his fists.

The long flat creature reappeared. The sequence of light blue eyes underneath it vacillated, and it started to hum.

"18 minutes," Rowni said, keeping his voice low.

"The creature says," Tamara whispered, "we must all stay here."

"Yes, I heard it too." Maashi took Rowni's and Tamara's hand in his. "We must show we are united. The creature is planning something. That's why it wants us to stay here."

"How long must we wait?" asked Rowni.

"Not very long," said Maashi, "but we should obey for our own safety."

As soon as he finished speaking, the door to their left opened, a Rodenegad stumbled in and crashed on the floor. Maashi and Rowni pulled his body in the room. Tamara saw a few other Rodenegad lying about in the hallway behind. Some on their backs, some face down. She counted six of them.

"What happened to them?" she asked.

"This one is in a deep trance," said Rowni.

"Maashi," Tamara squealed, "look at the screen! The dots are making a circle."

"14 minutes," said Rowni.

Maashi quickly reached the control panel. He explained his plan to Tamara as he set the parameters.

"Using the new device, I'm setting the ship on a collision course with the portal. I will eject the ship's reactor which is programmed to explode. Should it fail to explode on its own, I'll release a series of drones armed with explosive devices to blow it up." Maashi checked the levers for errors. "I must stay and make sure everything goes as planned," he said. "Precise timing is crucial."

"Is everything going to blow up?" asked Tamara. "Even this ship?"

"Yes. Everything. But if the reactor explodes, I plan to steer the ship away so we can retrieve the Rodenegad. They must be tried for the trafficking of sentient aliens." He bent over and took Tamara's face in his hands. "Please, leave now with Rowni."

"I don't want to leave you," said Tamara. She was trembling and thought her legs would give way.

"Go," said Maashi.

"But how will you get out?"

"I'll transport directly into your shuttle from here." He bent his head and kissed her hands.

Tamara's mind was swimming in anguish. *Was Maashi telling the truth? Was he really planning to join them or was he just trying to save her?*

She tried to say something. but her voice was gone.

How could she go without him?

"Twelve minutes."

She wiped her tears and turned to face Rowni. The guard had found a weapon on the Rodenegad. Weapon in hand, he nodded one last time at Maashi, and picked Tamara up. He opened the first mirror, then sprinted down the hall.

Rowni opened another mirror and they both saw a Rodenegad slipping through. Rowni set Tamara down behind him. The alien reappeared. He held up a weapon in his gloved hand and fired, aiming for Rowni's hand, sparing the life of a valuable prisoner. The Multi hissed and dropped his weapon on the floor.

Without any hesitation, Tamara jumped, grabbed it, and fired three times at the Rodenegad, hitting his shoulders and chest. He fell on his side and remained still.

"Stop," said Rowni as he got up. "We'll attract the others. We must reach the shuttle bay. Time is almost up. Follow me." He reached for the weapon. "I'll hold this."

Relief flooded over Tamara. She had never shot at a real live target before. As an emergency room physician, she left the hospital at all hours and used a small handgun for protection. She didn't stop to check if the alien was dead.

They found another route which proved to be a shortcut.

"This way is better." His hand was bleeding and he slipped it in his wraparound shirt to avoid leaving a trail.

"Are you all right?"

"My hand is fine. We can take care of it later."

They reached a hangar with two alien shuttles. The door to one of them was open and they quickly boarded.

Tamara settled in the seat Rowni pointed at. He quickly tied the oversized restraints in a knot so she wouldn't float about in the cabin once they lost gravity. He tore a piece of his pants and wrapped his hand with it.

"Do you know how to fly this thing?"

"Trained to operate any type of vehicle, including alien space shuttles."

Rowni took his seat and activated the ship's controls. Tamara saw through the open door three Rodenegad zip in and rush into the shuttle bay. They aimed their weapons at the shuttle.

"Hurry!" yelled Tamara. "They're shooting at us." The shots sounded like firecrackers exploding on the hull. Tamara tried to swallow but her mouth had gone completely dry.

"Please hurry," she whispered. "We need to leave now."

Rowni triggered a lever and shut the door. He opened the shuttle bay to the void of space. A booming alarm went off. He released the forcefield that blocked their way out. The shuttle lifted off the floor. They made their way out of the confines of the hangar.

"Shields at full strength. Thrusters on maximum power," he said as the ship zoomed out.

Tamara hated take-offs. The increased gravity of acceleration hit her hard. Her stomach churned. Nausea made her head spin. She gripped her seat, forcing herself to breathe in and slowly exhale. She bit her lip feeling grateful for the pain. It would distract her and prevent another panic attack. A tiny drop of blood floated for a few moments in front of her face then gently rocked away to the back of the ship.

Don't leave me again Maashi. Make sure you join us.

Chapter 28

Maashi checked the main screen in the control room: eleven minutes. He scanned the computer and found the sequence of orders needed to eject the nuclear fusion core.

Adjusting the levers, he expected everything to go through smoothly but 'Error,' flashed repeatedly on the screen.

"How can this be?" he muttered.

Frustrated, he searched the database and scanned a long list of irrelevant details until he figured it out. The computer needed physical proof the one giving the order was a Rodenegad.

Maashi's anger flared, he hissed long and hard. He spotted the Rodenegad lying on the floor a few feet away. He went to his side, grabbed the alien under the arms to drag him to the console. Its dull brown leather-like clothing reeked of rotten eggs. The Rodenegad weighed as much as two adult Chamranlinas. Impossible to lift the vile creature.

Maashi clenched his fists and muttered between his teeth. "Souls of my ancestors!"

The thought of severing the alien's hand repulsed him but nonetheless, he readied himself. He spit in disgust when, from the corner of his eye, he saw another Rodenegad slip into the control room.

As soon as the alien stepped in, he aimed his weapon at Maashi's throat. Rage filled Maashi's mind. He hissed and the ear-shattering sound echoed off the mirrors like a thousand drums.

The Rodenegad hesitated a fraction of a second, just long enough for Maashi to pounce on him like a Raah-Hazan, the huge black panthers from Maashi's world. He jumped on the Rodenegad with such force that the alien lost his balance and slammed into the mirror behind it, breaking it.

Maashi grabbed the creature's weapon and threw it across the room hissing with renewed vigor. His amber eyes glowed as if they were on fire. Maashi had never been so committed to a single purpose until now. That despicable creature was the only obstacle standing between him and his goal.

"If I have to kill you to destroy the portal, then so be it."

With one hand, Maashi tilted the head of the Rodenegad backwards to render it unconscious. With the other hand and the weight of his body, he pinned the creature against the broken mirror. The creature struggled and made some gurgling sounds. Then one of its gloved hands grabbed Maashi's throat and started squeezing. Maashi pushed the alien's neck with more force than he had ever harnessed before. The creature's grasp on Maashi's throat lessened and the alien collapsed. Maashi quickly pivoted the body and pushed it toward the console. He positioned the left hand on the main console and used it to move the levers.

The computer acknowledged the order to eject the core.

The sequence started to run, with a loud alarm blaring in the ship's intercom, and would be completed in two minutes. Another alarm was set to go off in five minutes. That's when Maashi ordered a series of phaser blasts from the ship to the ejected core. Then adjusting the levers one last time, he set the ship to autodestruct in fifteen minutes to give him enough time to escape.

Maashi dropped the alien's limp body on the floor and sped out of the control room as fast as he could. He took the main corridor which led to the back of the ship where all the equipment for extravehicular activities was located. He was grateful he only had to open a mirror once. Rounding the last turn, he inadvertently triggered a booby-trap. The laser, well-hidden in a small depression on the wall, zapped his legs with such intensity it felled him.

The ship shook from a massive explosion outside. The core had been destroyed.

That meant only eight minutes left before the ship exploded.

Maashi's legs felt like they were caught in a vice. Unable to move, gasping and moaning, his mind swam in pain.

Like all Sheffrous experiencing severe pain, he held his breath. Maashi fought the instinctive reaction with all his energy. In normal circumstances, this functioned as a cry for help to the other Chamranlinas. But without the presence of another Chamranlina to save him, the reaction would continue until he lost consciousness.

Little by little, his vision blurred.

"Must...breathe."

With great effort, Maashi willed his lungs to breathe. He struggled to visualize the pain in his mind. He saw it, contained it as if it were a ball of blinding light, and locked it in a dark box, away from his conscious thoughts.

His extremities paralyzed, Maashi used his arms to crawl the remaining distance to the storage room. Raising his upper body as high as he could, he opened the storage room door with his device.

The room was in the shape of a T. The first part had sections on both sides where a line of space suits hung from the walls with a lower shelf holding helmets. The suits were dark brown, the Rodenegad color, made of a stretchy material which didn't look sturdy enough for deep space. The connecting fasteners were a bright mustard yellow making the suit fast and easy to put on.

The escape pods were in the elongated part of the T. Oval with a wide berth to accommodate the large abdomen of these creatures, the pods were divided into several sections to secure the head and limbs and prevent movement inside.

Maashi took a quick look around and decided to forego the pods and reach for the spacesuits. He had to find one that would fit his height. The paralysis intensified. Leg movement became impossible.

He groaned. His body fought his every step.

"No!" he screeched. "Absolutely not!" He wasn't going to die here even if it meant using all his energy. He roared, pulled the suit off the wall and managed to slide his legs in the semi-rigid lower half. The upper part wasn't a good fit, but running out of time, he squeezed in and reached for the helmet on a low shelf. As he set the helmet on his head, he caught a glimpse of the elongated creature floating in the middle of the room.

What was it doing there?

He yelled at it, "You need to leave this ship! Go far away!" The helmet locked in place. A beacon to help locate the suit in space turned on automatically. The virtual signals inside activated. He punched the controls located on his lower arms for the proper gas mix.

Everything went white.

>———<‹ ‹ ● › ›>———<

Maashi opened his eyes. The lights in his helmet flashed yellow every few seconds.

Did he succeed and destroy the portal? Was he still in the asteroid?

The outer cover of the mask was closed, preventing any outside viewing. Remembering what the helmet looked like, he envisioned the side of the helmet. There should be a locking mechanism to release the visor to see outside.

Not happening.

With much effort, Maashi lifted his hand higher and found a toggle button. He pressed it, the visor slid upward, and the blackness of space lay before him. A field of debris of all sizes and shapes floated about confirming the destruction of the Rodenegad ship. He didn't see the portal. His mind filled with hope.

The yellow signals in his helmet turned red, catching his attention.

What did they mean?

He focused on remembering the Rodenegad language. He read, 'Alert, oxygen and nitrogen levels critical. Return to ship immediately.'

That didn't sound good.

Maashi tried moving. His arms moved but not his lower body. Flashbacks from his time as a prisoner of the Krakoran invaded his thoughts; being trapped in a close-fitting suit that enclosed all his body except his face and genitals. The fear and desperation he felt at the time threatened to overcome him.

The suit had no directional power whatsoever. Erratic thoughts floated in his mind like random objects. How funny. He was a sitting duck. One of Tamara's favorite expressions. Sitting like a duck. Swimming like a duck. Stuck like a duck.

Trying to analyze the dancing coordinates floating in his visor only caused more confusion. Exhausted, he closed his eyes and controlled his breathing to dispel the fear creeping inside him.

No worries. The shuttle should pick up his beacon.

Everything was tranquil. No sound at all. No pain, only growing numbness in his legs.

Tamara. Shapinka. Are you safe?

Chapter 29

Tamara fought the terror that had taken hold of her when she saw three Rodenegad burst into the shuttle bay. Shaking, she grabbed the armrests of her seat until her fingers grew numb. She sat very still. Held in place by an improvised knot of the seat restraints, but with the absence of gravity, her stomach contents sloshed around and threatened to go overboard. *Give me a critical trauma to manage anytime over this no-gravity nonsense.*

She gazed at the shuttle's virtual screen since the shuttle had no windows or front viewing area. A direct view of the world outside wasn't part of the Rodenegad culture.

"Do you think the outer hull is damaged?" she asked Rowni as she scanned the inside of the shuttle filled with odd-looking tools that reminded her of her dad's garage. He loved his power tools, and they were always perfectly hooked up on the walls.

Rowni just shook his head to one side in the odd Chami way. "Don't think so. The Rodenegad weapons didn't penetrate the exterior shell."

Tamara sighed. *We're lucky if we got out of this unscathed.*

"Plotting a course away from the ship. Aiming for the mouth of the asteroid." He adjusted levers.

The sudden acceleration slammed Tamara against her seat.

Rowni shouted, "Hold on! Turbulence in our rear."

Seconds later, they were engulfed in a shock wave. Debris blew the ship sideways and the small craft rocked like a rubber duck caught in stormy seas.

Rowni cried out, "We're being pushed off course!"

The shuttle swung widely from side to side.

"Oh, I don't like that." Tamara gulped, clenched her teeth, and held on tight to the seat's arm rests. *I should've expected this. A big explosion like the one Maashi planned was bound to create a gigantic disturbance.*

"Boulder coming right at us," said Rowni.

Something massive hit the shuttle and it lurched to the right. Alarms sounded. The lights went out for a few seconds, went back on, then out again.

She heard Rowni punching at the console in front of him. "Thrown off course again. Attempting to correct."

The ship was caught in a barrel roll. Round and round they went. She thought her brain would turn upside down in her skull if this didn't stop soon. There was no gravity, and her body didn't move much, but it was like being immersed in one of those interactive video games.

Tamara held her breath. *At least now the lights are back on.* She spotted a corner of the control room and kept her eyes on it.

"Are we done yet?" she shouted. "I don't feel good."

"We suffered minimal damage. Systems are rerouting." Rowni grunted. "Trying to steer a collection of random metallic parts the enemy calls a ship."

After a few minutes, the rotation slowed. The shuttle stabilized.

"The following waves should be a lot less severe," said Rowni in a calm voice.

"Ah. Good. Better. Ah… do you have any trash bags?"

"Bags? Why do you need bags?" Rowni glanced at her. "Your skin color is greenish. Your eyes are open wide. Are you ill?"

Tamara put her hand in front of her mouth. "I'm not sure. I might throw up, I mean vomit, if we go on this roller coaster again."

Rowni quickly faced his console and produced a virtual diagram of the cabin and its contents. "Found some. Here." He handed her a few brown bags with a large opening that seemed to be well suited for the intended purpose.

"Brown bags. That's the Rodenegad color all right," said Tamara. "I hope I won't need them. but I'll keep one close just in case." She clenched one in her fist and stuffed the others behind her back.

"How is it," she said, "that you speak English so well?" *Small talk will help keep my mind off this nausea.*

"I was part of Sheffrou Maashi's entourage. I learned the language from the Sheffrou himself."

"By kissing?"

"Yes. It is most effective. Close physical contact amplifies the telepathic pathways." Rowni flashed a rare smile. "And it is pleasurable."

Maashi had learned English and tapped into Tamara's intimate thoughts and emotions with that method. With a knowing grin, she asked, "I don't recall seeing you around. Where were you?"

"I was head of the security team when Sheffrous Maashi and Tomisho traveled." Rowni rubbed his brow and hissed softly. "I was captured with three others by the Krakoran on the night of the Great Eclipse Celebration." He paused. "The others didn't survive." He lowered his head. "May they join the Souls of their Ancestors."

Tamara nodded. "May they rest in peace."

Her nausea subsided. She put the bag she had been holding with the others and said, "What do you see out there? Is the portal gone?"

"For now, the sensors are overloaded by all the particles released by the explosion. But the turbulence is an indication it has been destroyed."

"What about Maashi? Any signs of him?" Tamara's voice caught. *Did he make it out in time?* She didn't want to put into words what she feared the most.

Rowni spoke in a kind voice, "I'm tracking the debris to detect any transport pod or any reading that corresponds to a Chamranlina. Most of it is comprised of very small particles. An event of great magnitude occurred." His expression hardened. "I don't know if he had enough time to transport out."

Tamara blinked back tears. A heavy weight pressed on her chest, and she couldn't take a deep breath. She recalled how in the ER, she used to ask the children experiencing an asthma attack for the first time, "Do you feel like there's an elephant sitting on your chest?"

Was Maashi alive? They probably wouldn't find out until later. There was nothing they could do. Just wait and keep looking for him.

"There is a ship up ahead," said Rowni.

Fear surged into Tamara's mind. "What kind of ship?"

"The scan shows humans."

"That must be *Innovation*, the human ship that was following the needle."

"It's too far to communicate with them," said Rowni.

"We'll need to let them know who we are as soon as feasible, so they don't mistake us for Rodenegad. Send your response in English," said Tamara. "Don't forget to mention there's a human on board. They won't fire until they can confirm whether it's true or not."

"Done," said Rowni.

He turned to look at Tamara. "Do you know why Sheffrou Maashi was on board the needle? Space travel is prohibited for Sheffrous."

"Maashi was kidnapped by a group of Black and Silver Guards who took him in space."

"Kidnapped by guards?" Rowni's eyes widened, and he tilted his head sideways.

"It's a long story." Tamara waved and she watched her arm make a full circle because of the low gravity. "Suffice it to say that the Black and Silver Guards found out about a trafficking ring aboard a space station. They kidnapped Maashi so he could impersonate another alien, a buyer. Maashi played the part so well his group retrieved two guards, Sheffrou Ashani, me, and two other humans."

"Sheffrou Ashani?" Rowni's eyes increased in size. "Was he kidnapped?"

"Yes. He was kidnapped by the Krakoran on the same night you were taken. Nobody knew his whereabouts, and everyone was excited, especially Maashi when they got him back."

"Is he well? Where is he now?"

"He's on another needle. He was quite thin, but I think he's okay. The Leader, Dennyvan, transferred him as soon as he could on another needle. He refused to keep two Sheffrous on board at the same time since Maashi's body was changing and becoming mature. He made a big deal out of that."

Rowni nodded sideways and his lips stretched in a knowing smile. "Yes. I saw. Sheffrou Maashi has changed."

Something slammed into the shuttle.

"Right thrusters are damaged. Attempting to compensate," stated Rowni. He punched on toggle buttons and adjusted a lever, but the shuttle zigzagged out of control. A piercing sound like a bullhorn went off.

"What's that sound?" cried out Tamara grabbing the sides of her seat. Bile burned her throat. *Not Again.*

"Fire in the back," said Rowni. He unfastened his seatbelt and propelled himself to the back of the shuttle by pushing on his seat. The control room filled with smoke. A moment later, the filters turned on and the smoke started to dissipate. Tamara heard Rowni grunting with pain.

The console crackled. Rowni held on to handles on the walls and slowly made his way to the front. He isolated the communication. "This is Captain Teaburg from the starship *Innovation*. Identify yourself."

Rowni opened a channel. "Emergency. Fire. Breach of integrity is imminent. Transmitting our coordinates now…"

Tamara yelled, "Mayday! Mayday!" She coughed and struggled to catch her breath. "This is Tamara Walsh. Beam us aboard."

The transmitter crackled one last time and went dead.

Tamara coughed several times. She bent over, held her chest, and finally caught her breath. They had been transported aboard *Innovation* and were confined in a chamber with a large opening. About ten feet away, a group of humans faced them. Rowni stood rigid at her side with an arm outstretched in front of her.

His brow dark and wide with concern, he said, "Stay behind me. The humans have weapons."

Tamara cleared her throat. "Hey," she rattled, "we're unarmed. Don't shoot."

The first individual with a navy-blue uniform and a well-trimmed beard, said to the two others, "Lower your weapons." Keeping a wary eye on Rowni, he said, "Who are you? Why were you in those aliens' shuttle?"

Tamara took a step forward. Rowni tensed. "It's all right, Rowni. They won't shoot."

"Don't come any further. You're in the decontamination zone. A couple more minutes and we'll lower the forcefield. I am Commander Sullivan, first officer."

A door in the back slid open and a dark-skinned uniformed officer walked in. As soon as he saw Tamara and Rowni he said, "Sir, they were on the Rodenegad ship. They are two of the three who freed us."

Rowni bent sideways and whispered to Tamara, "He is the human male who said he could pilot the shuttle." Rowni tried to straighten up but one of his legs buckled under him. He crashed on the floor with a low moan.

"Rowni!" Tamara cried out. "You're hurt."

Commander Sullivan took one step. "We'll move you both to sickbay as soon as the decontamination is completed. We will have ample time to discuss the details of your escape later."

The uniformed officer stepped forward and said, "Where is the other alien that was with you?"

Tamara opened her mouth to answer but her words choked in her throat.

Rowni said in a grave voice. "Our leader, Sheffrou Maashi, planned to join us in the shuttle. We have not located him." He lowered his eyes.

"He might still be out there," said the officer. "Without him, none of us would have survived."

Commander Sullivan looked at Tamara. "What should we be looking for?"

"An escape pod or a..." Tamara stopped, overcome by her fear for Maashi's welfare.

Rowni added, "A Rodenegad spacesuit without directional control."

Commander Sullivan nodded. "Search all quadrants within 10,000 km. Use all the men and equipment you need." Turning back to face the two, he said, "How should we address you?"

Tamara faced the commander. "My name is Tamara Walsh. This person is a Chamranlina called Rowni and is one of Sheffrou Maashi's guards."

"Are you the woman who was on the shuttle with Lieutenant Yoon and Shiva Patel?"

"Yes, I am."

"Lieutenant Yoon stated you're not a colonist."

"That is correct."

"We'll do everything we can to find your partner. Officer Markus," Sullivan indicated the other officer, "will oversee the search."

"Thank you," said Tamara. "Sheffrou Maashi is part of the elite of Chamranlina society. He fulfills a vital role." *And I love him.*

Chapter 30

After Tamara had been cleared by the doctor in sickbay and Rowni was taken care of, she relaxed in her assigned quarters. Her room, the size of a large master bedroom with an imposing en-suite, was furnished with a luxurious sofa big enough to seat three people, a side chair, and also featured a full-size bed. The decoration, including table lamps with art deco shades reminded her of the contemporary look of her time: muted unassuming grays and beiges with a splash of bright accessories.

Tamara plopped her tired body on the couch and raised her legs. Sparkling water in plastic-like bottles had been provided for her comfort. She poured some in a glass and took a sip. She savored the refreshing taste after smelling the disgusting sulfur smell on board the Rodenegad ship. Exhausted but too tense and worried about Maashi to sleep, she leaned back trying to empty her mind.

Tamara watched the bubbles in her glass rise to the surface one by one and burst. Her fingers drummed on its side. It was such a relief to know she had made it to the human ship. After all this time imagining how the ship would be, what the people would look like, she concluded that, although different than what she imagined, the ship had a true human vibe. For one thing, the furniture was designed for her size. Well, a little bigger, but she always had to deal with her small size even on Earth. She closed her eyes.

Where are you Maashi? Tears gushed to her eyes. Her chest tightened.

I'm not going to cry. I'm not.

She suppressed the sniffles and rubbed her forehead. Remembering what Maashi had told her a while back, "If one of us dies, the other will feel it." She grabbed her glass with shaky hands and took a long breath in. In her heart, she knew he was alive.

I must stay positive. The crew is searching all over. They will surely find him soon.

Someone tapped on her shoulders. She sat up and looked around. There wasn't anyone else in the room.

I really need some rest. I'm hallucinating.

She took another sip of the sparkling water and saw something move through the glass. She looked up. The long, flat creature floated above her, close to the ceiling. Its multiple eyes darted this way and that as if checking out the place. It undulated with a slow wave.

"It's okay. I'm alone. You're safe." Tamara said in a soft voice.

The creature slowly circled the room.

"Do you know where Maashi is?"

A musical hum played in Tamara's ear. Images of outer space inundated her mind. She saw the asteroid as if traveling in a spaceship parallel to it. A speck way out beyond the asteroid a little to the right floated aimlessly. The image zoomed on the speck. A Rodenegad spacesuit. She flinched.

"Is it Maashi? You're showing me Maashi?" she said, fighting to keep the enthusiasm out of her voice. Any shouting or abrupt movements could frighten the creature.

The humming stopped, replaced by an insistent, low-frequency sound. Fear and anguish filled Tamara's mind. The creature's appearance changed. A long dark blue stripe appeared on its edges, and it darted back and forth across the room. Hurry. Hurry. Then it was gone.

Maashi was out there, in danger.

Tamara sprang from her seat. Just then, she heard shouts.

"This is security. We're coming in." The door opened and Officer Markus and two others burst in.

"The computer detected an intruder in your room," he said. "Are you all right?"

Tamara waved her arms, overcome with excitement. "I know where Maashi is. He's in danger. I must speak with Commander Sullivan right away."

"I know it sounds crazy, but I saw him," said Tamara to the doubtful commander. "Show me a diagram of the area and I'll point it out to you. Maashi and I and have seen this creature before. Even Rowni has seen it."

"Yes, it is a remarkable being," Rowni, sitting beside her, confirmed.

Sullivan grumbled. "Is that all the evidence you have? We can't travel through space to find your leader without a specific target."

Tamara continued, "I can't contact the creature. It reaches in our minds to transmit information directly."

The large conference room with its plush burgundy armchairs surrounding a long oval table could seat twenty people. Commander Sullivan and Officer Markus were present. Lieutenant Yoon joined them a minute later. He nodded to Tamara as he came in.

Glass cases at one end of the room displayed detailed models of spaceships. At the other end, a large canvas depicting swirls of bright colors hung on the wall. The floor was covered by plush steel gray carpet.

"Show us a detailed hologram of the sector surrounding the asteroid," said Commander Sullivan to Markus. He tilted his head and added, "Strange occurrences seem to follow you, Ms. Walsh."

"It's Dr. Walsh, but you can call me Tamara. Back in my other life on Earth, I was an emergency room doctor."

Commander Sullivan frowned but remained silent. He pulled at his jacket and smoothed his salt-and-pepper beard.

A moment later, the door to the meeting room slid open and a new officer with stars on her shoulders walked in. Everyone rose.

Commander Sullivan did the introductions. "Captain Teaburg, this is Dr. Tamara Walsh and the individual beside her is Rowni, a Chamranlina guard."

The captain was a middle-aged woman with a few gray hairs in her dark brown locks. She had a serious expression but kind eyes. "It's a pleasure to meet you, Dr. Walsh, Rowni." She waved at the group and took her seat at the end of the table. "Please proceed."

Markus punched the toggle buttons on a control pad. A few dots appeared in mid-air, connected to each other, then progressed to an elaborate picture floating above the large table. The asteroid was clearly visible in the center.

"What do you think, Dr. Walsh?" said Sullivan.

Tamara scrutinized the image. "It doesn't look like what I saw. Can I see the other side of the asteroid?"

"Computer, project a slow 360-degree rotation of the picture and enlarge it by a factor of ten," said Markus.

"Rotate 360 degrees and zoom by a factor of ten as requested," said a female voice.

"Computer, refrain from repeating orders," said Markus.

The diagram proceeded to rotate, and Tamara kept her eyes locked on it. "There," she pointed at it, "stop it right there."

"Computer, hold picture," said Markus clasping his brown hands together as if in silent prayer.

Tamara blinked and said, "Is this a real-time projection? Can we see all the debris?"

"Computer," said Sullivan, "use same diagram and show the current positions of all debris over one meter in size."

Several dots appeared on the enlarged screen like pebbles strewn on a beach. Tamara took a step to the right. "Computer," she said, "zoom on upper right quadrant. Using a plane sagittal to the length of the asteroid, enlarge the area plus and minus fifteen degrees from the plane."

The picture changed completely, showing hundreds of pieces of debris.

"Computer," said Sullivan, "analyze debris two meters in length and search for any life signs."

"Possible life sign at the edge of sector, at plus 14-degree," said the computer.

Tamara gasped. "Computer, zoom in on area between 13 and 15 degrees."

"Zoom complete. Life signs confirmed at 14.236 degrees."

"He's there. He's alive," said Tamara, her voice suddenly infused with energy.

"Computer," said Sullivan, "pinpoint life signs and give us an estimate of the distance from *Innovation*."

A blurry image of a Rodenegad spacesuit came into view. "The image is 35,000 km from *Innovation*," declared the computer.

"Computer, display details of life signs," said Markus.

"Life signs are too faint to interpret," said the computer.

Markus turned to Commander Sullivan, "We must be careful. It could be an armed Rodenegad."

Commander Sullivan said, "Computer, how much time would be required to reach that area with the shuttle?"

"The shuttle would require 75 minutes at maximum speed," said the computer.

Markus frowned. "Seems a long time if the vitals are faint."

Captain Teaburg said, "Computer, with the data you have, how long will it take for the vital signs to become unstable?"

The computer responded, "Insufficient data available to estimate time before termination."

Rowni stood and said, "We must get there as soon as possible. If the life signs correspond to Sheffrou Maashi, it is imperative to retrieve him now."

Captain Teaburg glanced at Rowni and Tamara. "*Innovation* can get us there faster." She pressed on her watch and said, "Helm, plot a course to a target Commander Sullivan just uploaded on the computer. Get us there promptly."

"Yes, Captain," said a human voice. "Target entered. ETA in 10 minutes."

"Acknowledged," said the captain. "That leaves us just enough time to prepare. Commander Sullivan, as soon as the ship is within range, beam up the individual directly to sickbay. Have a security detail at the ready in case it's an enemy."

Commander Sullivan rose and said, "Yes, Captain."

Tamara stood. "Thank you for your help, Captain. Rowni and I want to be there when he's brought on board."

"I understand," said the captain, "but we must ensure adequate security for you and the staff. As soon as we can confirm that there is no danger, both of you will have access to sickbay."

They all left the room. Tamara's heart thumped in her chest.

Please, let him be okay.

Chapter 31

Nurse Arlene glanced at the doctor, her face tense with concern.

"I think we've done everything we could." The doctor threw the stimulator on the table. "it's almost like he's resisting our efforts to wake him." She looked up at the nurse, her face scrunched up in contained annoyance. She lowered her mask and stepped back. "The captain will be pissed. She really wanted to talk to him. We'll just have to wait." She took off her gloves with a scowl and threw them and her mask in the recycling receptacle by the door.

"Keep an eye on him. will you? He's unconscious but stable. I'll be in the hall."

"Yes, doctor."

Doctor Kowalsky inhaled a deep breath. "I'll let Dr. Walsh and the other alien see him although I don't expect they'll be able to do much to wake him." She shook her head and a few blonde strands fell out of her ponytail.

The nurse nodded.

The doctor stepped out of the room.

Maashi's muscles ached. He felt exhausted as if he had been swimming for days and crossed the Chanterra sea. His body throbbed like an avalanche of boulders had rolled down the side of a mountain and crashed over him.

His senses were dulled, barely registering the outside world. He felt a presence close by, but fear kept him frozen in place. What if he destroyed the portal only to be captured by the Krakoran? They would have strapped him solidly as he was now and kept him in a brightly lit room. The thought made him shudder with dread.

Did he fail his mission? Did the explosion destroy the Rodenegad ship only to open the gateway to the enemy? His mind sank with despair. His blood pressure plummeted.

Maashi struggled to move and breathe. The paralysis which had started after he got zapped when he tried to enter the storage room had progressed upward. Fortunately, he had the ability to absorb oxygen through his skin.

He waited for a long while, refusing to let his conscious mind take over, hoping his worst fears would be proven wrong and his remarkable capacity for self-healing would be sufficient to save him. With enough time, his body would mend if there wasn't any severe damage to his internal organs.

Something pulled at him, urged him to leave. As if watching himself from the outside, he saw his body float aimlessly in a whirl of pale clouds. This was a place where only muffled sounds could be heard and where pain couldn't reach him. He wanted to stay there and rest. He didn't want to go back but he knew he couldn't stay long. Life wasn't there. Life was filled with pain and misery.

It felt like a long time before he regained consciousness. At first, he could accomplish slight finger movements. Then his eyelids blinked and finally, he pulled his arm, testing the restraints.

Maashi heard the short beeps of an electronic device. He opened his eyes and turned his head to look. Human. Relief flooded his thoughts. Taller and slimmer than Tamara, the Fanella had a pale complexion and deep-set eyes as blue as a young Sheffrou's tongue. Another smaller female came to her side. She had an oval face with darker skin and inquisitive black eyes.

"Call security," said the first Fanella.

Maashi blinked then focused on her blue eyes.

"Right away," said the other. She punched numbers on a rectangular device that she slipped back in her side pocket.

As the paralysis waned, intense pain took over, like flames rising from his legs to his upper body, burning him from the inside. Unbearable scorching heat. Maashi tried to contain it but, in his weakened state, controlling the pain was next to impossible. "Help. Help me," he said in a hushed whisper. He moaned, a long soft wail. "Make it stop." His breathing became shallow. The pain obliterated the room, and he blacked out once again.

Chapter 32

S omething was wrong. Tamara had the strangest feeling, like the walls were closing in, sucking all the air of the waiting room. The sensation crept inside her, circled around her throat, choking her like a creeping vine. She had been waiting for two hours and couldn't wait any longer. She had to see Maashi now. She glanced at Rowni standing beside her. He held his breath. His eyes thinned to dark slits. She was sure he could feel it also. She rushed out of the waiting room into the hallway of the sickbay area looking for the doctor.

A security detail arrived at the same time. The doctor stepped out the treatment room where they kept Maashi with a grim look on her face.

"Doctor!" Tamara cried out, "I need to see Maashi. I need to see him now."

One of the security officers stepped in front of her. "Please control yourself, ma'am. This area is restricted."

The doctor said in a tired voice, "It's okay. Let her through. And the alien too."

Tamara stared at the doctor but didn't say a word. She bolted into the room with Rowni limping right behind.

Maashi lay unconscious on a gurney, his arms and legs strapped securely. The bright room was all white.

"This is wrong," said Tamara to the nurse. "You must lower the lights and get these restraints off him. He's going to panic when he wakes up."

Doctor Kowalsky had followed them in and nodded to Nurse Arlene. "Do as she says."

The nurse promptly lowered the lights and fumbled to release the restraints.

Rowni touched Maashi's face and took his hand in his own and held it. "Drowning in pain. The Sheffrou is too weak to fight."

Tamara kissed Maashi's other hand. She looked up at Rowni. "What can we do?"

"Only a Sheffrou can help," said Rowni. "Condition is critical. He has been exposed to Rodenegad poison."

Commander Sullivan and Officer Markus walked into the room.

Rowni turned towards the two men, his brow dark with worry. "I need to contact my people right away. Sheffrou Maashi is in grave danger." He pronounced the words slowly, his body still reeling from the burns he suffered in the shuttle.

Sullivan said to Markus, "Take him with you to a communication center. See if you can contact their ship."

"Come with me," said the tall dark-skinned Markus.

Rowni turned to Tamara and said, "Stay with him. Do not leave his side."

Tamara shook her head. "I'm not going anywhere."

Commander Sullivan brought the doctor aside and said, "What do you think?"

Doctor Kowalsky checked the readings on her recorder. "According to these, he won't survive the night. I've tried everything I can and he's not responding. He exhibits strong vagal reflexes and he's in excruciating pain, a bad combination."

Nurse Arlene sat at a computer and called out to the doctor. "Doctor, we just received the toxicology results."

"Let me see," said the doctor.

"Oh. This isn't good," said the doctor with a pained expression. Bending forward, she followed the numbers on the screen with a finger. A loose strand of hair hung in mid-air in front of her face. "The patient has been exposed to a nerve blocker, a neurotoxin, and a paralyzing agent. The three work simultaneously and when the paralysis wanes, the excruciating pain takes over."

"Can you do something to help him?" asked Tamara.

The doctor straightened up and said, "The pain is killing him. I tried giving him analgesic but he's too unstable to permit the administration of adequate medication. He could experience irreversible shock."

Commander Sullivan rubbed his jaw. "We must find a way to save him. I had a discussion with Lieutenant Yoon. He explained in strong terms that this individual is extremely important for the Chamranlinas." He glanced at Tamara who was caressing the patient's cheek then turned back to the doctor. "Do what you can, Susan." On his way out he said, "I'll inform Captain Teaburg of his condition."

A few moments later, Rowni came back. "News is not good," he said.

"What do you mean?" said Tamara still holding Maashi's hand in hers.

Rowni walked over to a couple of chairs against the wall. He motioned Tamara to come and sit down. Tamara came over, settled on one chair, and Rowni slowly slid down on the floor, his back against the wall.

The nurse walked over and offered them both some juice to drink in a glass with a straw.

Dr. Kowalsky stepped out to give them some privacy. The nurse hovered over Maashi, keeping a close eye on his vital signs.

Tamara sipped some juice. She felt drained. She watched Rowni's pale face. Fatigue was taking a toll on everyone.

"I should have stayed aboard the Rodenegad ship instead of the Sheffrou," Rowni's words came out strained. With eyes half closed, he lowered his head. "I should have insisted he leave."

Tamara whispered, "Maashi had made his decision. He wasn't going to let you stay in his place. He felt it was his battle to win or lose." She understood that. She had been in that kind of situation back on Earth. The ER sometimes required life-and-death decisions that required your own personal intervention. No one else could be trusted to do the job.

Tamara inhaled a long breath. No use dwelling on what was done. They needed to concentrate their efforts on the present, on saving Maashi. "Did you contact the needle?"

"Yes."

"What did they say?"

"They agreed that Sheffrou Maashi is in a critical state and that he needs the care of a Sheffrou."

Tamara leaned back in the molded plastic chair. "What are they going to do about it?"

Rowni repositioned himself on the floor beside her. The other chair was so small it was useless to him. "Nothing." He stared at his hands.

She huffed with frustration. "Who decided that? Was it Dennyvan?"

"Dennyvan consulted with the Council of Elders on Chitina. They refuse to risk another Sheffrou's life to save this one."

Tamara sat numb, speechless, like someone had punched her in the gut. She set her juice aside, her mind working on the problem, poking at it, grasping at straws. "What about Ashani? He's on the other needle traveling back to Chitina. He could come back and—"

"No."

"But he's a Sheffrou and he's Maashi friend, pupil, whatever. I'm sure he would agree to come."

"No."

"But why?" she said, raising her voice. Getting nowhere, she fisted her hands. Anger surged inside her like a tsunami wave growing taller with each swell.

"Sheffrou Ashani is weak from captivity. It is too dangerous."

Tamara fumed. What are friends for when you can't count on them to help you when you're in dire need? She stared at Maashi lying unconscious. There had to be a solution.

"There is an alternative," Rowni said in a hushed voice.

"I'm listening."

"You."

"Me? What do you mean?"

"You are Sheffrou."

Tamara said between clenched teeth, "This is not funny."

"I am speaking the trurth." Rowni touched her arm with light fingers. "You are Sheffrou. Maashi has said so many times."

"Come on. What are you talking about?" She shook her head vigorously and her hair flowed this way and that. She waved her hand dismissing the suggestion. "Maashi was just saying that. Sheffrous are Chamranlinas. They have the power to heal, and they can decrease pain. I'm human and female. I don't have any powers."

"You refuse to help?"

"Listen, I—"

"If you refuse, we will lose the Sheffrou."

Tamara blinked. Staring into Rowni's eyes, she realized he was dead serious.

A memory from long ago flashed in her head. 'Step up to the plate, if you don't, we will lose the patient'. Her teacher said it so often the words were drilled in Tamara's mind. The vivid memory pulsed in her brain as if the words had been spoken the day before. Tamara had attended a family picnic in a charming country setting when a young man stung by a bee experienced anaphylactic shock and went into cardiac arrest. Tamara was the one who spurred into action and performed CPR until the paramedics arrived. She saved his life.

She stared hard at Rowni. His suggestion was ludicrous, but they didn't have any other choice. Swallowing hard, she muttered, "What am I supposed to do?"

Rowni tilted his head to one side and said in a calm and measured tone, "Listen carefully. Sheffrou Maashi is overcome by fear and pain. Help him reduce the fear, he will regain control over the pain, and survive until tomorrow."

"Reduce the fear..." She inhaled, trying to visualize how she could accomplish that. "Okay. But what happens tomorrow?" A shiver of dread ran down her spine.

"A green Sawisha is on his way aboard Dennyvan's needle. Chopa, the Sheffrou's Chowli, left Chitina two days ago. They should all arrive tomorrow."

"I see." She swallowed. *Help is on the way.*

"What about Chari?"

"Who is Chari?" said Rowni.

"He's Maashi's first Chowli. He was on the needle with Maashi. I don't understand why they didn't send him."

"I don't know anything about Chari."

That was a puzzle she would have to figure out later.

She could do this. Yes. One night shift and the Chamis would take over. She grabbed her juice and took a long sip.

"What am I supposed to do? Specifically?"

"Reassure the Sheffrou."

"Give me details. I need to know how to help him."

Rowni didn't seem to understand the question. "Tamara," he said in a soft voice, "when Sheffrou Maashi and you are together in the Encounter room, what does he like to do?"

Not expecting that.

She glanced at him sideways.

"He," she scratched the back of her neck, "asks me to take off my clothes and likes to hold me in his arms."

"What else?"

"He likes to kiss me. On the face and chest and..."

"What do you do when he does that?"

She cleared her throat. "I, like to kiss him too," she paused, "I kiss his face, his chest, his neck."

"Does he enjoy anything else?"

"He likes to feel my skin and hold me skin to skin." Tamara felt her cheeks getting warm. "Is that what you want me to do?"

"That is what is necessary." Rowni grunted and rose from the floor. "And you must start now."

Tamara nodded.

He extended one arm and said, "Give me your shirt and pants."

Tamara wiped her hands on her pants then did as he asked. "I'm keeping my underwear."

"You can climb beside him on the bed and lay over him. I will tell the others not to disturb you. I will be standing outside the door. Call if you need me."

Nurse Arlene had been discreetly checking results on the computer. Tamara went to her and said, "Can you order a warm soft towel and a fuzzy blanket? I'll need both right away and then, you can leave."

The nurse promptly ordered the two items, retrieved them from the replicator, and gave them to Tamara. She whispered, "Good luck," and left. Rowni followed behind.

Remembering details from her past, Tamara took the warm towel, rolled it, and positioned it around Maashi's head. The anesthesiologists often did that to keep their patients warm but in Maashi's case, it would have a calming effect.

Using a chair, she climbed and settled over Maashi. Right away, she noticed his body felt cooler than usual. She took the fuzzy blanket she had thrown on the back of the chair and covered his abdomen and part of Maashi's chest.

"Maashi," she whispered. "It's me, Tamara. Can you hear me?"

No reaction from Maashi. Tamara licked her lips. The orange juice burned in her throat. *What if I can't do this?*

She reached out and with the tip of her fingers caressed his face.

"Maashi," she whispered, "I'll stay with you until you feel better. You must hang on until help is here." She readjusted her position and climbed a little higher on his chest.

"You have always been gentle and kind to me. When I first came to Chitina, I was so frightened, so lost. You were patient, understanding. You treated me like I mattered, like you cared."

A flood of emotions surged in Tamara's mind. "The day I started trusting you was the day I almost drowned in the lake by the Gorganna gorge. I fell into the deep end and fought hard to reach the surface, but the powerful current pulled me under. I thought for sure that I was done. My life flashed in my mind. My kids, my husband, Earth.

"You came to my rescue. You scooped me up in your arms and apologized for not paying attention to me." Tamara blinked. "Thank you for saving my life." She caressed his cheek and pressed her cheek against his.

Sensing no reaction from Maashi, she said, "Maashi. Don't be afraid. I'm here to help. Trust me." She hugged him and snuggled on his chest.

"Your friends are also coming to help. Just relax, and you'll be all right. I'll stay close. I'm not leaving."

She kissed his forehead, his nose, his cheeks. She lightly pressed her lips on his mouth avoiding a deeper kiss. He had warned her that as much as he could transmit pleasure through his kisses, he could transmit pain. She should never kiss him if he was in severe pain.

"When my children were small, sweet Maashi," she chuckled, "I always wanted to call you that. Just too shy to do it." She smiled. "I used to play music to help them relax and go to sleep. It worked every time. I know you're never heard classical music but I'm sure you would enjoy it." She bit her lower lip and said, "Computer, play *Clair de Lune* by Debussy. Play it softly."

The computer answered, "Searching."

A minute went by, and Tamara thought that the computer wouldn't find the piece, but then the music started playing. The familiar notes made Tamara's heart soar and she smiled as she rested her head on the Sheffrou's chest.

She saw no change in his breathing, not even the slightest movement.

This is harder than I expected.

Her brow knitted with worry, she said in a soothing tone, "I need you. I love you, more than anything. You probably already know that, but I wanted to say it anyway." Her voice broke. Tears poured and ran down her cheeks. "I should've stayed with you on the ship. Please Maashi, stay with me."

She rested over him, skin against skin for the longest time. Exhaustion took its toll. She put an arm around his neck and closed her eyes. An instant later, a dreamless sleep overtook her.

Chapter 33

Hours later, Tamara opened her eyes to the strangely familiar surroundings of the treatment room. The scent of disinfectants, alcohol, and plastic instruments filled her nostrils. Snuggled in Maashi's arms, her body pressed on his skin, Tamara noticed he didn't have the gorgeous caramel smell she was used to. The sickly alabaster shade of his skin had warmed to a golden tan but the quatay on his chest was so pale it was barely visible. She frowned in mild alarm. He wasn't back to normal yet.

With her arm resting on his chest, she traced the intricate design of his quatay with her fingers. He had always enjoyed that.

"Maashi," she called. "Maashi?"

No response.

Tamara felt her limbs starting to shake with fear. What if something was seriously wrong with him? She refused to consider that possibility. *Just give him time.*

"Rowni," she said. "Are you there? Come in."

The door opened and Rowni limped in. He approached the bed and squeezed Maashi's hand. Clicking softly, he bent his tall frame and deposited a kiss on his neck.

"He looks better," he said, setting gentle eyes on Tamara. "Thank you."

Tamara sat up and said, "I'm relieved he made it through the night but I'm afraid his condition is still guarded." She stared at Rowni. "How about you? How's your side?"

The door opened and a mixed crowd came in: Commander Sullivan in his navy-blue uniform with his broad jaw clenched tight, Doctor Kowalsky with her blonde hair pulled back neatly in a bun, her blue eyes holding a steady unfaltering gaze. Four Chamis followed.

Shonava Benshimu Hellowina, close friend of Maashi, entered. The powerful green Sawisha's muscular frame, a bodybuilder's dream, cleared the doorway by inches. He was followed by an equally impressive figure, most likely his first Chowli, a Multi with a sash remarkable for the many shades of green and red.

Behind them, Chopa, Maashi's Chowli, wearing his signature spotted brown sash entered the room with a somber look on his face. No doubt he had been briefed on Maashi's condition. The last one was a guard, part of Shonava Benshimu's personal security, recognizable by his green attire and multicolor sash.

In two strides, Benshimu approached the patient's bed. He nodded at Tamara with a solemn look. "It is a pleasure," he said.

Tamara climbed down from the bed pulling the fuzzy blanket off Maashi and putting on the shirt and pants Rowni handed to her.

Benshimu turned to the Sheffrou. He reached under his upper body, hugged him close, burrowing his face in Maashi's neck. He ran long fingers in his hair and clicked softly in his ears.

His genuine affection touched Tamara. She had no doubt he would try his utmost to help him.

After his initial contact, Benshimu deposited Maashi on the bed, straightened back up, removed his shirt, exposing his quatay, and handed it to his Chowli.

Commander Sullivan raised an eyebrow and exchanged a quick glance with the doctor at the sight of Benshimu's impressive green markings covering his neck, shoulders, and upper back like a cape.

Benshimu reconnected with Maashi, making sure to establish skin to skin contact. Tamara watched in awe as the green pressed his chest against Maashi. He lifted the Sheffrou's chin, and his lips pressed against his in a long kiss to transfer as much as possible of his saweya, his life energy. His goal was also to relieve Maashi's pain by sharing it with him.

In the meantime, Chopa joined Tamara. He hugged her and said, keeping his voice low, "How are you, Tamara? We have been quite concerned. I left a few days ago when we were informed you had been taken by the Rodenegad. I hope they didn't harm you."

Emotions welled in her. She realized how much she missed his calm and reassuring presence. Her voice cracked. "It's been like a roller-coaster."

Chopa said, his voice a soft whisper, "It's easy to get lost in someone dear's pain."

Tamara's lips stretched in a sad smile. "Thank you."

"I think it is best to leave and let Shonava Benshimu engage the Sheffrou," said Chopa. "We will be needed in a few hours. Now is a good time for you to eat and rest and for Rowni to get the medical attention he needs." Chopa put a light hand on the guard's shoulder and clicked at him.

Rowni cocked his head to one side and said, "We are both grateful you came. Our concern for the Sheffrou's welfare was foremost on our minds. It's difficult to tend to him in our current physical and mental state."

Tamara nodded. Truer words could not be spoken. 'Physician, heal thyself', an old Greek proverb came to her mind. "You're right," she said. "Chopa, you couldn't have come at a more opportune moment. For my part, I'm starving. I think I'll go to my quarters to shower, eat, and rest. Rowni and you obviously know each other and can get reacquainted during that time." She glanced at Benshimu and Maashi. "How long do you think it'll be before they need us?"

Rowni said, "At least twelve hours. Perhaps more."

Benshimu's Chowli suddenly went to speak to the doctor. Tamara sauntered over to hear the conversation.

Doctor Kowalsky's lips were pinched, her expression grave.

"What is it? Is there something wrong?" said Tamara.

"It's as I feared," said the doctor. "He is paralyzed from the waist down."

Tamara felt like all her energy had been drained. She covered her mouth in alarm and whispered, "Will he recover?"

Benshimu's Chowli looked down at Tamara. "It is too early to tell," he said in a low voice. "Forgive me for not introducing myself. My name is Tanshib, first Chowli to Shonava Benshimu." He bowed to Tamara. "I suspect it will take months for him to recover the use of his legs. I will develop a more accurate assessment of his condition after I have seen the toxicology results and conducted neurological tests. At this moment, we are attempting to stabilize his parameters so we can transport him aboard the needle."

"How are you going to stabilize him?" asked the doctor. "He doesn't tolerate pain killers. His blood pressure drops like a rock whenever I try to administer some."

"All Sheffrous respond to physical and sexual stimulation," said Chopa who had joined the group. "They use the energy produced to promote their charissa, their state of well-being. In the Sheffrou's case, we can share his pain and help him lower it by close body contact, including kissing and caressing him."

The doctor raised her brows as she listened to his comments. "An unorthodox approach. That certainly wouldn't work with my patients."

Chopa, unfazed by her reaction, continued. "Sheffrou Maashi is currently going through a phase in his life called Dompati, the process of attaining maturity. This will no doubt complicate his recovery. He will respond in an enhanced manner and will need to be under close observation for his own sake and for the sake of the ones surrounding him."

A low growl startled the group. They all turned towards Benshimu as he extricated his upper body from Maashi's tightening arms. His confident demeanor was gone. He cursed under his breath. He inhaled sharply and shook his arms loose as if to shake off bad spirits. His Chowli went to him, clicked at him, and stroked his back.

Maashi opened his eyes. He moaned and squirmed under the intense pain.

Doctor Kowalsky checked him with her tricorder and said, "His pressure is the highest I've seen so far. Can I give him some analgesia?"

Benshimu holding on to his Chowli for support, said, "Yes, please do."

The doctor grabbed a syringe, adjusted the dose, and injected medication in the Sheffrou's arm. A few seconds later, Maashi's tense body relaxed. His arms settled at his side. He regained some color. Benshimu and Chopa approached the bed.

Maashi blinked, then opened his eyes. "Ben," he said in a hoarse voice, "thank you... for coming." He turned his head slowly to the other side. "Chopa..."

"I'm here, Shonava," Chopa said. "We will help you heal."

Tamara came into Maashi's line of sight. "We're all here for you," she said.

Maashi moved his mouth but took a moment to speak as if his tongue was in the way. "The portal? What happened...to the portal?"

Rowni had stayed back. He came to his side and answered in a steady voice, "It's destroyed, sir."

Maashi's brow darkened with worry. "What about...the flat creature? The one who saved me?"

"What is he talking about?" said Commander Sullivan.

Tamara said, "The alien creature that gave me the information on his location. It also helped us fight the Rodenegad. It comes and goes without warning." Tamara turned to Maashi. "It's alive."

Maashi spoke with visible effort, "Must save the creature," he blurted. "Save the offspring...."

"Oh no. He's crashing again," said the doctor.

Benshimu pulled the stricken Maashi into his arms once more. Chopa also removed his shirt and pressed his chest on Maashi's back, anchoring his arms over Benshimu's.

Maashi's shoulders relaxed. He rested his head on Benshimu, his respiration became more regular. His color improved.

"It's going to take longer than I expected to stabilize him," said Benshimu. He looked at Commander Sullivan. "It seems we will be your guests for a little while."

Sullivan nodded his approval. His expression didn't show undue concern. "Understood. I sort of expected that," he said in a calm voice. He turned to Tamara. "I'll need more information on this creature. Is this the same one that appeared in your quarters?"

"They're going to be busy here for some time," said Tamara. "Give me a half-hour to shower and we'll discuss this further over a meal."

Chapter 34

Commander Sullivan reclined on the stylish ergonomic chair of level 6 forward. That's how they called the lounge where the crew could savor a meal and enjoy some R & R. Apart from a rich eggplant color as the dominant hue accompanied by a palette of shades of gray on the carpet and walls, the set-up reminded Tamara of a typical lounge; a small section in the back filled with tables and plastic molded chairs and a larger area up front with several sofas in groups of three or four to promote conversation. She loved the added touch of the Tiffany-like sconces on the walls creating islands of subdued lighting.

The few patrons chatted amiably among themselves with an occasional glance towards Tamara. Most wore the gray and white uniform with a colored band along the shoulders and arms, most likely indicating their function or rank aboard the ship. Some wore flowing clothes, shirts, and pants, but Tamara noticed the clothes were tied at the wrists and ankles no doubt to decrease the risk of them getting in the way should an emergency occur. Deep space, although considered empty most of the time, contained unknown and unexpected dangers.

After wolfing a full meal of real mashed potatoes, computer-generated meat, greenhouse-grown beans, and an avocado salad, Tamara reclined back with obvious satisfaction. "I'm full.

This is so good," she said, putting down her napkin. "I haven't eaten this much since... well," she chuckled, "let's say it's been a while."

"I'm glad to hear that," said Sullivan with a smile. He sipped a tall cup of coffee and smoothed his beard. "Tell me more about this floating creature that Sheffrou Maashi mentioned."

Tamara took a gulp of her latte then said, "There's not a lot to say, really. We don't know much about it." She glimpsed the striking expanse of space dotted with stars visible through the broad window on the far wall. "Originally, two of those creatures shared my quarters, prisoners of the Rodenegad same as we were, meaning Lieutenant Yoon, Patel, and I. Then, the Rodenegad killed one of them and tried to feed it to us as if it were crispy bread. I was beyond disgusted when I realized what they gave us to eat that day was the other creature."

She took a long breath remembering the overwhelming grief and despair she had felt. Taking an instant to compose herself, she added, "I've been told that when we were rescued and transferred aboard the needle, Captain Dennyvan's ship, the other creature flew in through the airlock door minutes before we left the space-station. Later, the creature followed me into my quarters and floated just under the ceiling."

"Yes," said Sullivan. "The whole story about your capture by the Rodenegad and their plans to sell you at the space-station was quite an eye-opener. If Lieutenant Yoon and Patel hadn't filed that report in all its gory detail, we never would've imagined this could happen under the very nose of the Alliance."

Tamara continued. "The creature is unlike anything I've ever seen. It communicates with Maashi and I telepathically and can also produce humming and musical sounds. However, if it feels threatened, it can create a sound loud enough to cause loss of consciousness." She stopped and decided not to mention the time when the creature intruded into her dreams.

"So, this creature is dangerous?"

"It looks harmless, but we shouldn't underestimate its abilities. As a matter of fact, I think it used sound to defeat a group of Rodenegad when we were aboard their ship. Rowni, Maashi's guard, found one of the aliens at the entrance of the control room. He was unconscious with no visible injuries. We suspected the creature was responsible."

"Where do you think it is now?"

"I have no idea. It seems to be able to travel through space and materialize at will and go wherever it wants. It was on Dennyvan's ship, left, and then reappeared on the Rodenegad ship."

Keeping his voice low, Sullivan leaned in and said, "What do you mean, left?"

"The ship's computer couldn't locate it anymore. We assumed it went out into deep space. At least that's what Chari said. He's Maashi's first Chowli. He was on Dennyvan's ship." Tamara took a long sip of her coffee. "This coffee is good, not as good as what I used to drink but it's quite acceptable, as Maashi would say."

Sullivan frowned. "How many Chowlis does the Sheffrou have?"

"As far as I know, Maashi has three, Chari, Chopa, and Rahma whom I haven't seen in a while. Sheffrous can have up to four Chowlis. They protect them and make sure all their needs are met."

"Why didn't Chari accompany the Sheffrou on the Rodenegad ship?"

"Humm, I don't know. Normally, he would've been by Maashi's side."

Commander Sullivan raised his hand, and a blue and white robot server came over. It appeared to be floating over the carpet. Its movement and slight hum reminded Tamara of a hovercraft.

"Nellie," ordered Sullivan, "coffee refill for both of us." The robot proceeded to refill both their cups then spoke in an overly sweet voice, "Sugar? Cream? Or both?"

"None for me," said Sullivan.

"Two sugars for me," said Tamara.

Nellie proceeded to drop two spoonfuls of sugar in Tamara's coffee and with the help of its robotic arm left a small spoon on a napkin for her to mix it. The robot then proceeded at a fluid pace to another table.

Tamara stirred her sugar and a little smile lit up her face. "Nice."

"There's something that I don't get," said Sullivan, his gaze searching hers. "How did the Rodenegad manage to keep the creature prisoner if it comes and goes as it pleases?"

"A good question. All I can say is that when we were brought to the space station to be sold, it was enclosed in a big, clear bubble. Maybe that's how they contained it."

The commander shook his head. "Interesting." He swallowed some of his coffee. "Tell me. How long have you known Sheffrou Maashi? I took a few minutes to read the transcript of the statement you made aboard Lieutenant Yoon's ship about how you came to this area of space. Impressive."

Tamara tilted her head to one side, a habit she picked up from the Chamis. "Thank you. I appreciate that you did so because, at first, Lieutenant Yoon and Patel refused to believe my story. They thought I was crazy." She paused. Her mood turned solemn. "I've been with the Chamranlinas, I call them Chamis for short, for over a year. I've learned a lot about their culture."

"What is the nature of your relationship with Sheffrou Maashi?"

"It's complicated," Tamara blurted out. She squirmed in her seat. "Maashi holds a high status in Chami society, almost like royalty. He is the first lord of the Central Compound, the most important one among the fourteen compounds in their colony. He is Sawisha which means he is fertile, a trait that only a few individuals share, and Sheffrou so he can only father female offspring." She paused. "We're very close."

"I see," said Sullivan, stroking his beard.

"Maashi has given me the title of Chimitanga, which translates to 'special friend of the Sheffrou'. She lowered her gaze. She frowned, looked out to the blackness of space, and chewed on her lips. "I'm concerned about his condition. I've never seen him like that."

The commander nodded. "We will support the Chamranlinas and Sheffrou Maashi in any way we can. They have been instrumental in liberating our men and women captured by the Rodenegad."

Sullivan's watch beeped. He took one look and said, "We must go to sickbay right away."

"What's wrong? Is Maashi all right?"

Sullivan's pinched expression conveyed alarm. "His condition is worse."

>———‹ ‹ ● › ›———‹

Mayhem had taken over sickbay. Her training kicking in, Tamara quickly assessed the situation.

Benshimu grunted with effort as he fought to extricate his upper body from Maashi's hold. The Sheffrou had clamped his arms around the big green like a drowning man clinging to a lifeboat. Thunderous clicks bellowed from Benshimu's chest as he finally pulled away with a throaty roar. His Chowli Tanshib steadied him as he wobbled over to one of the oversized seats the humans had brought for them.

"I can't help him," Benshimu growled, holding his head in his hands,his face and neck pale as choun. His raspy, labored breaths came out in spurts. "I can't bear this bone-crushing pain." Tanshib started to massage his back and shoulders with long firm sweeps.

Chopa held Maashi and struggled to keep him steady. Maashi moaned, turned his head from side to side, and flailed his arms like a long-limbed injured bird. Chopa clicked non-stop to quiet him without success.

Rowni stood, his upper body bent over the bed beside Chopa, his brow wide and dark. Tamara thought he looked worse than when she had last seen him earlier. He needed rest, not wasting his energy to help Maashi when there were so many others present.

Doctor Kowalsky moved to the other side of the bed and tried over and over to take Maashi's vitals. At one point, she got too close to the patient and would have been smacked by Maashi's swinging arm if it weren't for Chopa's quick intervention. He caught it just as it flew inches from her head.

"I don't understand it," she said with a voice fraught with frustration. Her wide eyes betrayed her anxiety at failing to comprehend the change in her patient. "He was so calm a few minutes ago."

Commander Sullivan went to her. "Maybe you missed something?"

She flicked a wayward strand of blonde hair and scratched her head. "I don't know. His metabolism is so different. His vitals keep changing."

Tamara stood, hands on her hips, worry creeping in her mind. Was Maashi's condition getting worse even with Benshimu's and his team's intervention? She rubbed her face, trying to wipe away her growing fatigue. Something moved up high. She looked up and saw the long, flat creature floating inches below the ceiling. A line of grayish eyes oscillated this way and that. Was it analyzing the situation?

Tamara moved over to the center of the room and waved her arms to silence the others. The others hushed when they noticed the creature. She looked up and whispered, "Are you trying to help Maashi?"

An iridescent wave ran along the creature's mantle.

"Be gentle," she said. "Maashi is in a lot of pain."

The creature's body changed to a thin, translucent membrane undulating slowly back and forth across the room reminding Tamara of someone tiptoeing.

Tamara felt a soft touch on her arm. Gentle. Gentle. She understood the creature's message. She went to Maashi's side, glanced at the doctor who stepped aside, took Maashi's hand and kissed it.

A musical hum filled the room. The soothing sound had an immediate effect. Everyone watched in awe as the patient's arms relaxed. His moans changed to whispers then he became silent. Both Chopa and Tamara set Maashi's arms down by his side.

After a moment, his face regained its normal color. His brow relaxed.

Doctor Kowalsky whispered, "His face is showing some color. He looks more peaceful."

Maashi's chest expanded with a long breath. He blinked a few times. His semi-transparent second eyelids opened revealing the warm amber of his eyes. He turned his head slowly towards Tamara. In a barely audible voice, he said, "Sweet one." He squeezed her hand, closed his eyes, and sighed.

"I think the pain has subsided," said Tamara as she let out her breath. "He's going to rest now." She raised her head. The creature was gone.

Benshimu squared his shoulders and said, "I don't know what happened. This incredible feeling of being crushed came over me. The pain was unbearable. I had no choice but to sever my connection to the Sheffrou." He looked in Maashi's direction. "How is he?"

"Improved," said Tamara.

He rose and got closer to the bed. "He looks serene, like the pain has disappeared." His eyes widened as he scanned the room. "There was a long flat creature above us. It made a strange rhythmic sound. I couldn't move. Some strange force held me down."

"Yes," said Tamara. "The creature was here. I'm convinced it helped Maashi."

"His vitals have stabilized," said the doctor. She rolled her shoulders as if a weight had been lifted. "They appear normal, as far as I can tell."

"They are quite normal," agreed Chopa who stretched and adjusted his shirt. "It is a remarkable change. His condition improved in a matter of minutes."

Commander Sullivan stared at Tamara and said, "Do you think it was the creature's doing?"

"I think so." She shrugged. "I'm grateful it has survived. It seems to have a special bond with Maashi." She nodded to Rowni who tilted his head to the side in agreement.

"It appears to be the case," said Benshimu. "Shonava Maashi informed me of the important role this creature had in helping him reach his goal of destroying the portal." His voice had regained its confident tone. "We can now make preparations to transfer the Sheffrou. We wish to bring him to safety as soon as possible. They are waiting for us aboard the needle. Hopefully his condition will remain stable long enough."

Just then, a voice from the ship's intercom resonated. "This is Captain Teaburg. Red alert. All hands on deck."

Commander Sullivan's watch beeped. He checked it and clenched his jaw. "No transfer for now. Three Rodenegad ships have just appeared. I'll be in the control room. Stay here. I'll keep you posted." With that said, he turned to leave.

All eyes landed on two Rodenegad aliens materializing right in front of the door.

Benshimu roared and dove to cover the Sheffrou with his body. Tanshib joined him.

One of the aliens' arms touched a metal table close by. His image flickered and he disappeared.

While a nauseating rotten egg odor spread across the room, the other Rodenegad shuffled toward Dr. Kowalsky.

Sullivan called out in a loud voice, "Computer, intruder alert, medical unit section five."

The alien grabbed the doctor, who screamed. She pulled away and kicked the alien to no avail. "Let me go."

"Susan!" yelled Sullivan.

The alien just held on tighter and put the other arm on his stomach.

Tamara understood he was preparing to leave. She grabbed a metal device on a table close by and threw it at the Rodenegad as his image paled.

The image of the alien flickered then came back.

Sullivan jumped forward to help the doctor, but the Rodenegad quickly caught him.

Tanshib left Maashi's side and rammed the Rodenegad. The door behind them shattered. Splinters flew across the room as Benshimu's guard crashed in like a bulldozer. He and Tanshib used all the strength they could muster to topple the alien over.

Maashi, awakened by all the commotion, emitted harsh clicks. Tanshib and the guard changed tactics and started to push the head of the Rodenegad backward to block his airway.

Chopa joined Benshimu and covered Maashi with his body to prevent his capture should another alien appear, while Rowni stood by Tamara.

After much grunting and growling from Tanshib and Benshimu's guard, the Rodenegad collapsed on the ground. They immediately released the doctor and Sullivan from the enemy's grasp.

"Quickly," yelled Tamara, "we need to put handcuffs on him!"

"Computer," cried out Sullivan, "a set of zip tie handcuffs!" He went to a corner of the room gwhere they had a replicator.

"No!" yelled Tamara. "We need metal handcuffs to prevent the alien from disappearing. Those ties won't do."

"Right," said Sullivan. He changed his order. "Here they are."

Benshimu's guard took them and clicked them on the alien's wrists just as it started to stir.

A security detail of three walked into the room stepping over fragments of the door. They eyed the scene with surprised looks.

Sullivan said to the head of the detail, "Take that alien away to the brig."

"Yes, sir," The officer answered. "Should I put him with the others or by himself?"

"Put him in solitary for now."

"Understood." The three guards approached the prisoner and beamed him directly to the brig.

Tamara stepped forward. She stared at the commander. "Others? Are you holding other Rodenegad prisoners?"

"We rescued three other Rodenegad before you came aboard. They were floating in space like Sheffrou Maashi. They're in the brig."

Tamara's mouth dropped open. "They're alive?"

"Yes, they had suits on like the Sheffrou."

They heard footsteps coming down the hall. Captain Teaburg walked into the room accompanied by Lieutenant Yoon. She glanced at the fragments of the door and nodded to the group. "I seemed to have missed all the action."

Benshimu stepped forward and said, "Captain, why were we not informed of the presence of Rodenegad prisoners on board this ship? This is not acceptable. Keeping them endangers everyone."

"The decision came from the admiralty," said the captain. "The plan was to use them to our advantage as bargaining chips."

Benshimu roared, "Rodenegad don't bargain with anyone except Krakoran, and this only because Krakoran are more ruthless than they are!"

"We noticed that," said the captain. "They haven't responded to our hails."

The big green paced the room with heavy steps. "You must understand. They are not interested in your ship, your ship's fusion reactor, or even your technology, just the individuals on board to sell and trade."

Chopa stared at the captain and Sullivan. He stated in a calm, cold voice, "Capturing the Rodenegad was a necessary step. They must go on trial and pay for their crimes. However, their detention must be secure. Strict parameters must be followed because Rodenegad ships in the vicinity can locate prisoners and rescue them."

Benshimu added, "Your shields are not designed to prevent the enemy from invading your ship. They will send more and more soldiers to grab your workers, especially the females and soon, you'll be overwhelmed. You won't be able to fight back."

"We wanted to strike a deal with the Rodenegad," said Sullivan. "We thought our shields were strong enough."

"You decided on a course of action without consulting us," said Benshimu. "Their technology has been designed to prevent retaliation and abduction. Your shields need to be modified to be effective. If you had informed us that you were detaining Rodenegad, we would have provided the specifications needed to avoid signaling their presence." Benshimu huffed in anger. "Cooperation is crucial to avoid unpleasant outcomes including being boarded, especially when there is a Sheffrou on board."

Captain Teaburg pressed on her watch. "Security, have we had any other intruders?"

"No, Captain. None have been reported."

"The Rodenegad are evaluating their next move," said Chopa. "Do not let your guard down. They will most likely make other attempts."

The group heard someone taking a deep breath. Maashi, head raised, upper body resting on his elbows, said in a low voice, "We must leave now while the enemy is assessing its next move," he paused, taking another breath, "We only have a short time before they appear." He dropped his head back on the bed, closed his eyes and moaned as if the effort had drained all his energy.

Benshimu's brow darkened. "I agree. We must leave right away. This ship is not safe." He faced the captain. "My guard can stay to help reconfigure your shields if this is acceptable to you."

The captain raised her head and looked as if she was considering the proposal.

Lieutenant Yoon, standing shoulder to shoulder with her, said in a soft voice, "We should take advantage of this opportunity, Captain. We don't have any other ships in the sector if things turn dicey."

The captain nodded. "I appreciate the offer. Let's do so. I don't like the idea that we're a sitting duck."

"Sitting like a duck. Swimming like a duck." Maashi chuckled to himself.

All eyes turned to Maashi.

Dr. Kowalsky's lips stretched into an apologetic smile. "I gave him another dose of sedative. He might have had a little too much this time."

Benshimu hmphed, his brow dark. He said in a booming voice, "It's a good time to leave." He nodded to his guard. "Stay and adjust the shields. Dennyvan will pick you up later. Tanshib and Chopa will come with me."

"Sir," said Chopa. "May I stay with Rowni to work on the shields? I have extensive knowledge of human technology. Together, we will recalibrate the shields faster."

"Sounds appropriate. You may stay," said Benshimu. "Tanshib and my guard will follow me."

"What about me?" said Tamara. "Can I come?" She couldn't just leave Maashi in this condition.

"I believe," said Benshimu in a surprisingly gentle tone, "the initial purpose of your trip was to rejoin your people. You must consider the options carefully before you decide to join us. Sheffrou Maashi's condition is unstable. His life might be in danger. We must go as soon as possible." He paused and glanced at Chopa. "Contact her before you leave."

Chopa nodded sideways.

Tamara bit her lower lip. She went to Maashi's side. No words could convey the loss she felt at that moment. She held Maashi's hand and kissed his palm. He had fallen back into a deep sleep and didn't seem aware of her presence.

Captain Teaburg addressed Benshimu, "Shonava, we cannot allow you to transport out at this time. We must keep our shields up even if they don't completely block the enemy."

Benshimu sent a signal to Dennyvan's ship. "I informed the other needle of our situation," he said. "We will wait until it's safe to transport."

Chopa eyed Sullivan and said, "I am ready to work on your shields."

Chapter 35

Tamara couldn't believe the turn of events. She knew Maashi had to leave, but so soon.... It was like he had been there for one minute and then he was preparing to leave. Her mouth went dry.

She stood in the middle of her quarters and stared at a stunning picture of the Milky Way, hanging on a wall over the couch. Earth with all its wonders was there somewhere, a tiny speck lost among millions of stars, like her, a little dot lost in time and space.

Her mind reeled with the sudden turn of events. Melancholy threatened to bring down her joy at finally reaching her goal of getting back into the world of humans. Trying to make sense of it all, she ordered a serving of chocolate mousse and a slice of turtle cheesecake with all its caramel goodness and plopped on the comfortable couch.

What she had missed the most on Maashi's world was food, especially fruits and sweets. Closing her eyes, she inhaled the intoxicating aroma of chocolate swirling around her. She had waited a long time for a chance to savor the decadent desserts.

Tamara let the mousse melt in her mouth while she recalled how she traveled through a wormhole and almost died on the surface of that awful planet. The memory of those first days would be forever imprinted in her mind. The surface of Chitina was a cold, unforgiving desert without any water. The big orange sun's merciless rays would have roasted her completely if the Chamranlinas hadn't found her.

Tamara wondered how the Chamis reacted when they first moved to Chitina. Maashi had often talked about their original planet called Chamtali. When he spoke of his original home world, Chamtali, his eyes shone with longing. It had taken a long time for Tamara to realize he had never been there. That world had disappeared long before Maashi was born.

Chamtali, with its big oceans, luxurious flora, and advanced life forms was in many ways a world like Earth. Sadly, a rogue planet modified Chamtali's orbit bringing it closer to their sun, creating instability that translated into incessant volcanic activity which transformed the planet's climate. After a few hundred years, Chamtali became inhospitable to life, and the Chamis were forced to leave.

The last spoonful of chocolate mousse lingered on her tongue. She relished the taste and swallowed. *Man. This is so good.* The silky smoothness of the mousse brought back the memory of Maashi's tongue and a smile to Tamara's lips. She set the plate down and picked up the cheesecake.

Much later she had found out about one awful truth about living on Chamtali: the Chamis' enemies, the Krakoran. Hunted without mercy by these ruthless creatures from a parallel world, the Chamis never stood a chance. Even in the glorious years when their culture flourished, they were plagued by kidnappings perpetrated by the Krakoran, never enjoying to the fullest the treasures of their mother world.

Tamara paused. *Why was there always a dark side to things? Nothing was ever perfect.* On Earth, a world of incomparable beauty, the population had to endure the woes of war and climate change. Similarly, the Chamis lived on a lovely planet but lived with the threat of kidnappings. They thought moving to Chitina with its barren surface would protect them from the enemy, but it didn't. Within a mere fifty years, the hunt was just as deadly as it had been before.

After a few bites of cheesecake, Tamara ordered a glass of mango juice, her favorite. *No mango? Humph. Pineapple? Yes. Pineapple.*

She took a long sip of the juice. *Sweet.*

Over the years, the Chamis found ways to fight their enemy, but the threat remained, and their population plummeted. The prime targets of the Krakoran were the fertile Pure Colors, including Sheffrous, with a unicolor tongue.

The Krakoran also kidnapped females. Their numbers tumbled. The few remaining had trouble conceiving, completing a scenario which made the risk of extinction of their species very real and at the forefront of the leaders' concerns.

Maashi spent all his life under the threat of the Krakoran. Captured by the enemy one sequence ago, two years ago by Earth time, tortured and tormented, he survived when few did. The Black and Silver Guards eventually rescued him, but to this day he lived with the scars of his experience as a prisoner.

When Maashi found a portal existed between this world and the world of the Krakoran, he didn't hesitate. He had to find it and destroy it, no matter what the cost. For him, there was no alternative. There was only one choice, risk everything, even his life, to get rid of the Krakoran threat.

Tamara took one more bite of her cheesecake. She stared at the lovely furniture, the floral arrangement on the chest along the wall, the splendid comforter on the bed on the other side of the room. These were important, yes, but they were all material things. Where was the love, affection, and tenderness she need-ed? Would she find someone special in the world of humans? A soulmate? What about the unbelievable joy of sharing her body with a partner that made her feel like she was the most important being in the world?

She set the last portion of the cheesecake on the table. She grabbed a thick pillow from the bed, got back on her recliner, and held it against her chest. So many questions, so few answers. Closing her eyes, sleep quickly took her.

Hours later, something startled her awake. She sat up and blinked.

I love Maashi. He's my reason for living. Why can't I go with him?

How could she abandon the one who had saved her life? She had to stay by his side until he was healed. That's what he would have done for her if the situation were reversed.

Tamara smiled. Suddenly, everything seemed so clear. She would go back to Chitina and stay with Maashi. After all, the human colony wasn't going anywhere. She could always join them later.

Satisfied with her decision, Tamara rested her head back on the pillow and let her mind drift back to sleep. There was plenty of time to inform Chopa.

Chopa watched as Benshimu and Tanshib wrapped each of Maashi's legs with white bandages soaked in a neutral electrolyte solution.

Benshimu made a low rumbling sound as he concentrated on his task. "I hope," he said, "this solution will keep his skin moist and will help alleviate the pain."

Tanshib said, "It is something that has been studied but has not yielded conclusive results. However, it is preferable over administering high doses of narcotics for a prolonged period."

"I agree," said Chopa. He had his doubts about the technique but preferred to keep his opinion to himself. He was convinced that a Tousanou like Sheffrou Chendor, a well-known healer who had previously treated the Sheffrou, would be the long-term solution to Maashi's pain.

"The sooner we bring him back to Chitina the better are his chances of recovering," declared Benshimu.

"Did you get any update on our situation in regard to transferring to our ship?" asked Tanshib.

"I finished the recalibrating of the shields two hours ago and have not heard from Commander Sullivan. I strongly suggested that he surrender the Rodenegad hostages to us, but the commander didn't seem inclined to do so and he didn't share with me Captain Teaburg's plans."

Benshimu straightened up and adjusted his cream shirt embroidered with green vines. He grunted. "I think we are at a stalemate. I will see the commander to get more information on their progress. This situation cannot continue. We must be allowed to transport the Sheffrou and leave."

Maashi made a soft moaning sound. He opened his eyes.

"Shonava," said Benshimu, "How are you feeling?"

"Better," said Maashi. He gritted his teeth before adding, "I wish to see Tamara before I leave."

"Of course," said Chopa. "I will fetch her at once."

Chapter 36

Tamara entered the treatment room where Maashi was resting. The familiar odor of soap and disinfectant reminded her of her life as an ER physician. Smells could be powerful reminders of previous places and events. She missed the adrenaline rush of treating trauma patients. Those cases stimulated her and pushed her powers of deduction to the limit. That part of her life was gone now. All that remained was a faint spark in the back of her mind.

Maashi turned his head when he heard her coming. His face was pale, and his matted hair looked dull and lifeless. Every breath required a significant effort.

His eyes smiled when he saw her. "How are you, Shapinka?" he said, his voice weaker than she expected. Benshimu's Chowli stepped aside and took a place by the door.

"I rested and feel better. And you? How's your pain?"

"Still there but not as intense. Come closer. Let me hold you."

Tamara stepped closer and took his arm in hers. She put his hand on her cheek and kissed his palm like he used to do to her. "Your holoma isn't the same."

"My saweya is low. It will take some time before I heal." He caressed her cheek and his lips thinned. "I wish I could kiss you, but I can't. The pain would quickly overwhelm you."

"Once you reach Chitina, I'm sure things will improve, and you'll return to your normal self again."

Maashi inhaled a long breath. "Always the optimist." His lips stretched in a timid smile. "You embody the light that chases away the darkness. I will miss you."

"I'll be right there, at your side. I want to make sure you'll be okay."

Maashi's eyes honed on her. "It wouldn't be appropriate for you to come." He stopped as if the words pierced his heart.

"Why not?" Tamara shook her head. "I can't leave you like this."

"Shapinka," Maashi strained with the effort of speaking, "I may stay paralyzed. My energy is low. I won't be able to give you the joy and pleasure you deserve."

"I'm going with you and that's final." A gush of sadness flooded her mind.

Maashi blinked and took a long breath. "The Elders have not revoked the punishment of 200 lashes. I might not survive that."

Horror crept into Tamara's veins. "That can't be. There must be a way to cancel that order." She raised her voice, "I won't let them. I'll find a way."

With her head spinning, she let go of his arm, bolted out of the room, and ran back to her own quarters without acknowledging Tanshib or anyone else. Bursting into her quarters, tears rained down her cheeks. Clinging to the wall, bent over with misery, she waited for the storm to fade. Minutes passed. She walked to the restroom, rinsed her face with cold water, and sent a signal to Rowni and Chopa.

Facing the mirror, having regained her countenance, she muttered between her teeth. "We'll see about that."

Chopa and Rowni came a few minutes later to her quarters. They walked in with questioning looks.

Chopa sat on a chair across from her and said, "Are you well, Tamara?" His brow darkened with concern. "Your face and eyes are red."

Before he could continue his comments, Tamara raised her hand and said, "Maashi told me that he still must get flogged with 200 lashes."

Rowni looked aghast. His eyes widened. He stared at Chopa and blurted out a series of clicks. Chopa clicked back just as fast until Rowni stood and paced the room.

"I sense grave injustice," Rowni said, "from the Council towards Sheffrou Maashi. We must find a way to block their edict." He pounded his palms together and hissed. "I can reach out to my contacts as soon as we land on Chitina. There are certainly several avenues we can explore to challenge the Elders' decision."

"I will discuss the details of the Sheffrou's abduction with Chari after we beam aboard the needle," said Chopa. "The matter is too sensitive to discuss on regular channels. Chari was abducted at the same time and can provide us with the precise information needed to exonerate the Sheffrou from any wrongdoing. Dennyvan can also act as witness on behalf of the Sheffrou."

"Not possible," said Rowni, still pacing. "The Council will indict Dennyvan for his kidnapping of Sheffrou Maashi and Chari. The law specifies that anyone accused of a major crime cannot be brought forth as witness for another case. His testimony will be rejected. Chari, being a victim of the abduction, may testify, but his testimony cannot be used to help the Sheffrou. We must find another witness."

"What about the guy that was responsible for the costume and makeup?" said Tamara. "Maashi told me how a Multi disguised him as an alien with black makeup like kohl around the eyes. I remember seeing a pile of discarded dark brown veils a few feet away from him when I woke up in his quarters." She frowned. "I forgot how they called the aliens. It was something odd."

Both Rowni and Chopa stared at Tamara in surprise.

"A Woo-Odong?" said Chopa, raising his voice. "An astute choice of alien species. They are always covered by long, opaque veils."

"Quite an interesting stratagem!" exclaimed Rowni. "Dennyvan must have had access to privileged information. I'm looking forward to meeting Chari Varian. He was at Maashi's side all along and involved in the deception." His brow widened. "I don't understand why he didn't accompany the Sheffrou on the Rodenegad ship." Rowni stopped pacing in the middle of the room. "Dennyvan's trial will certainly be an interesting one."

The other two looked at him as if he had uttered some profanity.

Tamara blurted out, "I'm not concerned about Dennyvan and his shenanigans. I can't stand the guy. He's an ass." She continued with a determined tone. "We must concentrate our efforts on finding a way to get Maashi out of his predicament."

"I agree," said Chopa. "I will check all the data available pertaining to orders from the Council as soon as I board the needle. Perhaps there is a loophole in the laws concerning flogging."

"There's another problem," said Tamara. Lowering her head, she took a long breath and cleared her voice. "Maashi doesn't want me to come back to Chitina. What should I do?"

"What did he say?" said Chopa, concern in his voice.

"He said he wasn't sure he would recover the use of his legs and he wouldn't be able to offer me joy. He said," she gulped, "he might not survive the flogging." Tamara covered her mouth and blinked hard to avoid the tears that threatened to flow.

Rowni sat down beside her and put a hand on her shoulder. "We will find a solution." A shadow covered his gaze.

Chopa took Tamara's hand in his and held it. "We will take care of this. I will contact Rahma and tell him to gather his supporters and be ready for our arrival. Together, we will challenge the Council."

Too overcome by emotion to say anything, Tamara nodded and wiped a few runaway tears with her fingers. She was surprised when they both took her hand in turn and licked her fingers, a common Chami gesture to access her thoughts without kissing her.

Chopa whispered, "I will talk to the Sheffrou. I will make him understand why it's important for you to come to Chitina."

Tamara jumped when the lights in the room changed to red and a deafening alarm sounded in the hall outside her quarters.

"Stay with Tamara," said Chopa. "I will find out what's happening."

"I'm coming with you." Tamara rose.

They all left together.

They reached the main concourse and watched as people rushed about in every direction. Officer Markus crossed the hall in front of them and stopped.

"Go to the medical unit," he ordered. "All the other Chamis are there."

"What's going on?" asked Tamara in a voice loud enough to cover the noise caused by the crowd and the sound of the alarm.

"Two other ships have appeared. They are armed and their shields are up."

"Rodenegad ships?" said Rowni.

Markus shook his head. "No. I think they're from the Interstellar Alliance. The captain is hailing them as we speak. You'd better go. I must join them in the control room."

"Keep us updated," said Tamara.

Chapter 37

Tamara, Chopa, and Rowni joined Benshimu and his Chowli at Maashi's bedside. The medical section had been cleaned and given a fresh coat of paint. Benshimu's guard stayed outside by the newly installed door.

The big Sawisha straightened to his full height and acknowledged the group. He finished tying a forest green sash around his waist. "I have just been invited to join Captain Teaburg and Commander Sullivan in the conference room to discuss current matters with representatives of the Interstellar Alliance. They have two battle cruisers standing by. Officer Markus has provided me with directions. Chopa, Tamara, you may come with me."

Tanshib glanced at Rowni. "Sheffrou Maashi has been sedated and should sleep for a few hours."

"I'll stay with you and the Sheffrou," said Rowni.

"Let's go," said Benshimu. "We need to conclude an agreement with the Interstellar Alliance and be on our way."

The group arrived in the conference room. Two new aliens were present. Chopa whispered in Tamara's ear, "They are Vizinem. I had the pleasure of accompanying a witness to a trial when I was a young Chamranlina, and they were the official representatives of the Alliance."

The Vizinem had a striking appearance. They wore orange makeup on their oval faces and a red headband with a crown of fluffy white hair on their heads.

Captain Teaburg, Commander Sullivan, and Dr. Kowalsky were present dressed for an official meeting in a gray and navy blue outfit. A neutral color choice, thought Tamara. The captain introduced herself and the other members of her delegation while Shonava Benshimu introduced his group and Tamara. Thumb-size universal translators were distributed to the ones who required one and everyone took a seat.

"We are honored to meet you. I am Clomatilde, official representative of the Interstellar Alliance," said the Vizinem sitting closest to the captain. "My colleague, Srilanta, is the official witness." He calmly made eye contact with each one in the room. Clomatilde wore a tunic with red stripes embroidered with gold thread and a black high collar with a golden trim. His colleague wore the same outfit with green stripes.

Clomatilde sat a foot away from the long conference table and folded his hands on his lap. "There are several matters we need to consider," he stated. "We wish to keep this meeting brief to avoid causing prejudice to the parties involved."

"Indeed," said the second individual. "We are here to address the matter of species trafficking, the murder of the Rodenegad in charge of the recent trading on the space station D7654, and the destruction of the Rodenegad ship inside the asteroid ND60-665."

Captain Teaburg frowned and put both hands on the table. "We are grateful for your assistance in these important matters. I understand there are standard procedures agreed upon by all members of the Alliance."

"All the involved parties," said Clomatilde, "must choose representatives who will be transferred aboard our cruiser where our security will fit a sleeve on their arm or an equivalent appendage, to prevent them from beaming back to their ships. The tribunal will be assembled, and the trial will begin as soon as the five judges are chosen and agreed upon by all parties. Be advised that the trial will take as long or be as brief as needed."

The second Vizinem said, "We understand Sheffrou Maashi stands accused by the Rodenegad of the destruction of one of their ships. Because of the Sheffrou's high status in Chamranlina society, we can, as stated in the Alliance's laws, accept another individual to act as witness on his behalf."

Benshimu said with a grave voice, "Sheffrou Maashi's health is in jeopardy. We plan to travel back to Chitina as soon as possible so he can receive the care he needs. We will designate a representative in his stead."

Dr. Kowalsky said, "As the ship's physician, I can attest to the gravity of Sheffrou Maashi's health condition."

"Thank you. Your statement will be kept in our records," said Srilanta.

"I will ask Sheffrou Maashi's guard Rowni," said Chopa. "He is qualified to represent the Sheffrou in matters concerning the destruction of the Rodenegad ship."

Benshimu added, "The Black and Silver leader called Dennyvan should be the one questioned about alien trafficking conducted by the Rodenegad. He may have pertinent information concerning the murder of the Rodenegad at the space station. We can ask him to serve as witness."

Tamara said, "What if Dennyvan doesn't want to come? I don't think he will agree to be held as witness."

"If the individual refuses to serve as witness," said Clomatilde, "he must appoint a representative to testify for him."

"To make matters clear," said Srilanta, "any refusal to cooperate or attempt at fleeing will result in his ship being seized by our secondary cruiser."

"I will personally inform Dennyvan of the rules," said Benshimu. "What about the Rodenegad ships? Rodenegad have penetrated this vessel and tried to kidnap its occupants. We fear for Sheffrou Maashi's life, yet we're unable to transfer him to our needle."

Clomatilde turned to the captain and said, "Captain, we have communicated with the Rodenegad, and they informed us that you are detaining four Rodenegad on board this ship. Is this correct?"

"This is accurate," said Captain Teaburg. "They are charged with kidnapping our men and a group of colonists and must stand trial for their actions."

"Has an official complaint to the Alliance been filed?" said Clomatilde. "If not, please do so as soon as possible. The prisoners must be handed to the Alliance pending an official investigation."

Commander Sullivan said, "What if we refuse to release them? We have all the proof we need to convict them."

"If you have ample proof then the trial will be brief," said Srilanta. "Acting any other way would be unwise. It may lead to a confrontation with the Rodenegad ships with serious consequences including but not limited to, loss of life and property. I urge you to send your grievances to the Alliance so we can process this situation without prejudice to the parties involved."

Benshimu nodded. "This matter should be resolved diplomatically since there has been no major conflict so far between this ship and the Rodenegad. We should strive to keep it that way."

Commander Sullivan nodded. "Captain, if you wish, I can prepare a statement for the Alliance. Once you approve it, we can send it."

The captain sat back and crossed her arms on her chest. "Proceed. You can work on it with the help of Lieutenant Yoon." She turned to face the two Vizinem. "As soon as the Alliance confirms the reception of our statement, we will release the prisoners to you. We will also select someone to represent our crew and the other individuals that were kidnapped."

"We thank you for your cooperation, Captain," said Clomatilde, "and we will ensure that all parties voice their opinions and bring the proof of wrongdoing they may have. The Interstellar Alliance is committed to justice and avoiding conflict. No species is willing to sacrifice members of their crew or contemplate the destruction of their assets. This includes software as much as hardware." The two Vizinem rose as one and Clomatilde added, "Thank you for welcoming us aboard. We will now return to our ship. Any further comments or concerns can be transmitted by the witnesses."

The two stood and were gone in an instant.

"I thought the shields were working," said Tamara. "How can they transport out with the shields up like that?"

Chopa tilted his head to the side. "It would seem the Rodenegad can't penetrate through the shields, but the Alliance has a different technology, a superior one."

"That's why we use speed and subterfuge to deal with enemies rather than confrontation," said Benshimu. "There are always unexpected happenings."

Captain Teaburg's watch pinged, and she said, "What is it?"

A voice said, "This is the helm. The three Rodenegad ships have moved away beyond the reach of transporters. They have lowered their shields."

"Contact the Alliance ship on a secure channel," said the captain. "Confirm these findings with them and inform them the Chamranlinas are preparing to leave." She glanced at Benshimu. "Shonava, it was a pleasure, but I think you want to depart as soon as possible. Hopefully, we can see each other again in more favorable circumstances."

Benshimu's lips stretched in a tentative smile. "I believe our paths may cross in the future and we can engage in productive discussion about our respective cultures."

"Thank you. I will be looking forward to that."

"We will return to Sheffrou Maashi's bedside and wait for your signal before we leave."

"Dr. Kowalsky will accompany you and let you know when it's safe to go."

As they all stepped out, Chopa lowered his voice and said to Tamara, "I discussed your desire to accompany us back to Chitina with the Sheffrou. I explained how difficult it is for you to remain with the humans at this time. The communication was telepathic and brief, but you may come. However, you will need to follow us on the other needle. Rowni should be finished with his statement to the Alliance in just over an hour and will accompany you."

"I understand," said Tamara. "I'll go to my quarters to get something done and get my stuff."

"Stuff? What do you mean?"

"Things I wanted to bring with me. It'll take me just thirty minutes."

Back in her quarters, Tamara grabbed a small device containing music downloads, one thing besides food that she had terribly missed. Perhaps Maashi would find listening to classical pieces as enjoyable as she did. She also took a fitted leather jacket, a dark mushroom color. She loved the soft leather feel and the confidence it gave her when she wore it, even though it was a synthetic equivalent of leather.

Then she spoke to the computer. "Where can I get a haircut?"

"A technician is available at all hours. Do you wish for one now?"

"Yes. Send someone over now."

A young man in his early twenties with long blond curls tapped at the door.

"That was fast," said Tamara.

"My unit is the next one down the hall," he said chuckling. "How short do you want your hair?"

Tamara explained how she wanted her cut and he sat her down and ordered what he needed from the replicator. Twenty minutes later, he was done.

"I don't have anything to pay you," she said.

"Haircuts are complimentary aboard the ship. Thanks for the opportunity to cut your hair. It's a rich auburn, a lovely color."

"Thanks for a great job." The young man waved at her and was out in a quick minute.

She was about to step into the hallway when she decided to take a personal tablet with loads of data pertaining to Earth's flora and fauna and thousands of pictures of humans. They would keep her company when loneliness threatened. With those in hand, she was ready to go.

This time, she could face Maashi's world with assurance. Her first task would be to find a way to convince the Council to revoke Maashi's flogging orders. Second task, she would help Maashi to heal.

Chapter 38

Although he was captain of his needle, Dennyvan couldn't give orders to Benshimu. A powerful Sawisha and First Lord of the Seventh Compound with close allies in the Council of Elders, Dennyvan had never been a fan of Benshimu. He held a high rank in Chamranlina society and had even been asked to sit for an ailing member of the Council at some point.

Dennyvan knew he would face charges and stiff sanctions from his bold kidnapping of Sheffrou Maashi. The sanctions would certainly be eased by his recovery of several Chamranlinas including the two Black and Silver Guards he had been searching for, Sheffrou Ashani, and the human female, Maashi's Chimitanga, who, for reasons he couldn't fathom, was quite popular in the media back on Chitina. He shone with anticipated jubilation as he surmised that Sheffrou Ashani's return might even be enough to reinstate him as section Leader among the Black and Silver Pure Colors.

Even though they had lowered their shields, he kept a close eye on the positions of the three Rodenegad ships. His duty consisted of guarding the other needle and bringing up the rear, so to speak. As requested by the Alliance, he had surrendered his Rodenegad prisoner. Surprised by the Rodenegad's lack of aggression, he suspected dark plans and wanted to escort the other needle back to Chitina as quickly as possible. When his pilot confirmed the three ships had moved further out in space and didn't show any signs of aggression, he applauded the move. Perhaps he would be able to leave soon after all.

When Dennyvan heard that Maashi had destroyed the portal to the Krakoran world, he secretly beamed with pride. He downplayed in his mind the fact that he had objected to Maashi's plan to infiltrate the Rodenegad ship and refused to help. The Leader envisioned coming back to Chitina with Sheffrou Maashi a hero. One who had saved his people from the enemy.

In a virtual contact with the green Sawisha, Dennyvan tried to convince him that his needle, called 011, was equipped with better weapons in the event of a Rodenegad attack.

Benshimu flatly refused to leave on the 011. "Do you honestly think I would trust someone like you?" Benshimu said, in a tone that countered any argument. "You took Sheffrou Maashi by force, used him, endangered his life, and he now faces the wrath of the Elders. He must suffer the indignity, not to mention the risk to his life, of the punishment the Council members have decreed."

His face dark with anger, he growled, "I can't think of any argument that will be strong enough to convince the Council to amend the order of 200 lashes. Since your clever deception, the Elders have adopted a firm stance against those who dare disobey. They will not alter their decision. The Sheffrou, through no fault of his own, has now accumulated a long list of enemies and the Sawishas don't take kindly to being made fools of."

Dennyvan grunted in mockery. "The Council of Elders will certainly change their minds when they learn that the Sheffrou has destroyed the portal connecting our world to the Krakoran."

"Do you think they're so easily duped?" roared Benshimu. "I had ample time to review the recordings from your ship that show you refused to help the Sheffrou because you didn't believe in the existence of the portal. You forbade him to leave. He disobeyed your explicit orders and left anyway." He added in a menacing tone, "How are you going to prove that the portal existed now that it's gone?"

"We're actively looking for debris as we speak," Dennyvan said, holding back his growing irritation. "We will find proof of the destruction."

"Perhaps," said the green, "the portal existed only in the Sheffrou's mind. No real proof of this portal has been found and no one on Chitina will believe testimony from the Rodenegad. It's unlikely any Rodenegad will divulge the existence of a coalition with the Krakoran. Also don't forget, between your involvement in illicit trafficking and the destruction of a Rodenegad ship, we have new enemies to deal with."

Dennyvan growled, "You forget that in the course of our operations, we have rescued two Black and Silver Guards and Sheffrou Ashani among a few others." Fisting his hands, he added, "I will find proof that the portal existed and that Sheffrou Maashi destroyed it. Dennyvan out."

Dennyvan stood in his quarters and fumed about Benshimu's decision. Powerless to change it and forced to send Kotian, his makeup artist and a trusted Black and Silver Guard to testify on his behalf, he had no choice but to wait until the Interstellar Alliance representatives released them.

Pacing in his quarters, trying to quell his anger, Dennyvan heard a *ping* from the ship's monitor. "What is it?"

"The human female is requesting permission to come aboard," said a guard. "Do you wish to speak with her?"

Dennyvan shook his head to one side. *Why did she want to come? Why wasn't she aboard the other needle with the Sheffrou?* "Open a channel."

"Channel open, sir," said the guard.

"Dennyvan, this is Tamara. I want to go back with you to Chitina. I have Rowni with me, one of Maashi's security guards."

"Let me speak with Rowni."

"This is Rowni."

"Are you the one Sheffrou Maashi freed from the Rodenegad ship?"

"Yes, sir. Sheffrou Maashi freed me and Sheffrou Tamara with fourteen other humans."

Dennyvan bristled at the mention of 'Sheffrou Tamara' but held back any comment. Multis like this one who called themselves guards were unworthy of their positions. He could see that Rowni had swallowed the prevailing rumors about the Chimitanga as reality. "Did you see the portal with your own eyes? Can you confirm its existence and subsequent destruction?"

"Yes, sir. And so did Sheffrou Tamara."

Dennyvan's mouth stretched in a wry smile. "Very well, permission for both of you to come aboard."

Redden brought Tamara and Rowni to see Dennyvan. His eyes bore into Tamara when he saw her. "So," he said, "Shonava Benshimu refused to take you. He didn't want to trouble himself with your presence."

Tamara returned Dennyvan's glare. *What an ass.* "They left earlier," said Tamara. "They said they wanted to go back to Chitina as fast as they could because Maashi's condition was unstable." She knew her comment would irk Dennyvan. His ship was surely just as fast, but she couldn't help needling him. The guy had been a pain from the moment she had been rescued the first time. "Rowni testified in Maashi's place at the Interstellar Alliance tribunal. That's why he's returning with me."

"I see you haven't changed," Dennyvan said in a sarcastic voice, "always prickly like a noola-noola bush." Turning over to Rowni, he added, "Welcome. We haven't been formally introduced but I'm told you were part of Sheffrou Maashi's security. I'm surprised that you haven't followed him on the other needle."

Tamara knew Dennyvan's comments were an insult, but Dennyvan's bullying didn't throw Rowni. He ignored the bait and stated calmly, "Before my capture by the Rodenegad, I was head of security for Sheffrous Maashi and Tomisho. After Sheffrou Maashi freed me, he instructed me to protect his Chimitanga. That is why I'm at her side and will remain so until I receive further instructions from the Sheffrou."

Dennyvan grunted, "In that case, you can share Tamara's quarters since we have limited space. As for your statement concerning the portal, I want you to meet with our chief engineer and describe everything you saw with as much detail as possible."

Tamara stepped forward. "How long before we leave?"

Dennyvan looked down at her with a smirk on his face. "We have a few things to complete. It will take a day or two." He turned and pressed on a control panel beside the door, "Redden, please direct our guests to their quarters."

"Yes, sir."

The door opened. Redden was standing outside with his usual hostile expression. Tamara hoped the trip would be short. She was thankful Rowni was there because she didn't trust the other two.

Tamara stood a few feet away from Chari in her small quarters with the gray walls, floor, and couches. She had forgotten how depressing the needle was. The Ghouli Ghouli looked out of sorts. He wore a dark olive shirt and a purple sash. Only purple. He had omitted the red, pink and yellow bands that were part of his normal sash, reminding Tamara of an officer who forgot to put the stars on his uniform. He didn't have the usual twig in his mouth. *Yep. There was something not quite right about him.*

"I am pleased to see you, Tamara," he said. "Can you tell me more about Maashi's condition? Rowni briefed me, but I wanted your opinion."

"How about we sit first? These last few days have taken a toll." *Why didn't he leave with the other ship?*

"Of course, I forgot that you're only human," said Chari.

Tamara's eyebrows raised. *What was that supposed to mean?* She thought he had lost that sarcastic attitude a while ago.

"All I can say is unless he's sedated or in close contact with a Sawisha, he's in terrible pain." Sadness swelled in her like a wave. She paused and took a deep breath. "There's also the fact that his legs are paralyzed. I don't know if this is a permanent condition." She bit her lip, worry getting the best of her. "Only time will tell."

Chari stayed silent. He rubbed his black hands over and over each other. His face hardened.

Tamara frowned. "Did something happen between you and Maashi?"

Chari's facial expression showed no emotion. "We had a disagreement about the portal."

"What kind of disagreement?"

"We argued. I insisted it was too dangerous for him to go."

"And? What did he say?"

"He let me know I shouldn't interfere with his decision."

"Did you have a fight?"

"Why do you say that?"

Tamara looked away then cocked her head and stared straight at him. "Maashi is different. Before he destroyed the portal, he reminded me of those powerful Sawishas I saw at the Great Eclipse Celebration, sure of themselves, bold, like they're invincible. I got the feeling he wasn't going to let anyone get in his way once his decision was made."

"For someone lacking telepathy skills, you understand more than I expected."

"It's just that you don't look like yourself." *Like a dog who got a beating.*

"It is not a matter that concerns you." He rose to leave. "Get some rest, Tamara." In two long strides, he was out the door.

That was odd.

She sat back and twirled a strand of hair in between her fingers. She had struck a nerve, closer to the truth than Chari was ready to admit. Something had happened between Maashi and him. Something serious.

Chapter 39

Ever since Maashi arrived on Chitina, everyone's attention was focused on him. Not a single moment went by without someone asking how he felt, if he was in any pain, did he need food, water, a softer pillow? Was his head propped too high, too low? Did he want to see anyone?

His patience had been stretched to the limit.

On that day, sitting in a lounge chair in his quarters, Maashi hissed with irritation. He raised his voice. "I want to be alone. Everyone leaves now."

"Of course, Shonava," said Sasha, the suave creamy white who was constantly at his side. "The controls, as you know, are—"

"Right beside me. I know," Maashi's voice was a low growl. "Now, all of you, leave me before I strangle someone."

"We'll be back in three hours for your pool exercises," said Rahma, standing a couple of feet away, his torso naked. His quatay was starting to show and he proudly displayed the intricate red markings of a Pure Color taking shape on his upper chest.

Maashi shot him a stare which would have intimidated anyone who didn't know him well. Rahma just laughed and said, "Get some rest, sir."

They finally left: Sasha with an engaging smile, Rahma, standing tall, two other Multis which just seemed to get in the way, and a guard.

Finally, some quiet.

He understood their concern, but he wasn't ready to face the inevitable. He planned to take as long as possible before pushing himself to take his first steps. It didn't matter that Sheffrou Dasho, his close friend acting as his personal physician, had explained to him more than once that his legs had healed completely and that there was no reason for him not to be able to walk.

Maashi found himself in a dilemma. If he took too long to walk, the conspiracy theories would start anew and grow under the hungry stares of the Multis. This phenomenon had blossomed in the last ten sequences and now anything the Sawishas and the Sheffrous did was the subject of tremendous speculation.

There would be rumors that Maashi was spoiled, a coward who loved all the attention, that he had been coerced by the evil Dennyvan to impersonate a series of aliens, that the Black and Silver Guards were ready to use him in exchange for other guards.... The list was endless.

In fact, Maashi had never been one to bask under the weight of the insatiable eyes of the Multis who relished the long list of theories. He much preferred privacy over fame. Unfortunately, his life in the last few sequences had been anything but simple and his name was on everyone's tongue.

The truth was that the Council of Elders had been deliberating and discussing his case. Maashi knew that the odds of changing a former ruling were extremely low. He expected that the sentence of 200 lashes would not be overruled and would be carried out as soon as he healed, i.e., could walk unaided.

For reasons he couldn't begin to understand, this seemed to escape the attention of the well-wishers who wanted him to heal as fast as possible. Maashi was in no hurry. Why on Chitina would he push himself?

Chapter 40

*F*inally, I'm home.

Tamara couldn't repress a big smile as she followed Rowni down the tunnels to the anti-gravity elevators. She took a few minutes to adjust to the subdued lighting of the underground world of the Chamranlinas. He led her to her old quarters, and she recognized the familiar hallways with oval sconces on the granite walls every twelve feet.

"Do you know when I'll be able to see Maashi? Do you know anything about his condition?"

Rowni slowed his pace and said in a soft voice, "You need to get settled in, then Chopa will come speak with you. All I know is the Sheffrou is alive, and his condition is stable."

"Right," said Tamara. "You don't know more than me."

"I will not be directly involved in the Sheffrou's care. I will be reinstated to my previous position and be debriefed on the events that happened in the last few months. One guard messaged me and said Tousanou Chendor oversees Sheffrou Maashi's everyday care. Do you know him?"

Tamara repressed a shriek. *Maashi must still be in a lot of pain if they called Chendor.*

"Yes, I know him well," she said. "He helped Maashi recover from being poisoned after he escaped to the methane fields."

Rowni stopped in his tracks and stared at Tamara. "What did you say?"

"It's a long story. The best is to get in touch with Chopa. He can give you all the details. I really don't want to talk about that. All I can say is Chendor is a powerful Sheffrou 6 who was attacked years ago by the Krakoran and suffered life-threatening injuries. He has recuperated and now dedicates his life to helping others." Tamara took a long breath and stated in a steadfast voice, "Many things happened after you were kidnapped. A lot of sad things."

Rowni nodded. He clicked something and continued down the tunnel. They entered a new section with double doors with Maashi's crest on each side, a gold shoshan on a royal blue background. Tamara had never seen these before. They had been newly engraved. The two went in and reached the third door on the left, connecting to Tamara's quarters. She entered and looked up at the sky-blue ceiling with the puffy white clouds. She smiled. "Those are my quarters for sure," she said. "Not exactly the same but very close."

Tamara plopped herself on the long couch with the turquoise and powder blue cushions. Grabbing a thick cushion, she held it against her chest. "I never thought I would miss this place so much."

"I will inform Chopa that you are here. Do you know how to access food and drinks?"

"I do. Thanks, Rowni."

"I will see you later." He turned and left with a slow heavy step. Too slow. He must be bewildered by everything that happened. Being a prisoner of the Krakoran for long months had deprived him of knowledge of important events in the lives of the Chamis. *Why didn't she ask him about his time as a prisoner? Maybe it was better that she didn't.*

Tamara tapped on the control on the floor beside her and waited for the juice to materialize. She took a sip of the cool toughi and sloshed it in her mouth. She finished the glass and set it aside. She rose and went to the water room.

She saw herself in the reflecting glass and tilted her head this way and that. There was something different about her, but she couldn't quite figure it out. She liked her haircut, but it wasn't that. She used the restroom and watched without thinking as the door to the water room slowly closed.

After rinsing her hands and face, she noticed that there weren't any towels to wipe. "Well, still missing towels." Making her way back to the receiving room, she touched the controls to open the washroom door. It didn't budge. She tried again and again. "Damn. Why doesn't it work?" Gritting her teeth, she banged on the door. "Can anybody hear me? Where is every-one?"

A half-hour later, Tamara heard Chopa's voice. "I'm here, in the water room. The door is locked."

The door slid open and Chopa peered in. "Are you all right?"

"Why did the door lock like that? No one was answering. These things freak me out."

Chopa took her hand and apologized, "I am very sorry. We were on lockdown for over an hour. Three Rodenegad appeared in this sector and the guards seized them. They're now in cus-tody."

"Is Maashi okay?"

"He is safe. Sheffrou Chendor is here to speak with you."

"Can you work on the door, so this won't happen again?"

"I will make sure the verbal command is working. Come, Sheffrou Chendor is waiting on the other side."

Tamara entered the receiving room and marveled at the Sheffrou's appearance. He was such an imposing figure, as big and powerful as a sumo wrestler. He had been admiring a water sculpture that stood against the back wall. Bubbles rose in a series of fine tubes symbolizing how life is closely linked with water. He turned and a big smile softened the long scar on his right cheek. He set his striking violet eyes on her.

"Tamara, Shapinka. It's a pleasure to see you." He walked over to her side and took her hands in his pudgy fingers and deposited a light kiss on her palms.

"It's so nice to see you too. You haven't changed," she chuckled. "Just as charming."

Tamara inhaled his holoma which had the sweet fragrance of the tea olive tree and followed his every move.

"Please, come and sit with me," he said, his voice like honey. "I want to talk to you about Sheffrou Maashi."

Tamara settled on the couch. She tensed at the mention of Maashi. Chendor eased his humongous frame beside her, crushing the thick mattress under his weight. He pulled the end of his long midnight blue sash from under him and set it on the couch beside her.

"How is Maashi? Is he still in a lot of pain?"

Chendor grew pensive. "He is experiencing moderate pain if someone stays by his side. When alone, the pain overwhelms his senses."

Tamara's spirits wilted like a plant deprived of water. An optimist at heart, she had convinced herself that Maashi was on the mend with the help of Chendor and the other Pure Colors.

"Is there something I can do?" she asked.

"Not now. Any intimate contact could hurt you," he said. His violet eyes looked solemn. He added, "You need to stay positive, Tamara."

Resentment flooded her thoughts. "Will he recover the use of his legs? Does he have permanent nerve damage?"

Chendor sat back and the couch sighed. "I have examined him carefully with two other physicians and we haven't found any significant nerve damage."

"How can that be? Why is he paralyzed?"

His answer wasn't what she expected.

"I understand you worked with Maashi to set up the explosives to destroy the Rodenegad ship. Is that correct?"

"Yes. I don't see where this connects with Maashi's paralysis."

"Humans process things and events differently than Chamranlinas."

"What are you trying to say?"

Chendor's brow widened. "I don't want to offend you," he said, keeping his voice low.

"I just want to understand. What do you mean exactly?"

"You are partially responsible for the deaths of several Rodenegad, yet, as far as I can assess, you're not unduly affected by that fact. The situation is not the same for Chamranlinas. Only Blacks, Silvers, or Reds can kill other sentient beings with minimal consequences. The others are deeply affected if they cause other beings' deaths."

Tamara was speechless. *Was Maashi's paralysis psychosomatic?* She felt like a boulder dropped over her head. The room started spinning. She realized she was crying only when she saw the wet drops on her arms.

Chendor pulled a small piece of material and handed it to her.

Tamara's distress increased. "I should've stayed with Rowni," she cried, "and sent Maashi away on the shuttle. At least he would've been safe." Her sobs intensified.

He held her close and kissed the top of her head.

Her face hardened. "Those damn Rodenegad. They caused sorrow and heartbreak to so many." She fisted her hands. How could she forget the flat creature they had killed to serve as food to the prisoners? "They deserved to die."

Chendor stayed silent, his face a mask of granite.

Tamara wiped her cheeks with the cloth and noticed Chendor's wet shirt. "Oh, I apologize. I put snot all over your shirt." She looked up at him. His face had paled.

"I guess you didn't want to hear that. You must think I'm the meanest person ever." This made her want to cry all over again. She blinked the fresh tears away.

"It takes just a moment to change a shirt," he said with a soft voice.

"Are you angry with me?" she said and sniffled.

He looked at her with gentle eyes. "You're a much more complex being than I thought, capable of immense love to the point of sacrificing your life for another being yet also capable of killing for revenge or to save your own life. Extreme behaviors that we only see in Pure Black and Silvers."

Tamara stared at him. "I am human. We can be extremely good or extremely bad. We live in a challenging world filled with potentially deadly creatures where sometimes you must kill just to survive."

"You are a fascinating being. Totally endearing yet potentially deadly. I understand why Sheffrou Maashi is mesmerized."

He tilted his head to the side. "It would seem you're just as spell-bound by him. The intensity of your emotions is remarkable. I love this about you."

Calmer as if the flood of tears had helped to find relief, she straightened and said, "So, what do we do now?"

"We?"

"Yes," she said. "There must be something I can do." Her stomach made a low rumbling sound that she pretended not to hear.

Chendor pondered his answer for a moment. "Can I rely on you to be my confidante? I need someone who knows Maashi well and understands him to bounce off ideas with. I find the others don't adequately fulfill this role."

Tamara glanced at him sideways. "Are you mocking me?"

"Not at all. I think you are a very astute and clear-headed Fanella which puts you at a great advantage over the other Chamranlinas."

Tamara nodded. "Thank you for the compliment," she said. "I accept your proposition. I would also like to make a request."

"I'm listening."

"Can we involve Rowni, one of Maashi's former guards, in our discussions? He is a level-headed Multi with green dominant. I find that since he missed the events of the last few months, he can bring a fresh perspective."

"Do you mind if I have a meeting with him first? That is important to me."

"Sure. That's a great idea. Shall we shake hands on your proposition?" Tamara extended her hand and waited.

Chendor took her hand in his oversized one. She shook it and he laughed.

"Thank you," she said with a smile. "Now, can you tell me what happened between Maashi and Chari?"

"At one condition," said Chendor.

"What?"

"Your stomach has been making a lot of noise for a little while." His mouth stretched in a one-sided smile. "Aren't you hungry? When was the last time you ate?"

Tamara chuckled. "I don't remember. Sometimes I just ignore my stomach. I can't let it control my life."

"That is such a Sheffrou trait," Chendor's eyes widened in amazement. "However, contrary to other Sheffrous, I listen to my stomach as you call it and seize every excuse to enjoy some good food. How about we join Sheffrou Maashi for a bite as you would say? I hear he is comfortable now."

At the mention of Maashi, Tamara couldn't help it. She took Chendor's hand and kissed it. "Thank you so much for helping."

Chendor clicked his approval. He opened his mouth as if he was going to say something then thought better of it. "I will spare you the meaning of what you just did."

"That bad, huh?"

"Yes," said Chendor with a twinkle in his eyes. "Can I ask Rowni to join us?"

"Sure."

"First, I must take care of something. Do you mind going ahead? Do you know where Shonava Maashi's quarters are?"

"Yes, of course. I'll go there and you can join me when you're ready."

Tamara's belly rumbled again with insistence.

Chendor roared with laughter. "You really need to eat."

Chapter 41

Tamara knocked on Maashi's door and entered. She looked around the room. Contrary to what she had been used to, there were no guards in his quarters. She smiled when she saw his favorite glass sculpture, a gift from Chendor, a shoshan stallion rearing on his hind legs. The beast had a fierce look with big black eyes and flaring nostrils. Chendor must have seen a wild streak in Maashi. The power, the elegance, the fierce look of the animal wasn't unlike him, especially now that he was changing into a mature Sheffrou.

Maashi wasn't in the receiving room. *Maybe she came at a bad time.* Stepping further in, she peeked into the bedroom. Not there either. She huffed. Turning about, she saw a hallway leading further back. She trotted over and entered the pool area.

"Wow," she exclaimed. The room looked sinister in the dim lights. The blue walls were now a dull gray, the water turbid, uninviting. "That's pretty sad," she said, shaking her head in disbelief. Why didn't the Chamis maintain it?

Maashi enjoyed diving in the clear pool, and she had spent hours swimming with him at her side, floating on her back, staring at the gold swirls on the ceiling. The blue lagoon she called it. She backed away from the dark water. Random bubbles floated to the surface. She turned to leave then stopped. Why were there bubbles?

Tamara walked back and moved closer to the edge of the pool. She frowned, squinted, then saw Maashi lying very still at the bottom.

"Maashi! Maashi!" she yelled as loud as she could. He didn't move.

She gasped and ran out to get help.

In her rush, she forgot there was a yellow panic button on the controls by the doorframe. She dashed along the hallway and knocked as hard as she could on the first door she saw.

"Help! Help! Maashi's in trouble."

The door opened. Chendor stood bare-chested and stared down at her with dark violet eyes.

Tamara gulped, taken aback by his formidable size and the deep scar running down his neck and right shoulder. She recovered and blurted out, "Maashi is at the bottom of the pool. He's not moving. Something's wrong." Realizing she could've gone to any guard instead of bothering the top-ranking Sheffrou, she added, "Forgive me for disturbing you."

"You can always ask me for help," he said with a gentle tone. "Lead the way, I'll follow."

Tamara nodded and covered the distance to Maashi's quarters in record time. As soon as Chendor got to the pool, he dove in.

Pain. Intolerable, excruciating pain. Will it ever stop?

Escape was impossible. Attempts at evading it were futile.

Maashi's only choice was to hide. Underwater, his screams could not be heard, his muffled sobs created no sound, didn't cause alarm. He didn't have to pretend the pain didn't exist.

Overcome with anguish, he was losing hope. He moaned with despair in the only place where he could hide the shame of his tears. He knew if he stayed too long underwater, he risked drowning, but then, there would be freedom from this horrible pain.

Maashi dreaded the flogging. The Elders' decision tormented him. He couldn't find the courage to fight more pain. He was still young, just reaching maturity, looking forward to a long life. He might succeed in controlling this pain by using all his willpower, but with the flogging, death would claim him.

He was beyond endurance. For a being whose whole purpose was to feel and give pleasure, a life stricken with endless pain was unlivable. Lost in hopelessness, he sensed his soul pulling away from his body, trying to slip into the tranquil waters of a narrow river that meandered in a deep canyon and spilled into an immense ocean. The river called him. The ocean beckoned to him. It meant peace and freedom from this horrid pain. Staying here in the world of the living one more second was intolerable. He was close to giving up, ready to join the river that fled to the ocean.

In the darkness of the abandoned pool, a long vine-like creature slithered at the bottom searching for a victim. It touched his foot and Maashi barely felt it. It slowly snaked around his legs making its way up to his thighs before he noticed anything.

When the vine tightened its grip on his legs, his soul slipped into the peaceful river. He struggled to call it back, to focus his mind and find the strength to fight the vine before it climbed higher.

I can't die. Not this way.

Despair. Tragedy. End of the world.

Maashi shuddered.

A moment later, a warm thought slid into him. With incredible gentleness, it lifted his soul, flooded his mind with love and kindness. Like a small, wounded creature, his soul nestled in the solace of the gentle thought.

"Sweet one," the thought said. *"Do not abandon hope. I am here with you."*

Outside, Tamara stood distraught at the edge of the pool. Wringing her hands and close to breaking down, she silently prayed for Maashi. Then, she saw with immense relief his Chowlis, Chopa, Rahma, and the new one Sasha, as they bolted into the pool area and dove in the water. They joined Chendor deep underwater.

A swarm of tender touches, as delicate as soap bubbles came and reached out to Maashi. They held him, shared his sorrow, drank his despair.

Maashi's soul blended with those thoughts overflowing with life and love. He sunk into their embrace and his soul soaked in the newfound energy. His charissa grew and expanded reaching every single cell in his body. The vine retreated. His pain broke into small shards and dissipated into nothingness.

Maashi stretched his long frame and broke the emotional ties that bound his limbs. He could feel the charissa spreading, releasing him from anguish and despair. He moved his legs with long, slow strokes and swam to the surface. Held by Chendor and surrounded by his Chowlis, he inhaled a deep breath and filled his lungs with life-giving air. Tears of joy and relief dripped down his face. He raised his head and cried out with happiness. The horrible pain was no longer.

Another cry echoed from the edge of the pool. The group held him and brought him to the little female who wrapped her arms around his neck in a tight embrace.

"You're safe!" she cried, "Welcome back, my love."

Chapter 42

Two days later, while Maashi was asleep under close watch by two guards and his newest Chowli, Sasha, Tamara gathered his three other Chowlis, Chari, Chopa, and Rahma and his guard Rowni. She had high hopes that the group would solve Maashi's problem with the Council.

Staring into the eyes of each one present, she said, "I'm glad you're all here. I don't need to remind you how important the situation is. We have only two days to find a solution to the flogging issue. In the light of the incident at the pool, we must act now."

Chari said, his dark eyes thinned to small slits, "I know for a fact that once the Elders have decided on a course of action, they will not change their decision."

Chopa was quick to agree, "I have personally checked all records for the last 200 sequences and have not found any instance where the Council modified their penalties."

"I thought Dennyvan could help," said Chari, "but he stands accused of kidnapping the Sheffrou and his testimony will be rejected."

Rahma chimed in. "We may have another alternative." Out of touch with the group for special training these last few months, he had changed to a more mature version of himself.

Tamara admired his muscular arms and his wide chest partially covered by a burgundy tunic with a crimson red sash.

"I will connect you to a friend of mine," he said with his warm voice, "a young purple who is passionate about the study of law and is proficient in its intricacies. He has found an interesting perspective concerning flogging." Rahma pressed on a device that produced a hologram of a young Chami with a long thin face.

Tamara remembered this young Pure Color when she saw the deep scar above his left eye. He had been instrumental in identifying the culprit responsible for the plague that killed Maashi's offspring.

"Go ahead," said Rahma. "Tell us what you found."

"Good day to you all," said the purple with an enthusiastic tone. He pushed back a lock of chestnut hair dangling over his forehead. "I have been studying prior instances of flogging and realized there is a way for the one penalized to dodge the punishment. It's called substitution. Simply put, a volunteer submits to the punishment instead of the one under penalty. It hasn't been used for decades but may solve our current conundrum. However, there is one caveat. The Council will accept the substitution only when the individual who has been condemned cannot bear the flogging for health reasons or a physical impediment."

The group erupted in loud clicks. Rahma said, pounding one large fist into his left hand, "That is a great solution. One of us can get flogged instead of the Sheffrou."

"I wish it was as simple as that, Rahma," said the purple. "The law states Chowlis and Fanellas are excluded as substitutes, and no one can be coerced to volunteer for the flogging or be lured by future gains."

"That's not good," said Tamara. "Who would volunteer for this without gaining anything in return?"

The mood of the group soured. Rowni grumbled. Rahma thanked his friend for his help and cancelled the hologram. They stared at each other.

"Still," said Rahma with a stern voice, "there is some hope."

The door chime rang and Chendor said, "I am glad you are all together. May I join you?"

Tamara smiled and said, "Of course. We were just discussing how we can help Maashi with the flogging problem."

Rowni stood and said, "Shonava, please take a seat."

"Thank you," answered Chendor. He pushed a big cushion aside and eased his massive frame onto the couch.

Chopa clicked to him to inform him of what they had discussed and Chendor said, "Substitution. Interesting concept. Let me contact a friend who has excellent knowledge of the law. Perhaps he can help." Chendor punched on a series of controls and produced a long series of clicks. Shonava Shitan Garavella, a respected Pure Color, in charge of the Western Compound, appeared as a hologram.

"Salutations to all," he said. His head, covered with thinning gray hair, was visible and his upper body was covered by a forest green tunic with a gold collar.

"Good day to you," said Chendor. "The group would like to ask you some questions about a penalty."

"I will answer to the best of my knowledge," he said. "I'm listening."

"Shonava," asked Chopa, "in the case of substitution for flogging, are there any specific rules?"

Shitan tilted his head, looked away then looked back at them. "I believe you're referring to Sheffrou Maashi's penalty imposed by the Council of Elders for evading the Draharma trial. As far as I can ascertain, the rules of substitution would apply in his case since he is recovering from injuries sustained while fighting the Rodenegad."

Chopa said in a somber voice, "Shonava, I must inform you that yesterday, Sheffrou Maashi has been involved in a near-death experience. We are extremely concerned about his health."

"I was not aware of this," said Shitan. "Is he recuperating?"

"Yes, Shonava. He has been sedated and is under surveillance," said Chopa.

Chendor added, "Of course, his condition hasn't been disclosed."

"I agree," said Shitan. "Your group's discretion must be absolute." He paused. "This qualifies as a serious medical event. In this case, I am sure the Council would accept any request for substitution."

"Sir, it's a pleasure to see you again," said Tamara. "Thank you for joining us. Are you saying that another Chamranlina could receive the 200 lashes instead of Maashi?"

Shitan Garavella smiled. "It is a pleasure to hear your voice, young Fanella." He paused. "Did you say 200?"

"Yes, Shonava," said Chopa. "The penalty is 200 lashes."

Shitan straightened his shoulders and rubbed his chin. "Let me make this clear. It is not necessary for one individual to bear the 200 lashes. The total number of lashes can be shared by several individuals."

Tamara moved to the edge of her seat. "Sir, what is the minimal number of lashes for each individual?"

"In most cases, one lash is sufficient. However, in the case of 200 lashes, I would recommend a minimum of two lashes per individual to avoid being in contempt of the Council's decision."

A murmured whisper went through the group.

"Thank you for your help, Shonava," said Tamara.

Chendor nodded. "As always, your counsel has been most enlightening. You have given us ample food for thought. I will not impose on your kindness any longer."

Shitan's expression softened, he ran a long finger through his gray hair. "It was a pleasure to see you all. I hope this will help your cause and I will meditate to support the Sheffrou's recovery."

The Chamis clicked their thanks in unison. Tamara said, "We are in your debt, sir."

The hologram faded, then disappeared.

"Well, what do you think?" asked Tamara. "What do you plan to do?"

Chopa and Rahma looked at each other, then at Rowni. They clicked between themselves and Rahma answered, "My friends know that you, the Sheffrou, and Rowni have destroyed the portal connecting to the Krakoran world. We owe him a great debt and we will ask everyone we know if they are willing to participate."

Chari, who had remained silent and aloof said, "I will also contact individuals who are grateful for the Sheffrou's help."

"Remember to be discreet," said Chendor. "We cannot divulge our plan before Sheffrou Maashi is officially summoned by the Council. On that day, when he faces the judges, each individual must step forward and ask for substitution and then state the number of lashes he wants to receive. Participation in the substitution is not required to show support for the Sheffrou. Also, I do not condone any form of pressure to increase the number of lashes per individual. This is not a competition." Chendor stated with emphasis on the word competition.

Tamara had never seen him so serious. He was warning the others. His imposing figure with the pearl-gray shirt and the midnight blue sash now seemed larger than life. Did he know about substitutions? Did Shitan confer with him before he spoke to their group?

Chendor's holoma filled every little space in the room. Pungent, intense. Alluring.

He cares about Maashi. He's worried.

Tamara watched as the group focused on him like moths attracted to a flame.

Chendor continued. "You may tell your friends and supporters that we do not recommend more than ten lashes per person. There is no reason for anyone to be burdened with more and require medical assistance."

He rose and left the room with heavy steps.

Tamara stood. With her hands fisted and her face set in a frown, she said, "You have less than two days to seek help. Good luck."

After everyone had gone, she ordered a glass of toughi and a pudding that tasted like pistachios. She ate slowly and tried to stop the unease that crawled into her mind. What if just a few Chamis showed up and Maashi collapsed under the whip?

Unable to stand the distress caused by these evil thoughts, she jumped off the couch and went to see Maashi.

Tamara wiped her sweaty palms on her khaki pants. Her emotions had been running the gamut between sedate and completely out of control in the last few weeks. She turned forty-five a couple weeks ago. She thought about perimenopause and how women's bodies changed. *Was this what she was experiencing?*

She tapped on Maashi's door and waited. She had almost changed her mind and was ready to leave when the door opened. The guard bowed to her and with a simple hand gesture invited her inside.

She walked in and found Maashi in his receiving room holding a lumi filled to the brim with choun. *How so like him to be lost in thought and forget to drink his glass.*

At first, he showed no reaction to her presence. When she came within three feet of his position, he looked in her direction and said, "Tamara, come. I missed you, Chumpi."

The familiar phrase, the one Maashi used to say when she first came to Chitina, made her heart race with emotions that she could not translate into words. She slipped into his arms, tears filling her eyes.

What if something bad happened to him? She bit her lip and held back sobs. She rubbed her cheek against his, set her hands on his chest, then rested her head on his neck.

His arms covered her like a shield against dark forces. "I know," he whispered. "I know it's difficult." He held her head in one hand and rested the other in the small of her back. He kissed her face with gentle lips then licked her neck with his long, luscious tongue. This close, she felt his wide chest expanding with every breath.

"Are you as scared as I am?" she whispered.

He hesitated a moment before answering. "My fears have lessened. I spent hours meditating over the last few days. I'm at peace with whatever happens. My conscience is clear. Destroying the portal was the most significant thing I ever did. I fulfilled my duty to my people."

"I wish I could say the same," Tamara frowned. "My heart is pounding with anger, and I have this horrible feeling something will go wrong."

"Hold on to me. Let me kiss you." His fragrant holoma floated around them like they were resting on a bed of roses.

"Maashi, I want you to know I love you with all my heart." Trembling, her breathing came in spurts.

"I know. I love you also, more than you can imagine." He played in her hair with his fingers. "I see you cut your hair. You look younger, spunkier." His smile was spontaneous, genuine.

His lovely fragrance warmed her. Her desire grew. Inhaling his holoma, she clung to him and rubbed her cheeks on his wide chest.

He slipped two fingers under her chin and pressed his lips against hers. She felt his energy seep into her pores as he glided his tongue in her mouth. She tasted the sweetness of his saliva.

"I want you Maashi. I want you inside me." She couldn't resist him. Lust burned her flesh.

"Shapinka, I..."

His tongue swirled inside his mouth. He was struggling to hold back.

Urging him on, she whispered, "I know you want me." Wild thoughts fought with any reasoning she still possessed.

"It is forbidden, sweet one," he said, his voice choking with emotion.

"What are they going to do? Flog you?" Her tone cut the air like a sharp blade. She held his face in her hands. "Make love to me. Now." She licked his quatay with delicate strokes and gently bit his nipples.

Maashi arched his back and opened his mouth. The tip of his royal blue tongue rested on the edge of his lips, fighting to stretch out. "I want you also." He licked his lips. "I've wanted you for a long time." He said the words in a soft tone close to her ear.

"Come, Maashi. Come inside me." She pulled at her shirt, and he helped her to remove it. He pulled her pants and underwear and promptly took care of his clothes.

Running his fingers over her bare skin, he moaned softly. His chest rose and fell with each breath he took. Kissing her thighs, his moans increased. "Oh.... I want to taste you, Shapinka." His eyes stared deep into hers. "Let me lick you." He slid his fingers deep inside her then licked the wetness and gasped.

"Now, Maashi. Now."

Tamara opened her legs wide and welcomed his long, silky tongue. She knew he was close to surrendering to his desire.

He licked her and gently nibbled the soft skin in between her legs. With his eyes closed, his holoma soared and the pungent fragrance made Tamara's head spin. She watched his hard member grow bigger than she had ever seen before.

"Come, my love."

He positioned her above him and slid just a few inches inside.

Shaking and rocking, Tamara cried out. "Oh, more. More."

Maashi went a little further and she sunk deep in him. Grabbing his flesh, she let him thrust gently until twinkling stars filled her mind and she drowned in pleasure. As she climaxed, her cries echoed in the room.

Tamara saw him fumble with the controls to cut off the sound on the monitors, but she knew it was too late and she burst in soft giggles. Everyone in the sector must have heard her.

He moved his member slowly back and forth and inhaled deeply. Release came swiftly. His color changed and his skin glowed a deep blue, proof of exquisite pleasure.

He stayed inside her for a long time. Wrapping herself on his chest, she inhaled his warm caramel aroma. Maashi, the one she knew and loved, was back.

Relief flooded her mind. Her heart lifted by his love; she had found happiness. She smiled, her thoughts were like rose petals floating on a clear turquoise ocean.

"Shapinka, I love you," he said. "Rest and sleep without fear. Do not let worries trouble you. I will hold you close."

It took just a few seconds before she dropped in a sea of dreams.

Chapter 43

The next day dawned with its ominous portent. Tamara woke up in her quarters in a sour mood. She dressed in khaki colors, grabbed her turquoise sash and wrapped it around her waist. Within seconds, its color changed to sky blue. *What the hell?*

Tamara heard a familiar chime and turned around to see who was at the door.

Chopa entered wearing Maashi's colors, a chocolate shirt with pink pearls, his sash tied with an impeccable knot, his face a mask of concern.

"This isn't funny Chopa. I'm not in the mood for games today," she growled.

Chopa tilted his head. "What is wrong, Tamara? Why are you making this noise?"

"What did you do to my sash?"

In two long strides, he was at her side and knelt in front of her. "Your sash is blue."

"It was turquoise when I put it on," she said. She picked up the end and shoved it in Chopa's face, "Maashi gave me this sash a while ago. It was turquoise and now it's blue. This is a bad joke." Tamara glared at the Chowli.

"Tamara," he said, "the sash is made of a material that adopts the qualities of its wearer." He bowed his head. "It is blue because you are Sheffrou."

She rested her hands on her hips. "I don't believe you." She wrenched the sash off and threw it on the couch. "I'm not going to wear a sash today."

Chopa's face softened. He whispered, "I understand."

Tamara muttered under her breath, "Why did the Council order Maashi to be flogged? Why did they do that to him?"

Chopa sat on the couch. He ran his fingers in his hair and his chest heaved with a long breath. "He is going through Dompati, and the Council wanted to assert their dominance over him."

She huffed in anger, struggling to regain her composure. "Do you know," she said in a more controlled tone, "how many have agreed to take Maashi's place at the flogging?"

"I do not."

"Why not?"

"We cannot ask. Everything has been kept secret." Chopa paled. His eyes shone with tears. "Perhaps a few. Perhaps a hundred. All I can say is he must submit to at least one lash."

"This is going to be difficult for you too," Tamara said in a softer tone.

He nodded and a lone tear escaped and rolled down his cheek.

She touched his face then kissed his cheek. "We need to stay strong. For each other and for Maashi."

Chopa held her hand and kissed her palm. "Thank you, Shapinka, for your kindness."

She squeezed his hand. "I guess we should go now."

At the door, Tamara turned and looked at the sash. Its color had changed back to turquoise. She shrugged and left, Chopa a step behind her.

>———————<‹‹ ● ›››———————<

The ceremony, as the Chamranlinas called it, would be held in the Rashandamora cave, an oval structure long and wide which could hold thousands of Chamis. Tamara had been there once on the night of the Great Eclipse Celebration.

She followed Chopa, Rahma, and Chari inside, her chest tight with angst. Tamara felt cold chills run over her skin even though the cave was warm. Today would be a day of infamy instead of a wonderful celebration.

The group marched in under the towering columns carved in reddish brown granite rising every hundred feet. Their steps filled the stadium with discordant echoes as they made their way to the front under the stares of Chamis already present. The cave had an overpowering musty smell. It has been neglected for months. There had been no reason to celebrate for a long time.

The Sawishas, the fertile Pure Colors, sat in the lower rows of wide seats on each side of the main aisle while the Multicolors sat higher up. Some Chamis stood as the group went by. All kept silent with unreadable expressions. A podium at the front of the cave held the fourteen Elders of the Council representing the fourteen compounds of the colony.

The Sheffrou section was located on the left side of the podium. The Fanella section was on the right. Well behind, a metal gong at least six feet in diameter was suspended in mid-air in between two tall, thin pillars. A Multicolor attendant stood by, holding a long club.

Few Sheffrous attended. Tamara recognized Tousanou Chendor, Sheffrou Ashani, and the tall Sheffrou Tomisho, Maashi's loyal friend. The Fanella section stayed empty since tradition dictated they should not attend the somber event. Tamara had been allowed in since she was Sheffrou Maashi's Chimitanga.

Tamara couldn't help but compare today's gathering to the last time she participated in the celebration of the Great Eclipse of Chitina's two moons, Ara and Kori. Contrary to the previous event where Chamis of all colors had come to celebrate, only Black and Silvers and Pure Reds were present. Few other colors came and there was only a smattering of Multicolors.

"Chopa," Tamara said, keeping her voice low, "is that Shonava Benshimu sitting over there? What about the Red beside him? Isn't he the one Maashi rescued in that swimming competition?"

"Yes, both came to support Sheffrou Maashi. It is a commendable gesture."

Rahma and Chopa sat her between them while Chari chose a row in front of them. Tamara surmised they worried their stratagem of substituting others instead of Maashi might face strong opposition.

Tamara understood a group of Pure Colors had manifested their discontent to the Council. A great amount of animosity churned among the Chamis since Maashi's return. They refused to accept the edict that said only Sheffrous could be picked as first choice for mating.

Many argued that Maashi had been treated with too much leniency and wanted to see him suffer. It was high time for him to receive an appropriate punishment after his wild antics including trespassing through the Fanella compound months ago and, more recently, refusing to submit to a Draharma trial.

On the other hand, Chari had often stated that Maashi possessed a large group of followers who had come to show their staunch support. Was there any chance the two groups could clash, and fighting would ensue? Was this something possible? In the last few days, Maashi's entourage seemed on edge. In these volatile times, were the Chamis likely to rebel against the authority?

Tension in the cave hovered above them like a black cloud. The crowd stayed eerily quiet. Few clicks or words were heard. The Black and Silver Guards were grim in the best of times and today each one of them had a sour expression.

The sound of the gong indicating the arrival of the Elders startled Tamara. Wearing long silver and gold robes with dark gray sashes, they walked over to their seats in somber silence. A few of them looked over to assess the crowd and acknowledged the spectators. The others sat with their backs straight and their faces inscrutable.

Soon after, the gong resonated for a second time and Maashi was brought in by two guards. He advanced with a heavy step. The guards led him twenty feet in front of the stage. He didn't look at anyone and stood facing the Elders, his face a portrait of sad calm. His chest bare, Maashi wore only steel gray pants.

The gravity of the situation hit Tamara. She had never seen him looking defeated. Even though she knew his life was in danger, she never truly felt it until now. She remembered the color gray represented death for the Chamis. Goosebumps crawled on her arms. *May the Almighty spare his life!*

One of the Elders, a tall and thin individual with silver strands in his hair, stood and raised his arm as if to quiet the crowd, but silence had already filled the room with a heavy hand.

Chopa bent over towards Tamara and said in a low voice, "I will translate his speech for you."

She nodded keeping her gaze riveted on Maashi.

"We are gathered today to comply with the laws established four hundred sequences ago by our ancestors. In the case before us, an order was issued to Shonava Maashi Torrenadanga to complete a Draharma trial because he is undergoing Dompati. He failed to fulfill the trial as ordered." The Elder paused and stared at the crowd. "No Chamranlina can disobey edicts of the Council with impunity. It is our duty to ensure that orders are followed. No excuse is acceptable, and pardon will not be granted to the offender." The Elder paused as some Multis in the crowd clicked their disapproval.

"We, Members of the Council," he continued, "are aware that the punishment seems harsh in these trying times, but we are bound by the laws as they have been written and followed for centuries."

A Black and Silver Guard stood and bellowed, "Laws can we changed."

The Elder ignored the comment. "Sheffrou Maashi Torrenadanga, the Council has decreed the following: You must receive 200 lashes or otherwise be condemned to hard labor in the mines for the next 40 sequences. Do you wish to make a statement?"

Maashi took a moment to respond.

Tamara waited and watched as the crowd grew restless. Some stomped their feet. Others yelled, "Let him prove his innocence."

Another cried out, "No more Draharma trials."

"Punish him," said a lone Red with a big voice.

A loud clamor followed from a group in the back.

A Multi shouted, "Find Dennyvan, he is the one who took Shonava Maashi."

The crowd hissed and stomped in unison.

The Elder raised his arm to request silence.

"Members of the Council, Pure Colors, and Multicolors," said Maashi. "I state that, on the day of the Draharma trial, I was kidnapped and brought on a ship bound for interstellar travel. This all happened without my advanced knowledge and against my will. My kidnappers are the guilty ones."

The Elder raised his chin and tilted his head to the left. "Your objection is duly noted."

His eyes thinned. He added, "We are prepared to proceed with the 200 lashes, or 40 sequences in the mines. Which do you choose?"

Maashi looked down at his hands then stared at the Members of the Council. "I choose the lashes."

"Shonava Maashi Torrenadanga, you will therefore submit today to 200 lashes. Let's commence." The Elder raised his arm and Maashi's hands were bound to a post in front of him.

The gong sounded once more. The Elder returned to his seat.

A heavyset Chami dressed in steel gray stepped forward. He held in his hands a long whip with thorns.

Tamara started trembling. Her breathing came out in spurts. *It's really happening.* She bit her lip and grabbed Chopa's hand.

The Elder dropped his arm.

The crowd stood still.

The executioner stepped sideways and tested the whip by striking the ground. Satisfied, he took a step forward and sent the whip flying. A zipping sound cut the air.

Tamara's breath hitched.

The whip slashed Maashi's back and small welts appeared. Pink blood oozed down his back. Maashi shut his eyes and lowered his head but didn't make a sound. Tamara squeezed Chopa's hand. Her skin prickled. Her stomach cramped.

The executioner took a step back to prepare for the second lash. He raised his arm to deliver the blow. Tamara clenched her jaw.

A Black and Silver Guard came forward and stood in his way. "Members of the Council," he said in a loud, unwavering voice, "By the laws of our colony, I request substitution."

A few Elders shook their heads. Some turned in their seats to confer with their colleagues. After a moment, the speaker rose and said, "This is a highly unusual demand. However, the laws permit substitution. Therefore, I will allow it. How many lashes do you request?"

"10 lashes, Shonava."

The Elder fisted his hands but refrained from commenting. "Proceed with 10 lashes."

The Black and Silver removed his shirt and turned sideways exposing a scarred chest. A post was brought, and his hands were bound to the post. That's when Tamara recognized him as one of the guards on Dennyvan's ship. Her mouth went dry.

Why would this one volunteer for substitution? Would he be the only one?

The guard received the 10 lashes without flinching. Once done, the executioner removed his binds. The guard grabbed his shirt and went back to his seat without a word. The executioner readied his whip once again.

A low hiss spread among the Sawishas.

The executioner waited for a signal.

The Elder gazed at the crowd. No one moved. He signaled once again.

Tamara's head spun. She bit her lip and tasted blood. Her eyes filled with tears. Chopa put his hand on her shoulder and squeezed it gently.

Another Chami stood and came forward.

This one was the Red who owed his life to Maashi. He stepped in front of the stage and asked for substitution for 5 lashes. The Elder had no other choice but to accept.

The Red received the lashes and moved aside.

Again, the executioner waited for a few minutes. The Elder gave the signal and sat back down.

Another Chami stood.

Tears rolled down Tamara's cheeks. Everything became blurry. She couldn't help watching, each time hoping another would volunteer for the dreaded lashes.

Every time the whip was raised, another Chami came forward. A few asked for ten lashes but most asked for two or three lashes. When the count reached 100, a group of Red Guards clicked and stomped their feet in protest. Ten Black and Silver Guards moved closer to the podium.

The Elder rose. "The laws are specific and allow as many substitutions as the number of lashes minus one." He stared at the crowd and waited.

The Reds sat back down. There were no more protests after that.

When the 200 lashes were completed, it was over.

As soon as the executioner announced the final count, the crowd yelled and the Chamis stomped their feet in unison. Some Reds looked stunned. A few grumbled, but the overwhelming show of support from the crowd lasted for several minutes.

At last, all the Elders rose, and the spokesperson said, "We have witnessed a unique event in the history of our colony. The penalty has been fulfilled by substitution. Sheffrou Maashi Torrenadanga is free to leave. His record has been expunged."

Before Rahma and Chopa could react, Tamara ran down to Maashi and jumped in his arms. Maashi held her close to his chest and kissed her hair. "It's over, Chumpi. It's done."

A group of Chamis joined Maashi and offered their wishes for a prompt recovery. The first guard that asked for substitution came and hugged Maashi. He said in an excited voice, "I would have gladly taken a hundred lashes for you, Shonava. But we had been instructed to ask for no more than ten. I am grateful that we have spared you from needless suffering. After the incredible feat you have accomplished, the Elders should celebrate you and elevate you to the rank of hero."

"I agree," said another Black and Silver with enthusiasm. "We are going to start a colony-wide petition to that effect."

"Hail the destroyer of the portal to the Krakoran world!" yelled another.

The group broke into spontaneous cheering and quite a few stomped with joy.

Some recognized Tamara and they clicked and kissed the hem of her shirt to show their respect. Chopa and Rahma quickly moved closer to prevent any inappropriate touching. Chari stayed by Maashi's side but permitted the ones who were anxious to kiss the Sheffrou to do so.

Shonava Benshimu accompanied by Sheffrous Tomisho and Ashani made their way through the many Black and Silver Guards and kissed Maashi's shoulders and neck.

Tousanou Chendor spoke to the crowd with a booming voice, "To all who have suffered for Sheffrou Maashi, come to Sheffrou Tomisho's and my quarters to receive care for your wounds. It will be a pleasure to receive you and offer you a taste of fine food."

Maashi received each one and hugged and kissed them in return. Pale but dignified, Tamara could tell he was delighted by the incredible response. He had never met many of the guards, but they were the ones who risked their lives daily in the tunnels and on the surface to protect the colony and especially the Sheffrous. They understood the significance of the destruction of the portal and were immensely grateful.

Tamara watched as the Elders left the cave one by one. Their faces appeared more serene and their steps lighter. Whether they knew it or not, this was the beginning of a new chapter in the lives of the Chamis.

Chapter 44

Three weeks passed. Life on Chitina regained a normalcy that it hadn't experienced in centuries. It was as if the whole colony breathed a sigh of relief. Tamara rarely saw a guard and if she did, the guard was polite, smiling, and eager to assist her.

It was wonderful to live in familiar surroundings. Tamara's quarters felt like home. She could write at leisure daily happenings and funny anecdotes on the new tablet brought with her from the human ship. Tamara did notice a bit of fatigue in the past weeks that she shrugged off attributing it to stress.

Sprawled on her favorite couch in her receiving room and expecting to see Maashi any minute, she dug in a ripe toughi fruit and chuckled when the juice dripped down her cheek. Such a delightful taste. She wiped her chin with a small cloth and smiled.

She leaned back and pondered on the recent events and at how much Maashi had changed, physically and emotionally.

His playful mood was intriguing. He would sit and stare in mid-air, laugh by himself, or provoke Chopa by messing up his shirt and untying his sash, just for fun. She couldn't fathom why he refused to wear anything else than a short blue sash and cream pants. She chuckled to herself. Little did he know that it was the type of fashion often worn at resorts on Earth.

Maashi also told Tamara that he had a productive discussion with Chari, and they were now on good terms. The Ghouli Ghouli expressed his wish to go back to the Burned Zone to work with old friends and improve their living conditions. He needed the Sheffrou's approval, and Maashi released him from his first Chowli's vows.

The rogue Black and Silver Guards including Dennyvan and his Multi assistant, Redden, faced a litany of charges but word was that they would be released on probation if they agreed to participate in the building of a new dome. More Chamis wanted to spend time on the surface and the new project was on everyone's lips.

Tamara liked this new Maashi, easygoing and smiling. They spent time together swimming in his newly renovated pool. The walls had been painted sky blue with gold swirls except for one which was all white. As he often did, he evaded the answer when she asked why.

The door chime went off. Maashi strolled in dressed in a chemcha, a grin, and mocking eyes.

"Look at you," she said. "Broad shoulders and rippling muscles. You enjoy showing off your body now that you're in shape," said Tamara, intent on teasing him. "Have you been training in secret recently?"

"Very little training. It is not my favorite activity," he said, shaking his head to one side. "I've attained maturity, and my body is changing naturally to a more muscular and taller form."

Tamara grimaced, "That's nice. You look fabulous and don't need to work out to look this way." She sighed, "I wish I could say the same for me."

"I think you look wonderful."

"Are you kidding me? I don't understand how I've gained some weight," Tamara said, pinching her waist, "my appetite is poor and all I want to do is sleep."

"Oh. I sense a bit of annoyance. Let me hold you in my arms. You just need a little TLC, as you call it." Maashi slid on the couch beside her, lifted her in his arms and nuzzled her ears.

"Better?" he asked.

Held close, she took a long breath and said, "Mm, yes."

"How about I remove that shirt of yours? It seems to be in the way." Maashi unfastened her shirt and pulled it off her. "The rest is also unnecessary. It can all go."

Tamara smiled and snuggled closer. "What are you doing?" she asked, knowing well that he loved to hold her naked in his arms.

"If you really want to know," he whispered in her ear, "I will confide that holding you this way is most pleasurable." Maashi's amber eyes glowed as he ran long fingers on her shoulders, back and buttocks. "Mm. What a blissful sensation."

She chuckled. "I agree since today you smell like a bouquet of roses. It's quite lovely."

"Let me kiss you, sweet one," he said. "I'm powerless to resist your charms."

Tamara giggled. "What is going on with you?"

Maashi tilted his head this way and that, his way of delaying his answer. "I want to ask you something, but I'm not sure how to ask without offending you." He held her face and gazed into her eyes.

"It's unusual for you to be bashful." She caressed his cheeks and dropped kisses on his lips. "What do you want?"

Maashi blinked a few times and said in a soft voice, "Would you ever consider carrying my offspring?"

Tamara's jaw dropped and she sat up straight. Recent details she had dismissed as inconsequential came into focus. How she craved for chocolate mousse like the one she tasted aboard the human ship, or wanting to sleep in every morning and, more recently, noticing her breasts were sore.

"Is this a 'fait accompli'?" she asked. "Or a proposition?"

Maashi face and chest paled. His lips were sealed.

"Oh my gosh. Is this for real?"

Maashi looked away and then looked back at her. "You're pregnant."

"Oh my...." She swallowed hard and stared at him. "But we've done it only once and at my age, I'm not supposed to get pregnant this easily."

Maashi's eyes widened. He made sounds that weren't words then caught himself and said, keeping his voice low. "I've always had a remarkably high sperm count even for a Chamranlina." Looking away, he stated, "Once is enough."

"What?" She feigned anger then started to giggle and kept on laughing. She laughed so hard she cried. She held her stomach and hiccupped. Finally catching her breath, she squealed, "This is fabulous."

Maashi erupted in a low rumble then the sound got louder and louder until he roared with glee. "I am delighted," he said, "that you're happy about the pregnancy."

"Oh," Tamara croaked, wiping her eyes. "I need a glass of water." She took the glass Maashi offered her and gulped down the cool water. "Maashi, I'm forty-five. There are increased risks for me and the baby. You know, chromosomal anomalies, increased risk of miscarriage, etc."

He nodded. "Chendor and I completed a comprehensive ultrasound evaluation, we took a sample of your blood, a little prick on your ear while you were sleeping, and the fetus is normal. Also, I must tell you Chamranlina pregnancies last only four months and you have completed the early period when miscarriages can occur."

"But the baby might be too big for me to deliver. You're big and tall. You must be close to eight feet now."

"Our offspring are born with a soft shell around them which eases the delivery process, and they weigh no more than four pounds."

"A soft shell like an egg?"

"Yes."

"Wow. I don't know what to say." She sat back and thought, "How long have you known?"

"I had a test done on your saliva the third day after our encounter and it was positive."

"What?" she punched his chest. "You could've said something."

Maashi hugged her gently and whispered, "I was afraid to tell you."

She frowned and glanced sideways at him. "Were you afraid I wouldn't want it?"

"I didn't know what to think." He lowered his head and spread his hands on his knees. "Losing a child is a great tragedy."

Tamara nodded. "I know," she said. Months ago, Maashi had lost many babies from a plague. She rested her head against his silky-smooth chest. "I will never see my children again. It's almost like I lost them." She wiped her face. She made a mental note to ask Chopa to verify in all the records they had acquired from the human ship to see if he could find anything about her children.

Maashi kissed her forehead and raised her lips to his.

Tamara snuggled against his chest.

"I still can't believe it, but I promise to carry your child and love it with all my heart." She couldn't wish for anything more.

The door chime went off again and again.

"Who is that?" said Tamara. "Don't let them in. I'm naked."

"I'll go see. Take the time you need to get dressed."

Maashi went to the door and stood facing whoever it was to shield her from view. He clicked a few times and strolled back into the receiving room.

"Are you ready?" he said. "We are supposed to see a few friends on the surface today. They're waiting for us."

"On the surface? Isn't it too hot out there?"

"It's much cooler at this time of the sequence. You should be quite comfortable."

"Is it safe to go there?"

Maashi looked at her with a mocking grin. "I wouldn't bring you out if it wasn't safe, Tamara."

"Okay, then." She slipped on her light blue top and pants. "I'm right behind you."

Tamara followed Maashi through the long hallway leading to the main elevators. He acknowledged the lone guard at the door who bowed and stepped aside. Maashi entered the cabin and Tamara followed him in. She had taken these same elevators several times and going up ten levels was a simple process. All she knew was that the mechanism was based on antigravity, and it was a smooth ride. They ascended and reached the surface in a few short minutes.

The door opened in a foyer with floor-to-ceiling windows flooded with the orange sun's light. Maashi stepped out through the sliding door and Tamara took her first tentative steps. She inhaled the dry desert air and the smell of burned toast tickled her nostrils. A light breeze ruffled her hair.

She scanned the deserted landscape, the low dirt hills, the boulders as big as cars on the right, and the Chizoo Mountains miles away with their snowy tops glistening under the merciless sun. The last time she was on the surface, she had watched a captivating shoshan race with Maashi as one of the jockeys. The memory made her smile.

"Coming?" said Maashi. "You'll see. It's quite comfortable."

A large yellow tent had been erected a hundred yards away. She picked up the pace and got a closer look at the tent which was much bigger than she first thought.

"Awesome!" she exclaimed.

At least fifteen feet tall with an elongated hexagonal shape, it was tied to sturdy posts and open at one end. This gave the occupants a spectacular view of the mountain range on the horizon and permitted the breeze to flow in. The walls were decorated with fourteen different kinds of gold swirls, each representing a compound, and the floor was covered by a caramel-colored rug with cream pearls. Big enough to hold more than two dozen Chamis, she recognized several familiar faces among the guests sitting on low couches overflowing with cushions of all shades of blue. Several Sheffrous accompanied by their Chowlis rose when Maashi entered and greeted him with affectionate hugs and kisses.

Then, each one came to greet her also.

Shonava Benshimu came first. Wearing a white shirt with green markings, the brawny green bowed and took Tamara's hand in his huge ones and kissed her palms. "It is an honor," he said.

Sheffrou Dasho came second. Although his face was distorted by scars incurred during the attack on the night of the Great Eclipse Celebration, Tamara recognized him right away. His sash was sky blue and his pearl-gray shirt with long billowing sleeves hid his mangled right arm.

He approached and knelt in front of her. With long slender fingers, he caressed her cheek and whispered, "I know I look quite different but I'm still the same person. I am most pleased to be here today to congratulate you on your pregnancy. It is a positive omen for the future. May the Souls of our Ancestors look down favorably upon you."

Touched by his kind wishes, Tamara said, "It's a pleasure to see you too. I'm glad you came to celebrate. I wish you a successful recovery."

Chendor came next. He wore a midnight blue sash embroidered with threads of gold to mark the occasion. A white shirt covered part of his chest revealing his elaborate quatay. He clicked softly and said, "Words don't convey the pleasure I feel as I set my eyes upon you, Shapinka. Rest assured that I am here for you and will be available to help you in any way or fashion during your pregnancy. Congratulations to you both." He bent down low and kissed her cheek then rose and gave a bear hug to Maashi.

Wearing a long gold tunic with cream pants and a royal blue sash, Tomisho followed and pressed his lips on her palm with a wide grin. "I just learned that congratulations are in order. I wish you the best pregnancy, Tamara. Can't wait to see that offspring."

"Thanks, Tomisho," Tamara said with a mocking smile.

Ashani came last. He was still quite thin compared to the others, but Tamara thought he looked outrageously handsome with his chestnut curls and deep thoughtful eyes.

"I'm so glad," she said, "something positive came out of the trade. Maashi couldn't have been happier the day he found you, and the others barely contained their joy."

Ashani took a knee in front of her. "I am grateful for all you have done these last few weeks. I know Maashi couldn't have succeeded without your help." He caught Tamara by surprise by planting a kiss on both her cheeks.

One by one, they settled back in their respective places with a smattering of clicks and 'sh' sounds reminding Tamara of when she first arrived on Chitina. Maashi sat on Tomisho's right and Tamara settled between Maashi and Chendor's huge frame.

Maashi waited for a moment of silence then said in a voice filled with emotion, "First, let's bow our heads and join our minds to give thanks to the Souls of our Ancestors. Centuries ago, they braved the dangers and unknowns of space and traveled to Chitina to establish a colony." He paused for a minute and then took a long breath. "We struggled for many sequences to make this forbidden place our home. Now, our hearts flow with newfound hope that Chitina will truly be our home."

Chendor took the lead from there. "Let's raise our lumis and toast Tamara and Shonava Maashi who made all this possible. Without their courage and determination, we would still be facing a terrible foe which has upended the lives of our people for centuries."

Maashi handed a lumi to Tamara and took one for himself. Tamara made a discreet head signal to Chopa standing in the background. He took a lumi after offering one to the other Chowlis.

Before they raised their glasses, Tamara said, "We shouldn't forget Rowni's contribution. Rowni was Maashi's chief of security before being kidnapped by the enemy on the night of the Great Eclipse. He helped us destroy the portal and brought me back safely to the human ship."

There was a murmur among the group. They all raised their glasses and drank.

Chendor raised his lumi a second time. "To our friend and Ishkibu Sheffrou, Tamara Walsh, in the name of all present here today, and all absent," Chendor suddenly stopped, overcome with emotion.

Tamara rested her hand on his arm.

Chendor lowered his gaze, inhaled a long breath, and said, "To Tamara, gentle and fierce, we thank you and wish you health and happiness for many sequences to come." He shot a grateful side glance at Tamara and took a long gulp of his drink.

"Thank you," Tamara whispered. Overwhelmed by a flood of emotions, she was taken by surprise by the sudden flow of tears running down her cheeks. "Sorry," she said.

Maashi gave her a small cloth to wipe her face. "It's all right, Chumpi. Young Sheffrous often shed tears. We should know."

He took her hand in his and held it close to his side. "For those of you that don't already know, Tamara is with child. And I cannot be happier."

Tamara felt her cheeks burn.

The Sheffrous clicked in unison to congratulate her.

Tomisho said, "Congratulations. Everyone is thrilled with the news." He put his arms around Maashi and gave him a bear hug and kissed his neck. Then, he bent over in two and reached Tamara's hand and kissed it.

Lovely floral scents from the Sheffrous' holomas soon spread and filled the tent. Tamara felt like she sat in a garden filled with fragrant flowers.

Chendor clapped his hands and in a manner of seconds, several Chowlis brought a fabulous assortment of colorful gels, mousses, aspics, and puddings including Chendor's favorite, an edible green jelly called Loola. A second group brought crackers of different shapes, triangular biscotti, fruits and nuts.

Tamara couldn't help giggling at all the food and felt sorry for the discomfited look of Dasho and Ashani who weren't used to eating in public.

Chendor, on the other hand, appeared quite pleased with himself. Tamara knew for sure he had orchestrated the feast. He raised his arm and a large, covered plate was brought and set on the low table in front of Tamara.

"My compliments to our youngest Sheffrou," he said and smiled. His deep facial scar faded completely when he smiled, warming Tamara's heart.

"For me?" she said, grinning. "I'm anxious to see what this is." She raised the cover just an inch and squealed. "Chendor. It's chocolate mousse!" She sat there with her mouth open and said, "How did you know I was craving that?"

Chendor had a mocking grin and looked sideways to Chopa who stood behind the guests as inconspicuously as he could with eyes glowing with joy. "Someone brought the recipe from the human ship."

Tamara beamed with a big smile. "Chendor, Chopa, thank you. This is so nice." She hesitated then said, "Chendor, can I give you a kiss?"

The huge Chami said in a soft, sweet voice, "It would be a pleasure."

Tamara rose from her seat to reach the gargantuan Chami sitting beside her. She hugged and kissed him on the cheek. "Thank you for all you've done for me and Maashi."

Chendor's face softened. "You are very welcome."

A guard appeared at the entrance of the tent.

Chendor grumbled, "What is this?"

The guard bowed to the assembly and said in a loud voice, "Sheffrou Maashi, there are two messages for you. One from the Interstellar Alliance and one from the Council of Elders. May I hand them over to you?"

Maashi got up and went behind the guests to see the guard and took the two small devices. "Thank you," he said in a low voice.

The guard left. The group fell silent.

"Do you wish to read them in private, Shonava?" asked Chopa.

Maashi's brow widened. "No," he said, waving his hand with long fingers spread out, "everyone present here today is a friend and, as you know, all news gets out eventually."

He pressed on the first device and read aloud. "The Interstellar Alliance wishes to express its most heartfelt thanks to Sheffrou Maashi Torrenadanga for destroying a complex structure known as the Portal and for helping in the dismantling of a major trafficking ring that has affected thousands of lives over the last decades.

"The accusations against Sheffrou Maashi for the murder of the Rodenegad Chairman of the trafficking ring filed by a group of aliens called Rodenegad have been deemed unsubstantiated due to lack of evidence and reliable witnesses. After examining all records available, the Alliance has concluded that the likely perpetrator of the Chairman's murder is a creature known only as the 'translucent creature'. This alien entity has not been seen since the murder and the only information we have on its whereabouts is limited since it is known to travel freely in space. Any sighting should be reported to our representatives.

"We deplore the deaths related to the destruction of the Portal. However, the Alliance will not file accusations since the removal of the Portal will sever the contact with the Krakoran and hopefully bring forth a new era of freedom for the multitude of species victims of their tyranny.

"The Alliance wishes to inform Sheffrou Maashi that it is grateful for his tremendous contribution and that all charges against his person have been dropped.

"Best Regards, Clomatilde, official representant of the Interstellar Alliance."

Maashi raised his head high and sighed. "I am relieved they dropped the charges." He came back and took his seat beside Tamara. He glanced at her and asked, "Do you think that flat creature killed the chairman?"

"We'll never know for sure," she said in a grave tone, "but I think it was capable of doing it."

"What about the other message?" said Tomisho.

Maashi looked at the device in his hands and hesitated.

"Would you rather I read it for you?"

"Go ahead," Maashi handed it to his friend.

Tomisho clicked and opened the device. "It says, The Council of Elders wishes to express their gratitude to Sheffrou Maashi Torrenadanga for demonstrating incredible resilience in adversity and for the destruction of the connection between our world and the world of the Krakoran. Therefore, by the authority bestowed upon us by the Council, we grant him total and unconditional immunity against all future punishments, including but not limited to, Draharma trials and floggings."

Tamara stood and started to applaud with gusto. All the others stood and stomped their feet in homage to Maashi who beamed with pride. His amber eyes glowed and he hugged Tamara.

"I'm not done," said Tomisho. He raised his hand and the group quieted down. "After due consultation and consideration, the Council recommends Sheffrou Maashi Torrenadanga for the honor of sitting as an active member of the Council with all due privileges and responsibilities."

"Brilliant!" Tomisho exclaimed, looking up with astonishment at Maashi and the other Sheffrous.

Maashi shook his head and laughed. "It is hard to believe they would say something like that," he said.

Nodding, Tomisho continued to read the last part, "Furthermore, it is the opinion of the Council that interbreeding with members of compatible sentient species is acceptable if there are no detrimental consequences to either species. The Council believes that doing so with the express consent of both parties will enrich the genetic makeup of Chamranlinas and decrease the risk of depletion and extinction.

"In light if this new opinion, the Council has decided negotiations are in order with humans to establish friendly relations that could lead to encouraging more human females to come to Chitina. We plan to do a survey to see if this option is acceptable to Chamranlinas. We recommend you, Sheffrou Maashi and your Chimitanga, Tamara Walsh, as ambassadors for this project. Signed by all the members of the Council of Elders."

Tomisho belted out, "Souls of my Ancestors, this is un-believable!" With a roar, he said, "Better than any gift they could've bestowed on you. Congratulations, Maashi." Tomisho embraced his friend and gave him a solid kiss.

The others rose with clicks and foot stomping. They fierce-ly hugged a stunned Maashi and kissed Tamara's palm.

Tamara leaned back and smiled, savoring the historic mo-ment. *This is the start of a new era of freedom for all the Chamis and hope for a better future.*

She took a scooper and tasted the scrumptious-looking mousse. *Fabulous.*

<The End of The Sheffrou Trilogy>

If you enjoyed **Sheffrou's Gambit**
kindly post a review.
Thank you.
Cami Michaels

Glossary

Ara and Kori: names of Chitina's two moons.

Black Creatures of the Korr Nebula: fearsome, carnivorous, winged creatures who have colonized several planets in the Korr Nebula.

Chamtali: original world of the Chamranlinas.

Chamranlinas: name the aliens call themselves.

Chanterra sea: large body of water that existed centuries ago on Chamtali.

Charissa: "joie de vivre", a feeling of well-being.

Chemcha: protective underwear worn by Sheffrous and Sawishas.

Chimitanga: Sheffrou's little friend.

Chitina: planet where the Chamranlinas live.

Choun: breastmilk.

Chowli: close companion to a Sheffrou or a Sawisha.

Chumpi: sweet one.

Dompati: state of becoming a mature Sheffrou.

Draharma trials: three trials all Sheffrous and Sawishas must complete to gain the right to mate.

Encounter room: small oval room designed for intimate meetings and sexual encounters.

Fanella: female, much smaller and slender than the male.

Ghouli Ghouli Chamranlinas: a race of Chamranlina characterized by copper color skin and black hands and feet, and black circles around the eyes.

Googlian: fungus found in deep caves, glows in the dark.

Holoma: fragrant aroma produced by mature Sheffrous when they feel pleasure.

Hooga plant: thin strips of this tall plant are treated and used for flogging.

Ishkibu: a special kind of Sheffrou who can travel through wormholes.

Kego plant: fragrant plant which has numerous twigs.

Krakoran: also called Untouchables, aliens, enemies of the Chamranlinas.

Loola: delicacy, edible green jelly usually presented as a mold.

Multicolors: also called Multi, refers to Chamranlinas with multiple colors on their tongues. Apart from a few exceptions, they are infertile.

Moran drums: used in war to signal troops to attack.

Pure Colors: Chamranlinas with a tongue with only one color. They are fertile and part of the elite.

Quatay: characteristic erogenous markings on the chest of Sawishas and Sheffrous.

Rashandamora cave: immense cave where the Great Eclipse Celebration is held.

Rue Kish: intense sexual desire.

Saweya: life energy.

Sawisha: part of the elite group of Pure Color Chamranlinas, their tongue is unicolor.

Schloppies: testicles.

Sequence: one year on Chitina or 712 Earth days. The sequence is divided in 17 months; 16 months of 42 days and 1 month of 40 days. One week is 10 days and one day is 26 Earth hours.

Shapinka: precious one.

Sheffrou: third gender, may be male or female. Sheffrous are Pure colors, their tongue is blue.

Shonava: lord.

Shoshans: large antelope-like quadrupeds.

Sliva: long kiss on the mouth to obtain or transfer information.

Talifante: the order given to the computer to stop recording.

Tinqua plant: leaves are used to add flavor to drinks.

Toughi: fruit which tastes and looks like a blend of pear and apple.

Tousanou: title given to a the rapist.

Vizinem: aliens allies of the Chamranlinas.

Whisli berries: ingesting these berries changes the voice, makes it high-pitched.

Woo-Odong: tall and slim aliens always covered by dark brown veils with talons on their feet.

Woo-Olong-Ti: alien impersonated by Maashi.

Yaccata tree: flowering tree found only under the domes with pink flowers like the Japanese cherry blossom tree.

Acknowledgements

I would like to thank my friends and family for their continued help and support, especially my daughter Melissa Sanchez, and my fellow writers, Trilby Plants and Richard Luthman.

A big thank you also to all the members of the South Carolina Writers Association, Surfside group and the Sci-Fi/Fantasy Virtual group for their generous advice and critique.

Meet the Author

As a child, I dreamed of becoming an astronaut and traveling to faraway worlds.

Born in Montreal, I currently live in South Carolina and enjoy reading, traveling, and I'm still fascinated by stories about alien worlds. After a successful career as an obstetrician-gynecologist and four children, I divide my time between my family and creating my own science-fiction stories. When not busy writing, I ride my tricycle around the neighborhood or work in my bee and butterfly friendly garden.

I would be delighted if, after reading *Sheffrou's Gambit*, you would consider leaving a review on Amazon and Goodreads or any website of your choice.

I hope you enjoyed reading The Sheffrou Trilogy as much as I enjoyed writing it.

Good Readings to all!

Cami Michaels

Website: CamiMichaels.com

Email: CamiMichaelsscifiauthor@gmail.com

Facebook: Cami Michaels Sci-fi Author